Ridgeway

Murder

Cyberworld Publishing

Cyberworld Publishing

www.CyberworldPublishing.com

Cyberworld Publishing
Jindalee St
Toronto 2283
Australia

Ridgeway Murder

Robin Hillard

CHAPTER ONE: SUNDAY AFTERNOON

Four o'clock on Sunday afternoon.

The Ridgeway Arts and Culture Centre's art show was nearly over and most of the visitors had gone home. In the small front office Marion Shea was manning the credit card machine.

There were still a few stragglers but soon the committee could close the doors, congratulate themselves on a job well done, and head for their respective homes.

Marion sighed. It had been a long weekend.

Behind her, in the cluttered office, Rowena McKendrick, the coordinator, slammed the cash box shut. "No sign of Benjamin Knowles," she said grumpily. "What's the use of a treasurer if he's never around?"

"He was here on Friday night," Marion said wearily.

"You bet he was. No way he'd miss the opening and a chance to swill champagne and fawn over the guests. He should have been here for the whole weekend. It's a trip to the night deposit box for me, thanks to that bloody man."

The last few weeks had been punctuated by Rowena's complaints. And now she was repeating her familiar song. "Some people think this centre runs itself."

Marion, who had spent the last week attending to the hundred and one small details Rowena had overlooked, bit back the obvious retort. While she was willing to agree the woman couldn't do *everything,* she thought the coordinator could fit some work into her paid hours.

Though, for once, Rowena had a legitimate grievance. It really was too bad of Benjamin, Marion thought. And he was the one who refused to employ extra staff.

The subject of hiring another staff member had come up at a meeting soon after she joined the committee, and Benjamin opposed the idea.

"We can't afford another wage," he had said.

At the time Marion didn't know anything about the organisation's finances, and she had not contributed to the discussion.

Rowena hadn't forgiven her silence, and whenever Marion came into the office, she assumed the reproachful expression of Caesar when Brutus pushed in the knife.

Unfortunately, Marion had become involved in the centre's most important fund-raising event, this annual exhibition of local artists. When Loretta Wheelwright, the elderly president, invited her to join the committee, she had remarked that the newcomer's experience, running a commercial gallery in Melbourne, would be "such a help with our little show." And Marion had found herself organising the event.

From then on every time Marion came into the office the coordinator glared at her accusingly over papers that had been sorted, unread, into piles on her desk. Every innocent question was seen as a direct criticism of Rowena's performance. And every request for action, or even information, was met with "The treasurer handles that," "You'll have to ask Benjamin Knowles," or "I haven't had time."

When Marion realised that Rowena was married to the committee member, William McKendrick, she wondered if the coordinator expressed her resentment at home. Did she treat her husband to the sulks that made life so difficult for everybody at the centre?

At the meeting, when Rowena asked for help in the office, Benjamin had responded to her complaint by offering to take on some of her duties, but he had not been involved in the art show. He worked during the day and always had an excuse if Marion asked him to meet her in the evening.

This afternoon Rowena treated his dereliction as a deliberate effort to inconvenience an overworked coordinator, though if anybody had a right to feel peeved, Marion thought, it was herself. She was the one who was landed with most of the treasurer's work.

Rowena was still muttering when her husband, William, came into the office. No matter how often she saw the McKendricks together, Marion found it hard to think of them as man and wife.

William was twelve years older than Rowena, and with his solid, weather-beaten face, he looked exactly what he was, a respected landholder. Although he wore the jacket and slacks appropriate for a secular social occasion, he managed to look like a farmer coming into town in his Sunday suit, for the weekly church service. Willowy Rowena, with her long blonde hair and green shadowed eyes, might have been a mermaid, netted by sailors and put on display for the amusement of insensitive land dwellers.

Marion allowed herself a moment's amusement as she remembered the source of the mermaid myth—the fantasies of sex-starved sailors watching sea cows on a distant reef—and mentally transformed Rowena into a lump of grey, grunting mammal flopping over the rough rock.

In an effort to suppress her giggles, Marion felt herself frowning and turned quickly to the window. In Rowena's present mood, she would read any change of expression as a response to her own complaints, and however justified those complaints might be, Marion did not want to encourage the woman's self-pity. She also suspected that if she were drawn into the discussion, anything she said would be repeated to Benjamin Knowles. Just because Rowena was not talking to him today didn't mean he would not be the companion of her soul next week, and any comments made about the treasurer would be repeated, with embellishments.

The window overlooked a parking lot at the side of the building, and for anyone involved in the centre, the scene outside was more satisfactory than the petty office drama. Marion was pleased to see how many people were loading canvases into their cars. The weekend had been a resounding success, most of the paintings had been sold, the artists were delighted, and the centre's commission would give its bank account a healthy injection of cash. Last year the event had barely covered its costs, and Marion knew she was responsible for the success of this year's show.

Not all the vehicles belonged to patrons of the art show. The centre was next to, one could almost say surrounded by, a wide stretch of parkland that bordered a branch of Ridgeway Creek. On the other side of the building, the windows of the hall overlooked a stretch of grass shaded by big, old trees. The front entrance of the hall opened onto the main route to the creek, and a procession of families straggled past the door, around the side of the building, and past a notice informing them that parking was provided for THE ARTS AND CULTURE CENTRE and to collect their illegally parked cars. This violation of the centre's private space was a constant source of annoyance to the committee, and they wasted an inordinate amount of meeting time discussing the problem.

Marion chuckled as she watched a young man trying to push a very large Alsatian into a very small car. She turned to share the joke, but the others were too obviously involved in their own affairs to care about the scene outside.

William was preparing to leave. Marion didn't think he had enjoyed the exhibition. Rowena had been in one of her sulky moods. Although she was all smiles for the more glamorous patrons, she had nothing but grumbles and grunts for members of the committee, and that included her husband.

"I really do have to go, love," he was saying. "You know I'm expecting a call. We're getting a load of heifers tomorrow," he told Marion. "Now we've had some rain we're stocking up . . ."

"For goodness sake," Rowena said impatiently. "Can't you talk about anything except your stupid farm?"

William glared at his wife. He started to speak but caught Marion's eye and clamped his jaw on the words. Whatever he was going to say was not for the newcomer's ears.

The knuckles of his clenched hands were white, and if he opened them, Marion was sure she would see marks where his nails pressed into his palms.

Rowena reached into the drawer for the cash box, slammed it onto the desk, and stared at her husband, as if challenging his silence. Whatever was going on between the two of them, Marion didn't want to be involved.

"You might as well go, too," she told Rowena. "If you'll deposit the cash on your way home, Loretta and I can lock up." And when I see Benjamin Knowles, I'll have a few sharp words for him, she thought.

"Wouldn't I hear about it afterwards if I did that? Loretta Wheelwright—our noble president—left to shut the door herself because the lazy coordinator went home," Rowena replied.

That was too much for William. "Loretta is not like that," he said angrily. He moved closer to his wife as if determined to have his say, no matter who was with them in the office.

Rowena picked up one of the flyers that littered her desk and frowned over a page announcing the date and times of the weekend event. William didn't move, and after a few uncomfortable minutes, she looked up, as if suddenly aware of her husband's presence.

"There is no need for you to hang around," she said. "It's not as if you cared about this artsy stuff."

Marion gasped at the unfairness of the remark. William had supported the centre for most of his adult life, while, according to Loretta, "that Rowena only joined the drama group a year ago. To catch herself a husband, stupid girl. After Agnes left, William was just waiting to be caught."

So Rowena was wife number two.

Somehow Rowena had become the paid coordinator and William, a conscientious member of the committee, tried not to get involved in her ongoing feud with the president. Was that why he was going home before the show closed instead of joining them at the end of the day, when they would congratulate each other on the success of the weekend? Marion wondered.

He nodded brusquely to Rowena and strode out of the office, almost colliding with the subject of their argument, Loretta Wheelwright.

Marion sighed as the president came bustling through the door. Loretta was not a large woman, but there was no denying the power of her presence.

"Sales have been good," she said, joining Marion at the window to watch departing cars. "This has been our most successful year."

"No thanks to Benjamin Knowles." Rowena launched, again, into her complaint about the absent treasurer.

"What with organising the art show and handling tickets for the drama group," she whined, "I'm worn out."

Loretta stood angrily erect in the small room. "That is your job," she said crisply. "You had a list of the coordinator's duties when you applied for the position."

"You didn't tell me I'd be working all weekend. Nobody on the committee realises how much there is to do. You all think the centre runs itself," Rowena said, glowering at them both.

Marion avoided Loretta's eyes. The president might be hoping she would make some comment about how little the coordinator had contributed to this weekend's event, but there was no way Marion would be drawn into the argument. Although she agreed with Loretta, she felt any criticism should be kept for a private interview and not made at a time when members of the public could wander into the office.

Marion made her escape.

She intended to cross the passage into the hall, which was the venue of the centre's public events. But as she left the office, she stumbled into another McKendrick, William's brother, Dennis. He was leaving the hall and almost knocked her off her feet. She steadied herself with a hand against the wall as he muttered a curse and strode after William.

Why was he so angry? Marion wondered, then, a disquieting thought; how much of the argument had he overheard?

Dennis was not on the committee, but he was a leading member of the drama group, and Marion wondered if Rowena took as little interest in their productions as she had in the art show. If so, he might share Loretta's opinion of his sister-in-law and be ready to second the president's complaints.

Or was there another reason for his ill temper?

Marion knew the McKendrick brothers worked together on the family property, but, unlike William, when Dennis came to town, he didn't look like a farmer. He could be taken for a

10

lawyer, or a businessman. Today he was very smart in a stylish jacket and an obviously expensive, open-necked shirt. That was one thing he had in common with his sister-in-law. Neither of them economised on clothes.

But he could be mean in other ways. Earlier in the afternoon, when William congratulated the artist of one expensive landscape, Marion heard Dennis remind him sharply of paintings bought in previous years. He had accused his brother of "throwing money away."

But Dennis might have good reason to discourage a purchase, Marion thought. These were tough times for farmers, and, after years of attending shows of local art, the McKendricks must have as many pictures as their walls could hold.

Whatever the issue Dennis intended to raise with his brother, it would have to wait. William strode around the side of the building to the parking lot, but Dennis was barely through the door when he was intercepted by another member of the committee, Walter Edridge. Walter was, as always, oblivious to the other person's mood and there was no way Dennis could escape before he finished his rambling narrative.

When his victim eventually broke away, Walter would come inside, looking for another audience. Marion moved quickly out of his sight. As she dodged through the stream of departing visitors, across the narrow passage, and into the hall, she reflected on the complications involved in running a family business. Whatever happened in the McKendricks' lives, the brothers would have to work together on the property.

She was glad her siblings were employed in their own fields and had not impinged on her career.

Marion found her husband, Stephen, in the hall, gazing through a window that should have been cleaned. Outside, shadows were lengthening over the parkland that sloped gently down to the creek. A couple of self-important ducks climbed purposefully out of the water and settled with some of their fellows on the grass.

"The ducks are knocking off early," he said, laughing. "They've had a hard day scrounging for scraps."

"Wouldn't they be safer on one of the islands?" Marion asked, referring to the rocky mounds that had been thoughtfully

11

constructed downstream, where the creek flowed into a lake, to provide a place where waterfowl would not be harassed by dogs or parties of late-night drinkers.

"You'd better go down and talk to them," Stephen said. "I'm sure they want your advice."

As if they had heard the discussion, the birds shook their wings and took to the air, heading for the lake. Stephen linked arms with Marion, and the two of them laughed.

"Wonderful show, eh Marion?" They were interrupted by the gravelly voice of Walter Edridge. In the weeks leading up to the show, his efforts to complicate the simplest arrangements had driven her to the pitch of desperation, but now he was wrapped in an aura of self-congratulation. Margaret Edridge, joining her husband, made a wry grimace before murmuring the expected platitudes. She had no illusions about her husband's contribution to the weekend.

"I hear the grant's come through," Walter said.

"Grant?"

"For Judith's multicultural do."

Please God, no, Marion thought.

Ridgeway had a sizeable population of Sudanese Christians, but their presence had not impinged on the centre until Judith Bostock, the secretary, attended a workshop run by the local church and learned how much money was available for any nongovernment organization running programs for the recently arrived migrants. She decided the committee absolutely had to get involved and persuaded them to apply for funds.

They were delighted with the idea. Judith's Multicultural Arts Program had all the attraction of novelty and discussion about the project monopolised meetings to the exclusion of other, less-interesting business.

"Margaret plays golf with Ray Gowd," Walter was saying. Gowd was the manager of the First Queensland Bank, where the centre had its account. "We bumped into him at the club, and he told us the grant has already come through. I felt a bit of a fool when he raised the subject. Nobody told me." Walter looked accusingly at Marion, who quickly disclaimed any knowledge of Judith Bostock's project.

"Ray was a bit put out because our treasurer has taken the money out of his bank. Apparently Knowles decided we should keep the funds separate, but why couldn't we open another account with the First Queensland?" A reproachful pause. Did Walter expect Marion to explain the treasurer's convoluted bookkeeping?

"I haven't seen Benjamin Knowles," she said firmly, "and I don't know anything about the government grant."

"That's what I said to Ray, 'The executive handles all that stuff,' I said. 'You should talk to Loretta or Judith Bostock if you can't get any sense out of Knowles.'"

If Marion had her way, the money would go straight back to the department. She thought the refugees had enough problems adjusting to their new home without being dragged into a program at the Arts and Culture Centre. But the committee would be delighted with the news.

Since the program didn't meet any of the departmental guidelines, she had been confident the submission would be dropped into a bureaucratic wastebasket. But the committee had been enthusiastic about the idea, and she didn't discourage them. What harm could come from talking about a project that, she was convinced, would never get off the ground?

The discussions had produced a problem she had not foreseen. After the submission had been posted and Judith had left for a holiday in Greece, Walter realised the funding included money for a project manager.

He came to the next meeting armed with the official guidelines and read the relevant passages with a flourish worthy of the drama group. "What are we doing about this?" he asked.

"Nothing," Marion had spoken up quickly. "We don't have to do anything unless we get the funds."

There was a murmur of disagreement.

"We must be prepared," Loretta said.

Her motion to advertise the position was passed with only two dissenters, Marion and Patricia Menkes. Patricia had nothing against the project but, as a matter of principle, opposed any motion raised by the president. Remarks made fifty years ago, when Patricia announced her engagement to Loretta's favourite cousin, still rankled. The other members of the committee were so used to Patricia's attitude that they discounted her opposition.

Nor would any of them listen to Marion's arguments against interviewing staff for a nonexistent program. They were too engrossed in the exciting business of composing an advertisement to be placed in the weekend edition of *The Ridgeway News*.

The only effect of her objection was to convince Loretta and William McKendrick that the new committee member's experience as an employer would make her a useful addition to a panel that would choose the prospective manager.

Marion agreed to be on the panel. At least she could warn the applicants that nothing would be done unless the centre got funding, and given the number of competing submissions, theirs was unlikely to be chosen.

After the interviews, she put the multicultural project out of her mind and concentrated on the immediate problem of the art show.

She had been too sanguine.

If Walter had his facts straight, the proposal had been accepted and the money was already in the bank.

"It looks as if Judith can go ahead with her program." Marion said and didn't realise how heavily she had emphasised the pronouns until she saw Margaret's mischievous grin. Margaret had been married to Walter for fifty years. Fifty years!

"And do you still expect her home on Saturday?" Marion asked. In time to organise her own project, she then thought.

Walter bobbed his head up and down. Did that mean the secretary was coming home, or was he making an affirmative response because he thought that was what she wanted? Amiability is an admirable trait, but over the previous weeks, as Marion had struggled to pry information from Walter Edridge, she had wanted to wrap her fingers around the man's scrawny neck and squeeze words out of his small mouth.

"I'm sure the program will be a great success," Walter said. "Judith is a very smart lady."

Marion hoped he was right, but she had no faith in the judgement of a woman who would commit the members of the

Arts and Culture Centre to anything more complicated than a garage sale.

"She will have our full support," Walter added. As a retired solicitor he still used the oracular tone that once filled his clients with false confidence.

CHAPTER TWO: LATER SUNDAY AFTERNOON

While Walter was giving Marion the latest news, Stephen watched members of the committee taking down the unsold canvases and stacking them against the wall. He had done his duty through the afternoon, providing husbandly support and giving appropriately affirmative grunts to comments about the high standard of the art and the wonderful work of the centre, but as an outsider, he felt he could be excused their final, self-congratulatory gathering after the show.

Marion agreed. "Off you go," she said, giving his arm a friendly pat.

While she moved around the gallery collecting empty glasses, he slipped out of the building and took refuge in the car, where the radio would bring him up to date on the weekend's sport.

As he had watched his wife during the afternoon, he hoped her smile signified a genuine pleasure in the show's success, because he knew how hard she had worked in the weeks leading up to the event. But when he met other members of the committee, he wondered if she should have got herself so involved with this particular group.

And she seemed to have put the coordinator off side.

Was that why she intended to stay after the others had gone? Was she hoping to have a cosy chat with Rowena while the two of them washed up? He wondered if that was a good idea. From what he had seen of the coordinator this afternoon, she was in no mood for a friendly, female gossip with anyone from the committee.

Stephen was worried about his wife, because whatever she might pretend, he knew how much she missed Melbourne. Before his fall from grace, neither of them had expected him to be transferred from the Victorian head office to a regional branch of the bank.

"One of our best men," they had said, until that unexpected visit from the auditor. "How could a manager be so dumb?" they asked after an examination showed how much money had gone with the vanished member of staff. The accountant, who had worked in the bank for twenty years and had been a good friend of the Sheas, was now a wealthy man. He was living overseas, in a country that wouldn't send him back to an Australian court. "But the manager should have known," they said. Stephen Shea, no longer one of the brightest men in the bank, was an embarrassment, to be shuffled out of the way.

Stephen shivered. The sun had gone down and there was a chilly edge to the air. The temperature was not what he had expected from Queensland, but he had forgotten the effect of altitude. Ridgeway earned its name by straddling a ridge of the Great Dividing Range. To the east there was a steady drop to the subtropical coast; to the west, a dryer, colder hinterland plateau. The Sheas had been pleased to find the inland city was cooler than the lower, coastal land; they would have found most of the north of the state uncomfortably hot.

As he reached onto the backseat for his coat, Stephen watched a young family, complete with tricycle and dog, climb into their large van. After a day at the park, they were heading home.

"Downshifting," "tree change"—terms used to cover the plight of workers forced out of the race—might sound credible in some romantically picturesque little town, but they hardly applied to Ridgeway.

Most people who downsized to this inland city were retirees attracted by affordable houses and the facilities they would need as they aged. Stephen's face twisted, his career might be in eclipse, but neither he nor Marion was ready for Meals on Wheels.

He must have drifted off, because suddenly the sky had darkened to an inky black. The streetlights had come on, changing the scene, and making darker shadows of the trees. And there was only one other car.

At the front of the building, a rectangle of light appeared briefly as Marion opened the door and shut it behind her. As she crossed the parking lot, Stephen saw something move in the bushes that bordered the asphalt square. A possum? When the children were young, the family would have all piled out of the car and watched while Stephen flashed a torch into the undergrowth, trying to spot the little animal. They still kept a torch in the glove box. He shrugged. It was probably a cat.

Marion's footsteps faltered, then quickened. She must have heard the possum/cat scrabbling among the fallen leaves. Stephen reached over to open the passenger door.

"So much for that," she said, climbing into the car. "Her ladyship can manage by herself, thank you."

"Apparently no reconciliation over the hot suds," Stephen mused.

"I thought the show went rather well," he said, reaching for words to acknowledge the effort his wife had made.

"The artists were on cloud nine, and for the first time in years we made a profit." There was nothing wrong with the words, but the sharp tone showed her annoyance.

The weekend should have had people talking about the talented Mrs. Shea, who had created a successful event after the fiascos of previous years, but Stephen knew his wife had been stuck with the treasurer's job, handling sales, while Loretta Wheelwright played hostess.

"At least the crowd enjoyed themselves," she said.

Stephen switched on the headlights and was about to start the car when a small figure came around the building, heading for the old Mercedes on the other side of the lot. Loretta Wheelwright.

The old woman stumbled. A crash of glass on concrete and the jagged edge of a broken bottle glinted under a street light. The president had tripped on the gravel path and dropped the bag she was carrying under her coat.

Stephen opened the driver's door and started to get out of the car, but Marion pulled him back. "Leave it alone," she hissed. "Do you want to embarrass the old girl?"

He was grateful for her quick thinking. Because Loretta had no business carrying bottles out of the building.

Loretta might be president of the Ridgeway Arts and Culture Centre and widow of that well-known businessman, James Wilberforce Wheelwright, but over the years her income had dwindled.

She still drove her ancient Mercedes and, thanks to her committee business, the centre paid for her petrol. Marion had

18

already noticed how, after a function, bottles of wine mysteriously disappeared and suspected they found their way into Loretta's kitchen. Other members of the committee copied the first wise monkey and managed not to see the bulging paper bags that left the building with the president.

As the old woman recovered her balance, she looked around quickly, turned away from the mess, and walked briskly over to her car as if the puddle of wine and scattering of broken glass had nothing to do with her.

The Sheas waited until she had reversed her ancient Mercedes and pulled out of the parking lot before Stephen also drove away.

None of them knew that another pair of eyes had also watched the president's mishap. Another witness, hidden in the darker shadows of the trees, waited for the last car to leave and the coordinator's head to move away from the lighted window of the small office, before it moved carefully around the building and waited quietly beside the kitchen door.

Rowena McKendrick, standing at the office window, had an excellent view of the parking lot. She watched two sets of taillights swing in a half circle as the last cars moved into the street and gave a long, relieved sigh. She thought she would never get rid of the Shea woman, and the way the president fiddled around, the old girl might have been planning to stay all night.

Loretta Wheelwright was a regular pest. She stuck her pointy nose into everything and fixed her bright little eyes on the coordinator's face as she rabbited on about "the way we do things here."

Hypocritical old bag.

She acted as if she was Lady Muck, because her family once owned land, and she had married into the Wheelwright business. But when the Menkes' land was sold, it had barely covered the family's debts. And as for James Wheelwright, if half the stories Rowena heard were true, Loretta's husband should have gone to jail.

Rowena knew why Loretta was the last to leave. The president always waited until everybody else had gone before she pretended to tidy up and took the opportunity to stick a couple of bottles under her coat.

That Marion Shea was worse. Gushing over her after the show, wanting to do her girls together bit over the washing up. As if Rowena would ever forget the way she had behaved at that meeting. Marion had not said a word when she had asked for help in the office. Not that Rowena would be washing up tonight—she had other plans for the evening, and wouldn't the committee get a shock if they knew what she was going to do in their precious centre.

With Oliver Bostock.

She turned to her desk, stared helplessly at the pile of paperwork, and frowned at the cash box. Just another bloody job.

She left the office and went down the passage past the meeting rooms and looked into the big hall.

All the pictures had been taken down and those that had not been sold were stacked waiting to be collected by the disappointed artists. Before the exhibition, chairs had been taken off the floor and piled on the stage, where they were hidden by the curtain, which served as the backdrop for a brightly lettered banner. Tomorrow's working party would have to disassemble the moveable display panels and pack them away for another year. The willing, or conscripted, volunteers would set chairs in rows and turn the weekend's art gallery into a theatre for the drama group's production of *Macbeth*.

Rowena frowned at the ladder she had left leaning against a wall after that interfering old busybody, Loretta Wheelwright, insisted she take down one of the big pictures and help its new owner carry it out to her car. The ladder, and the box of tools beside it, could stay there for the night. Tomorrow's mob would have to deal with them. If anyone turned up. If they didn't, Wednesday's drama group could clean up the mess. Rowena McKendrick was no builder's labourer, whatever Loretta might think.

William's brother, Dennis, was producing the next play, and he would be furious if he had to spend rehearsal time clearing the stage. Too bad! If Dennis wanted the job done, he could jolly well do it himself.

The fuss he made about his blasted play, you'd think she had nothing better to do than organise bookings and chase costumes.

She deliberately turned her back on the hall and continued down the passage to the kitchen.

She put the kettle on. Oliver was going to be late. He had rung earlier to say he'd been called out. A car had broken down on the highway and he would have to tow it into town. "It's all good money, love," he had said. With so many listening ears she could not answer in kind. Even when they were alone, she was always careful not to ask what was most important to him, his garage, his wife, or herself.

His wife, Judith, Mrs. Oliver Bostock, secretary of the Arts and Culture Centre, was coming home next week. That would make things difficult for Oliver.

Rowena frowned as she selected a mug from the collection of crockery piled in the sink and washed it. She left the rest. It would be no use tomorrow's working party asking for help in the big hall. If she couldn't find anything to do in the office, she would be ostentatiously occupied with the washing up. She might even ask a couple of the lazy buggers to give her a hand.

At the other end of the kitchen there was a cosy little room known as the nook, which opened onto the backstage area behind the hall and served as a dressing room when the drama group staged its productions. At other times, members of the committee used the nook for their own, more intimate, celebrations.

Rowena giggled as she carried her drink into the nook. The committee would never know how often their coordinator and their secretary's husband used the little room. But the lovers were careful. Rowena never left her car in the regular lot. She always parked under the trees at the other side of the building, where it couldn't be seen from the street, and when Oliver came to see her at night, he walked across the park to the back door of the centre.

At least William didn't hang around. He was too embarrassed by her job.

"I don't mind you working," he had said, when she told him she had taken the position, "but I wish it wasn't at the Arts and Culture Centre." Because he was on the committee himself and most of the members were his personal friends. Stupid man. The only reason she got the job was because she was William McKendrick's wife, and what was the use of having friends if they couldn't do you some good?

She would be late home tonight, and if William complained, she could blame Benjamin Knowles. She'd say there was a lot of business to clear up and her husband would not press her for details.

It was a good thing Dennis had left earlier. She didn't like the way he sometimes looked at her, as if he could see inside her head and knew exactly what she did after the others had gone.

"I heard you coming home last night," he would say, giving her a nasty grin. "You must have been working very late." Unfortunately, the track to the old homestead passed under the windows of Dennis', cottage and the dogs always made a row when they heard her car.

Dennis would love to make trouble. He never had liked her and made it very clear he didn't think she was worthy of the great McKendrick name. But he needn't sneer. She was not taken in by his smarmy ways. He might be Mr. Charming at the centre, but if everything didn't go exactly as he wished—watch out for Mr. Thunder-Face.

It made her wild to see how he took advantage of her husband, his brother. She had noticed the way Dennis juggled the cars so William was always the one to fill the tanks. And whenever there was cash to be forked out, he waited for her husband to pick up the bill. Dennis even made William buy his lunch today. "Temporary cash-flow problem," he had said and laughed, as if sponging off her husband was a joke. William, the dumb ox, paid for the three of them.

But it was no good talking to William. "That's just Den's way," he said, when she complained about Dennis' snide remarks.

What would William think if he came back to the building tonight? She almost wished he would. Just so she could see his face when he found his wife snuggled up to her lover in his precious Arts and Culture Centre.

There was a faint scraping noise.

Was it a floorboard creaking?

She stared at the small window that reflected the light of the nook. It was well above head height, but anybody passing would see a light and know the room was occupied.

Would they guess she was in the building by herself?

Rowena shivered.

She reached to close the door of the nook.

She was too late.

Footsteps had moved into the kitchen. There was a hand against the door, holding it open.

She saw who it was and stretched her mouth to a smile. She muttered an inane greeting as she moved past her visitor into the kitchen.

Told herself she had nothing to fear.

Until she was pushed back into the nook.

And saw the hammer.

It smashed into her face.

The blow knocked her to the floor.

The hammer was raised again. And again. Crashed down. Bashing the head until it lost all shape.

A hand reached up to turn off the light, filling the little room with a darkness that hid the body on the floor and the puddle of blood around its head.

Footsteps retreated through the kitchen.

The door closed with a sharp click, followed by a louder thud as something smashed against the lock, and a dark figure slipped into the blackness of the trees.

CHAPTER THREE: MONDAY MORNING

When Marion lived in Melbourne she was always at work by half past eight, but here she was still in her dressing gown after nine o'clock. Stephen had left earlier, looking the successful banking man with his suit and laptop bag.

The table was littered with the remains of their breakfast: plates streaked with smears of egg and a cloth dotted with toast crumbs.

She had dawdled over her breakfast. Later, she would drive to the centre to help change the hall from art gallery to theatre, ready for the drama group on Wednesday night. But she was determined not to be the first to arrive. She had made that decision the previous afternoon when she heard Loretta respond to some request by telling the woman, "Mrs. Shea will see to it," and realised if she were not very careful she would find herself with a full-time job as an unpaid assistant to Loretta Wheelwright.

"That's what happens when you volunteer," Marion could hear her mother's caustic voice. After Vivian retired from her own, very successful, photography business, she had been shocked by the number of organisations that tried to enlist her services in a purely honorary capacity. "If I wanted to work, I would have kept my job," she said indignantly.

Marion's mother would never have fallen for Loretta's act. She would have recognised the type—a president who enjoys playing hostess at social events but manages to delegate all the less-glamorous jobs.

Marion collected the plates. As she packed the dishwasher, she remembered a documentary she had watched with her daughter, a nature show about a monkey troop. Loretta with her small, wrinkled face and grey, frizzled hair was like the alpha female. And what did that make Marion Shea—a subordinate ape?

But she was not sorry to be on the committee. It provided an easy answer to Stephen's inevitable morning question, "What are you doing today?"

And her activities at the centre provided a stream of funny stories to share with her husband each night. They could laugh about Loretta's more outrageous suggestions, the muddle of preparations, and the problems Marion faced getting anything done. It is not like running a show at home, she thought, but it was something she didn't say.

Home was still the house in Melbourne, and it was always a relief when Stephen left for work. She could drop her cheerful face and have a short, self-indulgent wallow of discontent. But she mustn't be a grizzle-pot, she told herself.

She headed for the bedroom, where she chose the sensible slacks and businesslike top she considered suitable for the stacking of panels and arranging of chairs she expected to occupy her morning.

They were lucky to have this place, she told herself firmly. The Margraves, newly retired, were touring the world, and thanks to the recommendation of a friend of a friend, they were willing to lease their unit to the Sheas. It was comfortable, conveniently close to the city centre, and Marion couldn't fault the owners' taste. But it was not her home.

And beyond the carefully landscaped complex, she still felt a stranger in the Ridgeway streets. She compared herself to the Wheelwrights and McKendricks, who had grown up in the town. Even poor Walter Edridge belonged here. When he took his place in the family law firm, Ridgeway wrapped its history around him like a snail's shell.

But the Ridgeway evoked by members of the Arts and Culture Centre was not the city of the present day. They still saw themselves as an important part of a large country town, and if suburbs spread over rural properties and shopping centres sprouted like mushrooms in areas they remembered as paddocks, they chose to ignore such unpleasantness. New people poured in, their children grew up, and businesses expanded to meet the needs of a bigger population. But life, for Loretta and her friends, revolved around their own small circle and they were happily oblivious of the change. When they said "that's the way we do things in Ridgeway," they meant "that's the way we did things forty years ago and that's the way they should be done."

So Marion saved the committee's funniest comments to share with Stephen and he capped her stories with tales about his weirder customers.

Poor Stephen. Stuck in the limbo of not-quite-disgrace. However much they pretended it was a routine transfer, his colleagues knew why he had been shunted interstate. In its own way, the banking world was as small and self-engrossed as any geographically isolated country town. The story of Stephen's misfortune must have travelled with his move, but he filled his new position with conscientious pride, and if he suspected whispers behind his back, he kept his fears to himself.

And she hid her homesickness. She was coming out of the shower when she heard a scratch at the back door and a scraping of claws against the screen as a ginger cat peered through the wire, hoping for breakfast. Poor beast. It was as rootless as herself. It had been dumped by some former neighbour and made its way here, to a complex where pets were strictly *verboten*. Marion splashed some milk into a small plastic dish, which she put out on the step. Stupid to feed the animal. They would have to leave it behind when they went home, she thought.

She switched on the computer to check her e-mail.

The highpoint of her day.

A message from her daughter, Barbara—a hasty, *Hi Mum. Everything's okay here. Pete's team won on Saturday.*

Barbara and Peter, both at university, were "minding" the Melbourne house and Marion had to contain herself when she e-mailed her reply—no rambling screen full of questions such as she had typed when they first made the move. Messages that made her cringe when she remembered them and had her thanking heaven she had clicked *delete* instead of *send*.

She never sent an e-mail until she had a chance to read it over, and anything she composed in the heat of the moment was kept till the next day. That was a discipline she learned from the gallery, dealing with prickly artists and buyers whose inflated egos should have sent them floating into outer space. "I don't know how you do it," Philip would say on his rare visits from New York. "I couldn't manage without you, Marion," would be his comment. Phillip valued her skill—not like this mob of amateurs who thought she should be honoured to work for them.

She had left her mobile charging overnight. Why did she bother? Who was going to ring?

The kids used e-mail.

"Call me anytime," she had said.

"You too, Mum."

But neither of them knew when the other was free, or rather Marion didn't know what the children would be doing and she kept up the fiction of her own busy life. E-mail was more convenient, and also, for Marion, more disciplined.

But maybe tonight Barbara would call and Marion would carefully school her voice to cheerfulness as she described her weekend.

How was her beloved garden? In her busy Melbourne life Marion always found time for her garden, and in the e-mails she did not allow herself to send, she could have asked about the health of every plant. But even on the phone, she would not pepper her daughter with questions.

She hoped the cats were all right. Stupid. One thing was certain. While Barbara was looking after the house, Doh-Ray and Fah-So would be overindulged and the magpies would get their ration of mince every day.

* * * *

Marion might have been planning to distance herself from the committee, but the best of intentions can be thwarted by forces beyond human control. The instrument of fate, this Monday morning, was Loretta Wheelwright, the very person whose casually overheard comment had inspired her resolution to spend less time at the centre.

As Marion closed her e-mail and opened the two-pack patience game, an American programmer labelled *Spider Solitaire*, Loretta's ancient Mercedes nosed into the centre's parking lot.

Over the weekend, battered vans, polished BMWs, and clapped-out Fords had squeezed beside huge four-wheel drives. This morning the president's car was the only one in the lot.

It was five minutes past the official opening time, but the absence of Rowena's Toyota didn't mean the coordinator was absent. Loretta knew she parked her car on the other side of the building, where it was hidden from the street. "I leave by the kitchen door after I've locked up," Rowena said when Loretta objected to the Toyota's wheels ploughing up the grass. "So it's easier to have my car there. And nobody has complained."

Nobody complained because the car couldn't be seen from the street, but if Rowena thought Loretta was ignorant of the way the coordinator amused herself of an evening, she underestimated the president.

An empty parking lot might not signal the coordinator's absence, but Loretta did not expect to find her in the office. Whatever else Rowena might do, she never came to work on time.

Nor was she surprised to find the door still locked. She had taken her own key out of her bag before she even tried the brass handle.

She was glad to have the office to herself.

Somehow, in all the excitement of preparing for the weekend show, she had not done anything about Judith's multicultural arts program. Of course it was the secretary's project and Judith would be back on Saturday, but there had been some embarrassing moments over the weekend when Walter Edridge told members about the government grant, and she had no answers for the inevitable questions about the committee's involvement with the refugees.

With so much else going on, it had been easy to change the conversation, but suppose she bumped into Patricia Menkes in the bakery or met Marion Shea at the fruit shop? Loretta's original belief, that Marion would be a useful member of the committee, was more than justified by the success of the art show, but sometimes the woman was too efficient. She expected the centre to be run like a business. Now they had the government funds, she would want to know how they intended to use the money, and as the secretary was not available, she would direct her questions to the president. And if Loretta couldn't tell her exactly what was going on, Marion would raise her carefully shaped eyebrows and wonder why they had committed themselves to such an ambitious project. So Loretta had decided to come into the office before the others arrived, read a copy of the original submission, and ring Benjamin Knowles at work to find out how much money the department had provided for the program.

She frowned at the mess of papers on the coordinator's desk. Ever curious, she rifled through the pile and saw an envelope from the bank. It was postmarked the previous Monday, but Rowena had not opened it. What was the matter with the woman? This letter should have been forwarded to Benjamin Knowles.

She tore the envelope open and was about to extract its contents when the phone rang.

"The Ridgeway Arts and Culture Centre, the president speaking." Loretta liked answering the office telephone and always gave the caller the benefit of her title.

"Raymond Gowd, from the bank." The manager's voice was unusually brusque. His questions were sharp and, to Loretta, totally incomprehensible. Cash transfer? Uncomfortably low balance? Problem meeting the monthly expenses? The coordinator's salary?

"I'll have to ask the treasurer." She choked down the words "I don't know."

She jammed the telephone under her chin and picked up the letter from the bank. A statement of their account that showed a negative balance. That was impossible. What had Benjamin told the committee at the last meeting? Their funds would cover ongoing costs, even if the organisation couldn't afford an extra member of staff.

She looked at figures and sat down, her legs suddenly weak. "I'll call you back," she said shakily, "I have to consult the treasurer."

She read the balance again. The figures had not changed.

Benjamin would be at work. Unlike the coordinator of the Arts and Culture Centre, the manager of the white goods department of a mega store had to be punctual. As a general rule, Benjamin discouraged the committee from calling him at work. Too bad. This business had to be cleared up. Loretta dug in the top drawer of the desk and found the list of committee phone numbers.

But Benjamin Knowles was not at the store. A woman answered the phone. She must have put the receiver on the counter because Loretta could hear her calling for "Ben—Ben Knowles!" The answer came from a younger, male voice. "He's taken a sick day."

The receiver was picked up and the message relayed as "not in the store."

Benjamin's coworker might have used the term "sick day" as a sarcastic alternative to "holiday," but Loretta took it literally. The treasurer must be ill. But she was determined to talk to him, even if it meant dragging him out of his sick bed.

* * * *

In a small, low-set brick house, in a street of similar dwellings, Diana Knowles answered the phone. No, Loretta could not speak to Ben.

"Why not?"

"He isn't here."

"Where is he?" Loretta demanded an answer. "Where is Benjamin?"

"In Brisbane. He had to go on Saturday. On business," she added, trying to end the conversation.

"What business?"

Diana ignored the question. She didn't share the old woman's belief that the president was entitled to know everything that happened in Ridgeway. But when Loretta pressed for more information, she found herself admitting that, yes, he had intended to come home on Saturday.

He had called on Saturday night. "I'm staying with Luke," he told her, "See you tomorrow." But he had not come home.

"Something came up," she said, trying to sound normal. "He is spending a couple of days with Luke, his brother. Family problems."

Loretta was not satisfied. "When will he be back? I need to talk to him."

Did she expect him to drop everything and come running because she wanted to speak to him? "Benjamin will ring you when he can," Diana said, putting the receiver down while Loretta was still talking.

Family problems usually meant elderly parents in trouble, and that had to be more important than some stupid committee affair. Diana was as angry as if her words had been true, and her husband was at his brother's house, the two of them struggling with a desperately ill father. As if Luke had not responded to her call last night with a bewildered ignorance.

* * * *

Loretta stared at the bank statement and wondered what to do. It was the treasurer's job to manage the finances, but Benjamin Knowles was not available. If Judith were home, she could handle Raymond Gowd, but Judith wouldn't be back till the end of week. Who else could she call? Which members of the committee would be available on a weekday morning and capable of dealing with this business?

Walter Edridge was retired and would be happy to come into town, but Loretta dismissed him at once, along with several other elderly members. William McKendrick? He would be a match for Gowd, but William had said he would be busy today. Something about a load of heifers. What about the most recent addition to their number, Marion Shea? Marion was a business woman. She'd know what to do. Loretta reached for the phone.

* * * *

Marion was moving the red queen, along with her son, to a new place under the king when the phone rang. She picked up the receiver.

"46 3 . . ."

"Marion?"

Loretta Wheelwright! Marion let the silence stretch. She should have checked the number before answering.

"Marion?" Questioning again. Did the president expect a more enthusiastic response?

31

"Yes?" Marion reached for the tone that, in her former life, she used to discourage importunate clients, the ones that never paid their bills. "Your voice would freeze the balls off a brass monkey," Philip had complained, but it stopped his behind-the-dateline habit of phoning in the middle of the night. Marion Shea, indispensable manager of a profitable gallery, could afford to set her own terms. If Philip didn't like it—tough. Marion Shea, undistinguished newcomer in a provincial city, also intended to set her own terms, which did not include dancing attendance on her majesty, Loretta Wheelwright.

"Marion, I'm at the centre. You have got to come. It's awful. Rowena isn't here."

Marion glanced at her watch. Nearly ten o'clock! When had Rowena ever been on time?

"I wanted to talk about the new project."

So you turned up, right on half past nine, to catch the coordinator coming in late, Marion thought.

"I'm sure you can manage, Loretta," Marion said firmly. "The work party's due at eleven." And I'm not going to be the first one there.

"Marion!" A screech of indignation. When the president commanded, her subjects should obey, but the newest addition to the committee was not impressed.

Then a small shaky voice, "Marion please—please come. It's awful. And I can't talk over the phone."

Loretta Wheelwright begging Marion Shea! Marion pictured the wrinkled, monkey face crumpling in distress and the bony, age-speckled hands shaking around the phone. She heard a sound like a small hiccup. "Please, Marion."

"I'm coming, Loretta," she said gently.

* * * *

As Marion walked across the parking lot, she noticed jagged edges of glass glinting in the sun. So Loretta didn't think it necessary to remove the evidence of her mishap. There were some things a Wheelwright does not do, and sweeping up pieces of a broken bottle is one of them. Fortunately for the Lorettas of this world, providence usually provides other hands to do the menial chores.

The front door was open. Marion went inside. What was the great emergency? Why couldn't it wait till the end of the week when Judith Bostock would be back? Or, if it was about money, why didn't Loretta ring the treasurer? Not that Benjamin Knowles would offer much support. Whenever there was a problem, he cited the importance of his own affairs and left "you girls" to sort it out. Marion objected to being "you girled" by a man younger than herself.

The office was a mess. Rowena's desk was littered with papers she had not bothered to file, and in the harsh morning light, Marion noted that the carpet was filthy. Somebody should ring the cleaners, she thought. Last week she might have put it on her own to-do list, but today she decided that somebody else could take responsibility for the condition of the building. If Loretta wanted the carpet cleaned, she could use the phone herself or push Rowena into making a call.

The old woman was bent over the desk, her hands twitching as they stirred the clutter of papers into even greater disorder.

"I've had a phone call from the bank!"

As she gave a garbled account of the manager's words she waved the balance sheet in Marion's face. "It doesn't make sense."

What was it Walter Edridge said yesterday? "Gowd was quite put out . . . Knowles moved the funds . . ." Did that explain the manager's call? Marion settled herself behind the desk, noting, as she did so, that the coordinator's swivel chair was the only decent piece of furniture in the office. The desk had been marked by years of service and the filing cabinet was a paint-chipped, wooden dinosaur, a relic from an earlier time when the centre was run from a small timber cottage on the other side of the park. At the end of her second week, Rowena had complained about her back and demanded a proper office chair.

Marion read the balance sheet several times, but the figures didn't change. There were no funds to cover the organisation's ongoing expenses.

"It's just not possible. Ray must have made a mistake," Loretta insisted.

"Ray" must be Raymond Gowd from the bank, Marion thought, but she didn't think his figures were wrong.

She knew roughly how much they should have in the account. The finances of the organisation were simple. Membership fees and revenue generated by hiring the hall and meeting rooms should cover the usual expenses. The annual art show, run by an enthusiastic gang of volunteers, was a thirty-year tradition that once provided a small, but steady, increase of capital that could be used for building renovation or other special projects. Over the last few years, money from the art show barely covered the cost of putting it on, but the regular performances of the music and drama groups should have made up for this. And there was a yearly grant from the Ridgeway Council.

According to the statement, a series of inexplicable withdrawals had taken all the capital, leaving them with a large deficit.

What about the government grant? Judith Bostock's program. Where was that money?

Even without the grant, when Benjamin Knowles presented the financial statement at the Annual General Meeting, it showed a good balance. That meeting had been held a few days before the secretary left on her trip, and Benjamin had responded to Judith's pointed questions by flourishing the auditor's report.

"We are right for another year," he had said, rattling off a list of figures and sweeping the papers into his folder.

Marian looked at the statement again.

"What about the money we took from the show?"

Loretta brightened. Of course, the weekend's takings had not been included in the statement. She pulled out the bottom desk drawer. No cash box. For once, Rowena had done the right thing and gone to the night deposit on her way home. "The bank will have that money now," she said. As if the centre's percentage of the weekend's takings would solve the problem, Marion thought crossly. "What does Benjamin say?" she asked. "And why isn't he here, to sort out the mess?"

"I haven't spoken to Benjamin," Loretta explained. "Because he wasn't at work. And of course I rang him at home, but he wasn't there either. Diana said he went to Brisbane on Saturday; something about the business."

Business. What business could he have in Brisbane over the weekend, Marion wondered. And why didn't he come home on Saturday night? Money was missing from their account and Benjamin Knowles, the treasurer, had left town. She stared at Loretta, but the old woman shook her head, refusing to see the connection.

"Nothing like this has ever happened to us," Loretta said. "Not in my thirty years as president." Then, suddenly helpless, "Marion, dear, what are we going to do?"

"I'll talk to the bank myself," Marion said firmly.

She checked the number for the First Queensland— making sure she got the local branch.

A timid female voice answered the phone. Mr. Gowd was not available. Marion insisted, using a tone that, in another life, had suppliers sending their consignments on time and customers paying their outstanding bills. Raymond Gowd came to the phone, but he wouldn't discuss the problem with Marion Shea. He would only talk to a member of the committee whose signature was filed with the bank: the secretary, Judith Bostock, the elusive treasurer, Benjamin Knowles, or the president.

Marion reluctantly handed the phone to Loretta, who opened the conversation with a rambling account of the weekend's show that included a canvas-by-canvas description of the pictures they had sold. She followed this with Judith Bostock's European itinerary, as a preliminary to informing the manager that their secretary would be home at the end of the week. After ten minutes, Gowd reconsidered his position, and when Marion took the phone from Loretta, he was happy to talk to her.

But however succinctly Marion tried to summarise the committee's position, it was a complicated problem and he suggested she come to the bank with Mr. Knowles, so they could clear things up. She chose not to explain that the treasurer was unavailable.

It was as well for the women's peace of mind that they left by the front door and didn't know what was lying, undiscovered, in the small back room.

CHAPTER FOUR: MONDAY MORNING

Marion didn't like going into a bank. Not anymore. She imagined the lowliest clerk in the most isolated branch had heard about Stephen. A manager so blind to the depredations of his accountant that it took a team of auditors to discover the crime. And now Shea's wife was involved in another financial mess!

Thank God the centre didn't use her husband's bank. The manager's name on the door, brass against varnished wood, was *J. R. Gowd*, not *Stephen Shea*.

J. R. Gowd was a large, square man, with floppy jowls that quivered when he moved his head. At home, in casual clothes, he might be a large teddy bear, at a party, that hostess' delight, a happy extrovert, but at work he crouched over his desk like a bad-tempered toad. Loretta greeted him as Ray, asked about his health, and tried to introduce him to Marion. He answered her brusquely and waved the women to chairs set, with mathematical precision, in front of his desk.

Loretta took the seat directly facing the manager, her proper place as president, but J. R. Gowd turned his head to stare at Marion.

"You have a regular monthly withdrawal," he said, "for Rowena McKendrick."

"Our coordinator's salary," Loretta explained, forcing his attention back to her. This was a question for the president. "We arranged to have Mrs. McKendrick's salary transferred directly into her account."

"You haven't got the funds to cover it." The Gowd jowls shook and hard blue eyes stared at the old woman, demanding explanation and apology.

Marion was pleased to see Loretta straighten her back. The president refused to be intimidated. No doubt she considered herself a match for any bank manager. "You must have cleared our government funds by now," she said sharply, her tone warning him not to try his tricks on her. "You've had the money for over a week."

Marion's own hands were clammy, and her mouth was suddenly dry. What had Walter Edridge said on Sunday afternoon? "The treasurer moved the money . . ." and Benjamin Knowles had business in Brisbane.

The manager's voice was cold. "We don't have those funds. Your treasurer explained your decision to transfer the grant to a different financial institution so the program money would not be confused with your other finances. We could have set up a separate account." He made no attempt to hide his resentment.

Marion didn't blame him. It might be a good idea to open a new account for the special project, but why had the treasurer used a different bank? She could think of one very good reason. Please God let me be wrong.

Loretta, no longer President-In-Charge-Of-Everything, shook her head "I don't know anything about that."

"I'll check with the treasurer," Marion said. "I assume you have some record of the transaction?"

"There would be the usual forms signed," the manager reminded them, "by two members of the committee."

There were several files on the manager's desk. He opened one and pulled out an official-looking document. He handed it to Marion, obviously promoting her to spokesperson.

She scanned the page quickly and passed it to Loretta, pointing to the signature.

"But I never saw this," Loretta protested. "I don't do the business stuff, that's for the secretary and treasurer . . ."

How did they manage while Judith was away? Marion wondered.

"Isn't that your name?" J. R. Gowd took the paper out of her hand and slammed it onto the desk.

"But that's not how I write," she stared at Gowd, daring him to contradict her. The manager twisted his mouth into an unpleasant grin. She might have been some stranger off the street asking for an unsecured loan.

Marion had another look at the document. The scrawl under a frighteningly large number bore no resemblance to Loretta's lovely sloping hand.

Gowd fiddled with his keyboard and figures marched across the computer screen. Marion wouldn't twist her neck to read them. Instead, she pulled a copy of the statement out of her bag. There had been huge outgoings every month.

"Of course you always check the signatures?" Brown eyes can never be as cold as blue but Marion did her best with the face she was born with, raising her chin and forcing her mouth into what she hoped was a hard line.

"Perhaps I should speak to your—ah—treasurer," a pause not lost on Marion, who spoke firmly to drown Loretta's burbling response.

"Benjamin Knowles is not available today. You have the executive's signatures on file, we would like to see them." She leaned back, dropped her hands onto her lap and willed Loretta to silence. Nothing was going to be discussed until this arrogant creature got off his big backside and produced the specimen signatures.

A few words on the phone brought a girl with the required card.

"Bettina, dear," Loretta gushed at the familiar face. "How are you enjoying your new job?"

The manager scowled and Bettina-dear's cheeks flushed as she looked at the floor. "Your mother didn't tell me you were working in the bank," Loretta chatted to the girl, who mumbled a reply and, at a nod from her boss, scuttled away.

Gowd studied the card, cleared his throat, and picked up the transfer authorisation with its version of the president's signature. He put it down and read the card again. Loretta and Marion waited.

"This is most irregular," he said, and blinked several times before managing something not quite as intimidating as his original glare.

Yes, the funds had been dwindling for some months. Yes, the bank had written to the treasurer but not, Marian noticed, to their regular box number. When there was no reply, somebody eventually found the correct address.

Marion straightened her back as J. R. Gowd stared at her, ignoring Loretta's hysterical insistence that the statement could not possibly be right. He had obviously decided the old woman could not be trusted to buy a loaf of bread without help and saw no reason to hide his opinion.

Two could play the accusation game. Marion took the statement and ran a finger down the page, pausing at each withdrawal.

Gowd still glared at her.

She forced herself to meet the manager's eyes, daring him to deny his bank's responsibility.

He did not. He did, however, need time "to gather all the paperwork."

"I'll ring you later today," Marion said. "To arrange our next meeting." She spoke firmly, determined to show it was Marion Shea, not J. R. Gowd who would set the agenda for that meeting.

* * * *

Marion drove back to the centre with Loretta huddled on the seat beside her. The old woman was shivering, and her red-daubed cheeks stood out, garish circles of colour on her white face.

What had she said on Friday night, when she welcomed visitors to the art show? "In the thirty years that I've been president . . ." Loretta had been the public presence of the Arts and Culture Centre for so long she was as much part of the landscape as the old town hall. Nobody would dream of replacing her, but while she regarded herself as the titular head of the organisation, Marion knew she depended on the other members of the executive committee to handle the actual business of running the centre. In her eyes, Judith had committed an act of desertion by dropping her secretarial duties and going to Greece.

Loretta had been badly shaken by the events of the morning. At some point in the interview she must have recognised the full significance of the situation. Her beloved centre was in trouble, and with the secretary in Greece and the treasurer unavailable, she would have to deal with it.

Marion had watched her growing horror as she acknowledged each fresh revelation of Benjamin's perfidy and had admired the effort she had made to hold herself together in front of J. R. Gowd.

But once she was in the safety of the car, the façade crumbled.

The old woman looked ill as she sank into the seat and Marion searched for a topic to get her mind off the problem. With a carefully chosen comment, she launched into the president's favourite subject—the inadequacies of Rowena McKendrick. The diversionary tactic worked, Loretta stopped shaking and there was a healthy colour around her rouge-reddened cheek as she talked about Rowena's unpunctuality, her notorious inefficiency, and, the juiciest conversational titbit, rumours of scandal.

"She sees too much of Oliver Bostock."

There was a notice propped up by the side of the road—black words on yellow. ROADWORK AHEAD.

When a guardian of the road, grand in his orange jacket, waved his sign, Marion stopped the car to let a large truck rumble past in the single, open lane. It was followed by a line of smaller vehicles.

The notice turned from STOP to SLOW and Marion inched forward, manoeuvring around men, machines, and wooden barriers.

There was another enforced wait as a huge earthmover dragged itself across the single lane. An impatient horn behind them broke the thread of Loretta's reminiscences, and the president was jerked back to the day's anxiety.

"We've got to go back to the centre," she said. She must be thinking of the work party, Marion decided, but the president was still brooding over the interview. She listed members of the committee and used her fingers to mark off the names. "Patricia Menkes," Loretta said with a touch of her old acerbity, "She won't be much help . . .Walter Edridge," her tone softened, "We'll need his legal mind. . ." Any committee depending on Walter's mind—legal or otherwise—was in big trouble, but perhaps, Marion thought mischievously, he and J. R. Gowd deserved each other. "And there is William. William is such a staunch committee man." Loretta took obvious comfort from the staunchness of William McKendrick and Marion could understand her feeling. There were stormy waters ahead, and they would need his steady hand.

William, with his sun-weathered face and deep, slow voice would not rush into action. He would give the problem thoughtful consideration and weigh the facts with the same care he weighed out feed for his stock.

Marion used William's name to divert Loretta with a question about the McKendricks. The old woman was happy to talk about the family.

"William has always been good looking, but the younger boy, Dennis, he's the handsome one. James always said he should have been in films." James Wheelwright found his way into most of the president's conversation and the committee were often given the benefit of his opinion. Marion wondered what the redoubtable James would have to say about their present situation. As far as Dennis McKendrick was concerned, the man had a point. Not many people would consider somebody in his late thirties a boy, but Dennis was handsome enough to please a Hollywood director.

He was active in the drama group. In their last production, the Sheas had seen him throw himself into the character of a pirate chief, and Marion thought the role suited him. Even out of his costume at the party afterward, he looked like the buccaneer hero of an old-fashioned adventure film. His blond hair had a natural wave, and she marvelled at the way his skin kept its gloss in spite of the ravages of the Queensland sun.

There was no doubt that Dennis was the star of the group, and had he been willing to leave Ridgeway, he might have had a stage career. But his soul was with the land. At the party, while the rest of the cast were reliving the evening's triumph, he had grabbed Marion, a fresh audience, to talk about the family property. "Our great grandfather moved into the district when all of this," he waved a hand to include the centre, the park beside the building, and the street in front of it, "was swamp."

"Don't you wish the old man had taken his acreage here?" Karen Francis pushed herself into the conversation. Karen was the Ridgeway community development officer and the council's representative on the committee. In the following weeks Marion would see her cast herself as a modern woman of business, but that evening she was the besotted admirer of the pirate chief. And no newcomer was going to monopolise her hero.

Unfortunately for Karen, in her effort to get Dennis' attention, she had spoken thoughtlessly, and the scowl that marred her hero's face would have terrified a pirate crew. Marion was amused to see how strongly he resented the suggestion that any piece of land was better than his family's property. He launched into a description of the wonderful views from their old house and the magnificent soil—perfect for raising their high-quality cattle.

Marion thought of that conversation while Loretta chattered happily about the McKendricks and the earthmover rolled cumbersomely across the single lane, to settle its huge treads on the gravel shoulder.

"We were worried about William when Agnes walked out," she said, as Marion manoeuvred around the machine. "He had always been the quiet one. Agnes organised their social life and without her pushing him, he hardly ever left the property."

"Wasn't he involved with the centre?"

"He was on the committee. Agnes had been the treasurer, but she resigned. She thought it would be embarrassing to have them both at the meetings, and she wanted William to stay with us. As she said to me, it was his only outside interest, and he had to go to the drama group parties." Loretta paused, as if wondering whether to say more, and evidently decided Marion, as a member of committee, was "one of us" and could be trusted with their darker secrets. "He had to be there for his brother. Dennis is a good lad, but sometimes, if he has too much to drink." She paused, as if trying to find the least-offensive description. "He can be difficult. And, of course, he should not drink and drive, so William has to take him home. That's how William met Rowena—at a drama group party. None of us knew her very well, and we were pleased to see him marry again." Was Loretta suggesting that, had they known Rowena better, they would have been less happy about William's choice of wife?

What a pity they had not recognised her shortcomings before appointing her to a position for which she was so obviously unfit.

A more competent coordinator might have noticed something wrong with the bank account. Marion refrained from voicing this thought, and the president burbled on happily.

What was it Stephen had said, when she decided to accept Loretta's invitation to join the committee? "You'll get to know people. Make contacts."

Contacts! A lot of old fogies—a president who could barely sit through meetings without nodding off, an absent secretary, and a treasurer who never bothered to come to the office and treated questions with a condescending brusqueness, which, she realised now, should have raised their suspicions. What a god-awful muddle. If Benjamin had absconded with the grant money they were in big trouble. And none of the other members would be much use.

Marion inched forward to pass the END OF ROADWORK sign and then pressed her foot down as if, by returning to the centre, she was not committing herself to even more involvement with the muddling committee.

* * * *

While Marion and Loretta were facing J. R. Gowd at the bank, an angry work party stood outside the Arts and Culture Centre, waiting for the coordinator to arrive with a key to open the door.

"Isn't Rowena supposed to start at nine-thirty?" Karen Francis raised her arm, so everybody could see her looking at her watch. She had used her position as the council's representative to take a morning away from juggling statistics. She would be happy to spend a few hours packing up pictures and arranging chairs if Denis McKendrick was running the work party, but Dennis had not arrived and she vented her disappointment by complaining about the coordinator.

A tune sounded from her bag. Even before she pulled out her phone she knew who was calling. Dennis. Something had come up. "I can't get away," he said. "You'll have to cope with the mob." Damn the man. He took it for granted she would leave everything else to get the hall ready for his drama group. Which was exactly what she had done, she thought bitterly.

"It's not much use, us hanging around." That was Shane Furnell. As if he had anything better to do with the day. Shane claimed to work odd hours in some undefined artistic field. Odd as in nonexistent, Karen thought. No employer would want to add Shane's unkempt ponytail and straggly beard to his workforce. She scowled at him and moved quickly to the back of the group, determined to prevent them from scattering. "Rowena won't be long."

"The president should be here to open the door." Marion would have been amused to hear Patricia Menkes take the opportunity to blame Loretta for their problem.

"The two of them are worse than alley cats," she had said to Stephen after her first committee meeting. "And neither is much use when there is work to do." She had caught the asperity of her own voice and added a carefully indulgent laugh.

Nor would she have been surprised to see some members of the work party taking the coordinator's absence as an excuse to change their plans.

Like recalcitrant cows determined to lead the herd astray, Shane and Patricia headed for the parking lot. A few of the others joined them.

Karen foiled the incipient rebellion as, working like a well-trained cattle dog, she moved in front of the group, blocking their path. She knew if they managed to get away, none of the truants would come back and, on Wednesday night, the drama group would have to clear the hall. And Dennis would be furious

Walter Edridge supported her effort. "There are pictures to be collected today," he insisted.

Karen was glad of his help and reminded the group of the trouble, two years ago, when a purchased painting was sent to the wrong address.

"Dreadful affair. Dreadful." Walter shuddered at the memory.

For once Karen didn't object to his fussing, as he fixed Shane with an awful glare and laid a bony hand on his arm. There were times, she decided, when silly old Walter was exactly what the group needed

* * * *

45

In spite of bank managers, earthmoving machines, and three consecutive red lights, Marion and Loretta eventually arrived, to be met by the accusing eyes of the work party.

"Rowena must have decided to take the day off," Patricia Menkes said, making it clear she held the president personally responsible for the coordinator's misdeeds.

Loretta didn't respond to her cousin-in-law's barb.

She fumbled in her bag for the key.

Marion took it out of her hand and, ignoring questions and complaints, opened the door.

As the mob moved into the building, Karen continued her cattle dog act. She herded her party into the big hall and set them to work dismantling the panels. Once she had everybody organised, she joined Marion and Loretta in the office.

"You're going to have to do something about Rowena McKendrick," Karen said, settling herself into the coordinator's chair. Marion was reminded of J. R. Gowd as the council's representative glared at them across the desk. What was it about an official position that turned ordinary people into bullying robots? "She must have decided to take the day off," Karen repeated the accusation Patricia Menkes had voiced earlier. "Thanks to her, we've wasted half the morning. And you know how much we have to do, to get the hall ready for Wednesday night."

Loretta might be intimidated by J. R. Gowd at the bank, but in the office she was very much the president. She moved purposefully towards the desk. For a horrible moment, Marion thought she would try to physically remove the council's representative from what she obviously saw as the official seat, but either she recognised the impossibility of tackling a fit young woman or, more probably, decided that such behaviour was below the dignity of a Wheelwright. Instead, she turned her back and would have left the office if Marion had not been standing in her way.

Marion pulled up the remaining chair and presented it with a flourish that acknowledged the importance of the president. Loretta accepted the seat with a gracious nod.

"We have a bigger problem than a slack coordinator," Marion said, kicking the door shut with her foot. "We've just been to the bank."

Her words brought Loretta back to the realities of the morning and the emptied account. The imperious president changed before their eyes into a frightened old woman. She slumped in her chair and looked helplessly at Marion.

Marion responded with a reassuring smile for the president followed by a frown that silenced Karen's complaints. This was no bumbling amateur to be patronised by the council's representative, but an experienced manager who had been negotiating, bluffing, and bullying her way through meetings while Karen was still at school.

She reduced the explanation to a few succinct words, cutting through Loretta's burble to show Karen the bank statement. Karen checked the figures with a bookkeeper's eye.

"Couldn't you see something was wrong?" she asked.

What did she mean by "you"? Marion thought. Damn it, the woman was a member of the committee. She had been to meetings with the rest of them.

Marion stood up, reached into the filing cabinet, and pulled out the notes from the last Annual General Meeting, including the treasurer's report. Karen snatched them out of her hand and shuffled through the papers as if the catastrophe had vested her, as the council's representative, with an extra authority. "What about the auditors?"

Sheffield and Dunn had not found anything wrong with the books, but Marion was not surprised when she saw the almost undecipherable signature at the bottom of their statement. The words might be W. N. Dunn, but the writing looked horribly like the scrawl the bank had accepted as Loretta's name. It appeared that the auditor's report was a product of Benjamin Knowles' fantasy.

Karen, like Loretta earlier, hunted through drawers, looking for the cash box. And like Loretta, she was relieved by its absence.

"At least Rowena banked the weekend's money," she said. "That will be in our account."

Why would Rowena take the whole cash box?

47

They could have been characters in a very bad play, mouthing their predictable lines. Marion wished she could walk out, but she was trapped on the stage with the rest of the cast.

"Judith is coming home on Saturday," Loretta reminded them. "Benjamin must know she'll check the account."

Judith Bostock, the secretary who had taken off to Greece, leaving her husband to his assignations with Rowena McKendrick and the committee at the mercy of its treasurer!

"If Judith knew something was wrong with the financial report, wouldn't she have spoken before she went away?" Marion objected to Loretta's reasoning.

Karen shook her head. "Judith didn't *know* anything, but she was always complaining about the way things were done. She thought the financial records were a mess—and so did I," she added virtuously.

"What a pity you didn't share your ideas," Marion said.

The door opened and a head poked into the office. "Who's taken the hammer?" Walter asked.

Karen grunted a reply as she hunted through files.

"We need the hammer."

"Rowena might have used it in the kitchen or the nook." Marion couldn't imagine the coordinator filling her evening with carpentry, but her suggestion served its purpose and the head disappeared.

"What about the grant money?" Karen asked as Walter scuttled off to hunt for the essential tool.

"That has gone," Marion said. She gave them the gist of Walter's conversation with J. R. Gowd but vetoed Loretta's suggestion they ask him to join them, to discuss the encounter.

Karen supported the decision. "There's no need to broadcast your problem," she said, "until you know exactly what Knowles has done."

A series of thumps across the passage told them the working party was getting on with the work. All the panels would be packed away, the stage cleared, and chairs set in their proper rows in time for the rehearsal on Wednesday night. Patricia's voice could be heard directing the activity as, in Karen's absence, she appointed herself the group's captain.

A scream came from the back of the building. "God! Oh my God!"

Walter Edridge. What was wrong with the man? Marion thought irritably.

She made her way down the passage. Members of the work party spilled out of the gallery, but she elbowed them aside and pushed into the kitchen.

The first thing she saw was Walter leaning against the wall. White faced.

Jostled by people behind her, Marion was pushed past him, and saw what was in the nook.

A bundle of clothes on the floor.

Rowena McKendrick! In her green mermaid dress. Splotched with brown. Her head . . .

CHAPTER FIVE: MONDAY MORNING

Marion's stomach heaved. She clamped her jaws together, swallowing bile.

She backed out of the little room, reached to close the door, and then pulled her hand down. She found herself thinking, "Don't touch anything."

She dropped to the kitchen floor and sat, leaning against the wall. Walter sat beside her. He didn't speak, but Marion clung to the idea of another creature. Breathing. Alive.

This isn't true, she told herself. It can't be true. Rowena went home last night. After the exhibition. She didn't stay behind. She is not a corpse, spread out on the floor. She is not, Marion repeated the mantra in her mind. She couldn't scream. The sound that should have shrilled in her ears was stuck in her throat.

She was horribly aware of her own body. Chest tight. Arms dragging like lumps of lead—fingers suddenly cold.

Somebody gave her a glass of water. She wet her lips and then gulped it thirstily.

People crowded into the passage. Voices shrill. Asking each other what was happening. Telling each other to wait for the police. Not to touch anything. Somebody said Rowena's name. It was repeated, mouth to mouth, like the cawing of crows over a roadkill.

"For God's sake ring the police." Shane Furnell called down the passage, not leaving his station by the kitchen door.

Marion stood up shakily and tottered out of the kitchen. Walter moved with her and, in an unusual display of good sense, shut the door behind them.

She pushed against the bodies, ignoring questions, and staggered down the passage into the office. She dropped onto a chair.

"Police," she whispered shakily.

"They're coming," Karen said.

She must have called from the office, with Loretta listening. The old lady was moaning softly, her hands pressed against her mouth in an effort to stifle the noise.

How efficient of Karen to ring the police, Marion thought. But Karen didn't look efficient. She had rubbed her eyes, smearing mascara down her cheeks, and clenched her fists so tightly the knuckles were livid white lumps.

Sirens.

Cars.

Police.

Marion lost track of time.

Men in suits and women in dark slacks moved down the passage with firm, determined tread. They were followed by more police in uniform.

Marion knew what was happening in the small back room. She had watched forensic teams at work—on TV. There would be cameras, measurements, body suits. But this was real. Rowena McKendrick. She had been in the office yesterday, talking to Marion, and now she was dead. Oh, God. It couldn't be true.

The police had shuffled most of the work party into the big hall. A young woman, looking comfortingly efficient in her uniform, helped Loretta out of the office and into a small meeting room. Karen and Marion went with her.

Marion stared at the window. Police cars were followed by an ambulance. It should have been here last night. It might have saved Rowena's life.

More vehicles drove through the parking lot, turned around the corner of the building, and stopped by the kitchen door.

There were thumps and voices in the next room as the police established themselves. Beyond that, in the office, Marion could hear the scrape of filing cabinet drawers being opened and closed. What were they looking for? she wondered.

There were more noises, footsteps, and bumps coming from the kitchen and from the nook, but she tried to block them out.

Somebody shut the kitchen door again, mercifully muting the sound, but it was impossible not to know what was happening. They were taking Rowena away.

Loretta was still shaking when one of the young constables came in. He looked very large standing in the doorway, a reassuring bulwark against all the awful activity. He held a glass in his hand. "This might help Mrs. Wheelwright," he said.

More water. In time of trouble, when there's nothing else, they offer you water, Marian thought bitterly. She put one arm around Loretta's shoulder and held the glass to her lips. The old woman took a few sips, nodded her thanks, and tried to stand up.

"We'll have to tell William," she said. "We'll have to go out to the McKendrick's place."

Please God! Don't let her ask me to drive her!

"William McKendrick," Marion answered the constable's question. "Rowena—the murdered woman," she choked over the words, "William is her husband."

"We have to tell William," Loretta said again. Her face was white around her roughed cheeks, but she knew what was expected of her as a Wheelwright and William McKendrick's friend.

The young policeman patted her arm.

"Better let us do that, Mrs. Wheelwright. We'll send one of our people. They'll know what to say." And, as Loretta tried to protest, "They've had training."

What kind of training would help you share that news, Marion wondered. Once, in her teenage years, she had thought of joining the police. Thank God she chose a different path.

"Are you up to answering questions?" The constable asked Loretta. She nodded, stood up, and tottered out, leaning heavily on the young man's arm.

After a very short while, he brought the old woman back to her friends. "We won't keep you much longer," he promised them. "Could you," he nodded to Marion, "talk to our sergeant?" Even in her shocked state, Marion recognised the politely phrased request as an official command.

She followed the constable into the room next door, which the police had chosen for their interviews. A sergeant, nearly as large as the young constable, was settled behind a small table. He gave Marion a name that slid straight out of her mind. In the following days, when she was questioned by detectives, more intimidating in their plainclothes than these uniformed men, she struggled to remember the details of that first interview.

"When did you last see Mrs. McKendrick?"

Marion had a sudden picture of green material, dark patches, and Rowena's bloody face. She started to shake. She gripped her wrist, pressed her nails into the flesh of her arm, and willed herself to speak slowly, describing the events of the previous afternoon.

She told him about her trip to the kitchen with the coffee cups.

"You didn't stay very long?"

Had the sergeant seen the state of the kitchen? Was he voicing a criticism of the committee that had gone home, leaving their poor, overworked coordinator to clean up by herself?

"I offered to help, but Rowena—Mrs. McKendrick—told me to leave the washing up. It was quite late," she added, "and some of us were coming back today."

If he noticed the weak self-justification, he chose to ignore it. "Was there anybody else in the building when you left?"

She said she didn't think so.

How did she recognise the victim? Marion heard herself describing Rowena's mermaid dress.

After the sergeant had finished with her, it was Karen's turn to talk to the police.

The door was open and Marion and Loretta could hear a rumble of voices from the big hall and heavy footsteps moving down the passage.

Karen didn't come back to the meeting room but joined the crowd in the hall. To Marion's surprise, the constable returned. His sergeant wanted to see her again.

He asked her about Benjamin Knowles and the trouble at the bank.

Marion tried to keep her answers brief. Yes, there was a problem with the bank statement and she had gone to First Queensland with the president to get it sorted out. The officer wrote down her response.

After the detectives were finished with her, Marion went back to Loretta and responded to the old woman's question with a shrugged, "Nothing much."

There was a noise under their feet as men scrabbled beneath the building, looking for—who knew what? Marion expected to see the boards erupt and a head to appear, followed by a dirt-stained uniform, but when the constable came into the room, he used the door.

"We found a blanket under the building," he told them. "It looks like somebody has been sleeping rough. Do you know anything about it?"

"It must belong to that horrible boy," Loretta said. "You know, Marion, the one who is always hanging around the parking lot asking for money."

Marion had seen the youth several times, but she had always quickened her stride to avoid his begging pitch.

"He might have been looking for cash," the constable said. Money from the art show that had not been banked. The cash box that had disappeared. Words tumbled out of Marion's mouth in her eagerness to describe this theft. She wanted to give the police the information that must clear Benjamin Knowles— at least of the murder.

Loretta also found relief in a torrent of words. She talked about drunkards, druggies, and layabouts, and repeated every story she had seen on her old TV.

After the constable left with his prize, Marion and Loretta were sent to join the others in the big hall. It looked strange in its half-dismantled state. All the panels had been taken down and were stacked against the back wall, waiting to be packed away for another year. Members of the working party had dragged some chairs off the stage and were sitting uncomfortably under the stolid stare of a uniformed constable. Marion had a sudden urge to leap in front of him, yelling something totally outrageous in an effort to force some expression onto his face. She resisted the impulse.

Please, God, don't let William come here, she prayed.

CHAPTER SIX: MONDAY AFTERNOON

Detective Senior Sergeant Thomas Erbacher and Detective Constable Gregory Shaw were driving to the McKendrick property.

Shaw wondered why.

Usually the unpleasant duty of telling the family about a death would fall to a uniformed constable—probably female. But to the younger man's surprise Erbacher had decided to talk to Mr McKendrick himself. "It's a rotten business," the senior man said, climbing into an unmarked car.

Shaw grunted agreement. He was new to criminal investigation, but during his time in uniform he had seen the aftermath of other, equally horrible crimes.

The woman's husband had to be informed as soon as possible, but he wondered why a senior sergeant was taking time out of the investigation to make the journey himself.

"I want to talk to William McKendrick," Erbacher explained as Shaw manoeuvred around the collection of official vehicles and into the street. "Have a look at the man and see how he reacts to his wife's death."

Shaw knew how often members of the supposedly grieving family were responsible for murder, but surely this one was easily explained. "Some druggie broke into the building," he said. "The woman disturbed him and he bashed her." Shaw shuddered, thinking of his own young wife.

"Are you sure it was a bungled robbery?"

"What else? We saw the back door and the broken lock. Young thugs looking for money. For drugs," The younger man continued. "He thought he was breaking into an empty building, and when the woman came into the room, he bashed her."

It could have been a private house. His house. Some night when he was working. And Janey was home by herself. He clenched his jaw and glared at the grey surface of the road.

That was a nightmare they all shared. Members of the force saw too much of Ridgeway's darker side. Too much alcohol. Too many drugs. Too many bashings. Killings. No policeman could trust the illusion of orderly suburbs or believe that, whatever happened in the lurid pages of the local newspaper, his own family was safe.

Rowena McKendrick had been unlucky, in the wrong place at the wrong time. Somebody wanted money and she was in their way.

"There was blood on the outside surface of the door," Erbacher said.

Shaw was puzzled. "I didn't see any blood."

"You wouldn't, it was only a speck. But I was looking at the lock. Where there shouldn't have been any blood at all."

"The fellow must have touched the door as he left."

"No. It was in the splintered wood. The killer used something heavy to bash Mrs. McKendrick, and it looks as if he used the same instrument to smash the lock. And the blood means it was done after she was killed."

Shaw was silent as he considered the implications of that discovery. What would forensics learn from a tiny sample of the victim's blood? Would there be fingerprints at the scene?

"Unless the killer wore gloves," Erbacher said.

If the killer had worn gloves, that would quash any theory of an unpremeditated murder by a drug-crazed intruder looking for cash.

They turned off the road onto a narrow, dirt track that wound between paddocks, green from the spring rain. Although they were barely thirty minutes from the centre of the city, they were already driving through farmland.

Shaw had grown up in Ridgeway. He had seen streets spread across pasture and shopping centres sprout on newly flattened land.

Originally the town had been the business centre for the surrounding properties, but over the last three decades the population had trebled as industrial development changed the nature of the inland city. The McKendricks were a remnant of the older time, when Ridgeway was a prosperous country town.

Before they left, Erbacher had taken the number of William McKendrick's mobile phone, and as they approached the property he punched it in. Shaw listened to the carefully chosen words and steeled himself for the interview ahead.

Erbacher had not given a reason for his visit, and there was no further conversation. So McKendrick had not asked why the police wanted to talk to him. Wasn't that a little odd?

Shaw opened his mouth to comment and closed it again.

Erbacher's grim face didn't encourage conversation. He might want to see how the woman's husband reacted to the news of her death, but he must be dreading the encounter. Talking to the victim's family was always the worst part of their job.

The detectives were first to reach the meeting place and they waited, in silence, for the dead woman's husband.

A battered truck pulled up and a solid man in work-stained clothes climbed out to open the gate. William McKendrick. He waved to the officers as they drove through. They didn't wave back, but after they had stopped, climbed out of the car, and introduced themselves, McKendrick glanced at their identification and waited for them to explain their business.

An elderly heeler nosed the strangers' legs and William spoke to it sharply. The dog backed away.

"Can we go up to the house?" Erbacher asked. Another man might have pestered them with questions, but William motioned his dog into the truck and climbed in after it.

He led the way, stopped to open another gate, and after driving through, waited to close it again behind the detectives.

Car and truck pulled up behind the old McKendrick house, and William led them across a patch of rough grass to the back door. It opened into the big kitchen where earlier generations of McKendrick women had cooked huge meals for the working men.

Erbacher gave him the grim news.

In words that seemed to hang in the air.

William stared at the officers. His face like stone.

"Dead? Rowena. No!"

He stood up, turning to an interior door, as if, Shaw thought, he could turn the statement into a lie by producing his wife.

Erbacher stopped him with a quiet word.

He sat down.

His head moved, in nodding answer to their questions. Yes, his wife did work in Ridgeway, at the Arts and Culture Centre. Yes, she was there last night.

The head was still. William sat, blank faced, staring at the floor.

After a few minutes Erbacher spoke again, quietly repeating the words. "Your wife was killed last night, in a back room of the building. She was bashed to death."

William stared at the old wood stove, and Shaw glanced from it to it to the modern gas oven that Rowena McKendrick would never use again. Her husband rubbed his eyes. Did he think the officers would disappear if he could shut them out of sight?

Shaw wished they could disappear.

"Did your wife stay in town last night?" He heard his own voice harshly dissonant in the quiet room.

William shook his head. "I thought she had come home. Late. After I had gone to bed."

So they slept in separate rooms, Shaw noted.

"You know about the art show?" The detectives nodded. "My wife had to stay back, after it was over, to tidy up. My day starts with the sun, so I don't wait up when she's working late and she tries not to disturb me when she comes in."

"And today?" Erbacher asked.

"Sometimes she sleeps in. It was a hard weekend." And, as if he thought more explanation was needed, "I didn't see her this morning."

The man had not even put his head around his wife's door for a quick good morning. Shaw couldn't imagine coming home late and going to sleep in a separate room without even looking at Janey. Or leaving for an early shift without giving her a quick kiss.

"Did Mrs. McKendrick often work at night, by herself in the building?" Erbacher asked.

William shook his head, nodded, and shook it again. As if their words made no sense.

"She can't be dead." he said it again.

Erbacher repeated the question.

"No. Yes. When there were things she wanted to clear up."

"Did Mrs. McKendrick have enemies?"

"Of course not. A few small problems at work, with the committee, nothing serious"

Erbacher continued questioning.

"Any unpleasantness in town? Stalking?"

"No."

"Had she ever received any threats?"

"She never mentioned them."

There was nothing more to say and the detectives left.

* * * *

"Funny set up there, with separate rooms," Shaw remarked, as he turned the car onto the track that twisted past a small cottage that predated the big house. A pair of worn dungarees had been pegged on a rope stretched between two trees. Somebody still lived there.

Erbacher disagreed. "The McKendricks might not be the district's most devoted pair, but I've been around long enough to know that marriage can take many forms. Separate rooms, separate towns, I've even heard of families where one of the couple lived overseas."

He climbed out to open the gate and closed it carefully behind the car.

As Erbacher settled back into the passenger seat, Shaw considered the older man's words. His own first child would be starting school next year and he thought himself an old hand at the marriage game, but beside his senior sergeant's years of wedlock, he was little more than a bridegroom.

"McKendrick couldn't even tell us if his wife came home last night," he persisted, determined to get a reaction from his superior. "Although he did seem badly affected by his wife's death—if it wasn't all an act."

He had been in the force too long to believe a long face and broken sentences always showed a genuine grief.

Erbacher grunted, and Shaw had to concentrate on driving as they turned onto the road and found themselves behind a large caravan that slowed on every rise and swerved dangerously around the bends.

"Bloody tourists," he muttered, dropping to an almost walking pace. Then, as they reached a passing lane, pressing his foot down to speed around the swaying van.

After they raced ahead of the lumbering obstruction, he returned to the subject. "I wouldn't mind a look at McKendrick's clothes."

"I guess not," Erbacher said dryly.

Shaw noted the tone and wished he had kept the last comment to himself.

If the break-in had been staged to cover a murder, the husband was an obvious suspect, but, of course, they had no right to search the place. Not yet. And not without a warrant.

Did Erbacher wish he had an older, more-experienced partner sitting beside him?

* * * *

When they got back to the station, the medical examiner was waiting to discuss the case. Henry Jamieson was a small, wiry man who had worked with the police for a number of years, and Erbacher respected his opinion.

More than he does mine, Shaw thought ruefully.

"It's my impression the woman was killed by the first blow," Jamieson said,

"So, the killer was a male?"

"Not necessarily. The attacker wouldn't have to be particularly strong. It could have been a woman, if the weapon was something heavy, like a hammer. We'll know more tomorrow after the postmortem."

Shaw shuddered. During his time as a uniformed officer, he had seen a lot of death, but this was the first time that as a member of the CIB, he was one of the team investigating a murder.

Had the killer come back to the centre because he (or she) knew the coordinator would be alone in the building, or was he after something else? Shards of broken china in the small back room suggested Rowena had made herself a drink. The forensic team would fit the shards together, but as Shaw visualised the scene, he was sure they would only find enough pieces to make one mug.

He had an image of Janey, as she had been that morning, in her blue dressing gown, laughing as she cut her son's toast into four carefully equal triangles.

He made a fist under the table as he forced his attention back to the discussion.

"Grudge killing?" Jamieson was asking. "How did the murderer get in?"

"He probably had a key." Erbacher said. "As far as I can make out, the committee passed them around like lollies at a kids' party."

Shaw groaned. He would be given the job of tracking down those keys. If that were possible. But nobody seemed to know how many there were. As the president had explained, "Most of the groups meet at night and the facilitators are supposed to come in during the day, but that isn't always convenient, so we let them keep a key."

"The killer must have used the front door," Shaw said, but Erbacher shook his head. "Would you believe they use the same key in all the locks? Because it makes things easier."

"They're a funny mob," Shaw said, and Erbacher, rifling through pages of interviews, did not disagree.

CHAPTER SEVEN: MONDAY EVENING

Stephen called a cheerful greeting as he opened the front door. There was no welcoming response. No light in the hall. Where was Marion?

He knew she had been planning to go to the centre, but the coordinator always locked the door on the stroke of five, and even while she was organising the art show, Marion never stayed in the building by herself. In Melbourne he often came home to an empty house. Marion frequently worked late, just as he did himself. But this was Ridgeway, where he kept more regular hours, and when he came home, his wife was always waiting to greet him. With this new routine, they were able to have a glass of wine before their meal, as people must have done in an earlier, more leisurely time.

There was no light in the sitting room.

A flick of the switch showed his wife.

Curled in a chair.

Shivering.

God! Something was wrong. The kids?

He reached out, pulling her into his arms. Holding her.

"Rowena. Rowena McKendrick. She's dead!" The words came between hiccupping sobs. "B-bashed to d-death."

He was shamed by his own relief that it was not his family but after the first, guilty reaction, he shared her horror as she told the story in short, disjointed sentences. Rowena. Murdered. Last night. At the centre.

"We shouldn't have left her there, by herself."

"If you had stayed you might have been killed too," Stephen said, clamping his jaw against the words. He held his wife in his arms as she buried her face in his shoulder, her body shaking with the sobs.

After the storm had passed, he poured Marion a brandy and, perching on an arm of the chair, held one of her cold hands.

"The police asked me about Benjamin Knowles," she said, "because of the money."

"Money?"

Marion told him about the letter from the bank and the interview with J. R. Gowd that had been overshadowed by the awfulness of finding a body.

"Benjamin wasn't around on Sunday night," Stephen reminded her. "Remember the fuss Rowena made, because she had to go to the night deposit box."

Marion gave a chuckle that ended in another hiccupping sob. She blinked back a tear and went on with her story.

"Somebody smashed the door, but the police kept asking about the keys—as if they thought the killer had let himself in."

"They have to ask their questions, Mari-love," Stephen said quietly.

He recognised a shadow from the previous year, when he was the one the police were questioning. The afternoon he had come home shaken and sick to the stomach, and struggled to describe his shattered world.

"I had no idea," he had said, and today, almost a year later, talking about Benjamin Knowles, he heard his wife using the same words. "We had no idea . . ."

Antonio had gambled with the bank's money—he had juggled withdrawals from customers' accounts until he could no longer cover his tracks. Was that what Benjamin Knowles had done—borrowed money from the centre's account, believing he could pay it back after one big win?

A year ago Marion knew nothing about embezzlement and had bombarded him with questions. So much money had been taken, and over so many months, how could Antonio get away with it?

By exercising his detailed knowledge of the system, Stephen had answered, so that even the auditors had trouble unravelling the complicated procedures he used to transfer funds.

The accountant had hidden his crime with clever bookkeeping, but Benjamin had not been nearly as smart. If anyone had looked into the centre's finances, they would have known something was wrong. But who would check a treasurer's accounts? Certainly not a committee of volunteers. Weren't they all friends together, working for the community?

"Perhaps Rowena got curious," Stephen suggested. "She might have looked at a bank statement."

"And he hit her over the head to shut her up?" Marion shuddered "But Benjamin hadn't been near the centre on Sunday. He was away from Ridgeway all weekend. And this morning, when Loretta rang his wife, he had not come home."

Stephen could see she was clinging to that thought. If the treasurer had been away the whole weekend, he could not have gone to the centre on Sunday night. He might be a thief, but not a murderer.

"He must have been milking the funds for ages—before I joined the committee," she said, answering Stephen's carefully phrased questions with the added reassurance that "I'm not on the executive committee."

"Why did you go to the bank?" Stephen asked.

"Because Loretta needed my support. She was in the office when he phoned, that horrible Gowd from the bank. She didn't know what to do, so she called me. Somebody had to talk to the awful man."

As a banker, Stephen had some sympathy for a manager who had to sort out the financial mess. An expert would examine the signatures more thoroughly, but he accepted Marion's judgement, that Loretta was not responsible for the scrawled names.

Another question the police had asked them all, did they know what the coordinator was doing in the building, after everybody else had gone home?

"Loretta said Rowena had stayed behind, to clean up after the show," Marion said.

Stephen shook his head. For weeks he had listened to his wife's complaints that the woman wouldn't do anything that was not specifically included in her job description. She even refused to look at the bank statements, saying, loudly, that they were the treasurer's responsibility.

"Rowena wasn't one for extra work." Marion put her hand over her mouth, as if to choke back an opinion often expressed, but now so horribly inappropriate. "I don't know why she was still at the centre. I only knew it was her because—because of the green dress."

Last night Stephen had laughed at the metaphor, mermaid or sea cow. This evening he pictured the green dress, a puddle of blood, and a face his wife could not recognise.

* * * *

Detective Senior Sergeant Erbacher might refer to members of the Arts and Culture Centre as a "funny mob," and Marion's attitude veered between sympathy and annoyance, but neither an Erbacher nor a Shea could anticipate Loretta Wheelwright's response to the tragedy.

After she had talked to the police, she had huddled in a corner of the hall. She was so obviously unfit to handle a car that the sergeant wanted to have her driven home. The offer was met with an indignant refusal. She had her Mercedes, thank you very much. All she needed was a little time.

But she couldn't stop shivering.

A young policewoman approached her most respectfully. Perhaps she had not heard the sergeant's offer because she was surprised to find Loretta still in the building and expressed her indignation at this official neglect.

"They should have arranged to drive you home," she said, and when the suggestion was expressed in those terms, Loretta decided that, as president, she was entitled to some consideration after her horrible experience.

She allowed herself to be helped into the police car.

Even in her shocked state, Loretta would have enjoyed racing through the streets at crime-chasing speed with all the importance of siren and lights, but the constable drove cautiously through the afternoon traffic.

The girl had not been happy about leaving her. "Are you sure you'll be all right, Mrs. Wheelwright? Is there someone who could stay with you?"

In response to the young policewoman's concern, Loretta had promised to phone her cousin, who lived just down the street. There was no need to tell this sweet lass that Patricia Menkes had been with them at the centre that morning and was probably having hysterics with her own family. No way would Loretta call on her!

There was nobody she wanted to talk to. Except James.

She picked up her husband's photo and sat gently stroking his face. What would he think of her, leaving their Mercedes in the parking lot? James had loved that car, but, after such a dreadful day, he would have wanted the constable to drive her home. "Better safe than sorry, Lottie-girl," he would have said.

Safe in her own sitting room, she began to feel more like herself, the Loretta Wheelwright who had gone to the centre this morning, expecting to read a copy of Judith Bostock's submission to the department and to spend a few happy hours bossing the work party.

She tried to make sense of the day.

Rowena McKendrick was dead.

"She was bashed to death." Loretta said the words aloud, as if that would make them more believable.

And that trouble with the bank.

She gripped the photo in a shaking hand. James would have dealt with the horrible Gowd. No bank manager would sneer at him.

And all those questions the sergeant asked, James could have answered them.

He would have sent police about their proper business, catching the killer. And he would have stopped that stupid Karen Francis from talking about Benjamin Knowles and the money that had disappeared. As if the police were interested in their finances.

They wanted to know about the treasurer, Loretta thought. A nasty little fear niggled its way into her mind. It was easily silenced. He had been in Brisbane all weekend. Karen shouldn't have told them about the money.

And there was something else they didn't need to know.

When the sergeant asked why Rowena was still in the building, Loretta told him she had stayed behind to clean up after the art show. There was no reason to mention the woman's relationship with Oliver Bostock—that had nothing to do with her death.

But she knew the police had Oliver's name on their list of people who had been at the show on Sunday afternoon, and he might be interviewed.

Suppose he had not heard about Rowena's death? The news would come as a dreadful shock and when the police spoke to him, who knew what he might blurt out? What unnecessary information he might give them.

What would James do about Oliver?

You have to talk to him, Lottie girl, she thought. That's what James would have said, and he would have added his favourite piece of advice, "You have to manage the world or it will manage you."

Oliver Bostock had been good to her. He worked for hours on her old car and never took a cent for his trouble. Now it was her turn to do something for him.

Loretta picked up the phone and called the Bostock garage. But when Oliver answered she started to cry. Somehow, between the sobs, she got the story out.

"Somebody must have broken into the building. They took the cash box." She paused to collect herself, and chose her next words carefully. "It happened after we had all gone home. Rowena stayed behind to tidy up."

She did not refer directly to Oliver's relationship with Rowena, but she hoped he would hear the warning behind her words, that he must be careful when he talked to the police. He should show only an appropriate grief for the loss of a friend and fellow member of the drama group. And it did not matter why Rowena was still at the centre. It was the coordinator's job to clean up after the show, and as far as the police were concerned that's what she was doing when she was bashed to death.

They all knew who killed Rowena—that horrible creature who hung around the cars. Begging. He had broken into the building looking for money, and when Rowena disturbed him, he bashed her.

After making the call, Loretta sipped a cup of cocoa to settle her nerves.

But she was still restless.

She was worried about that business with the bank and furious with Karen for telling the sergeant about their small problem. Suppose the policeman got the wrong idea and thought the missing money had something to do with Rowena's murder? What would happen to Benjamin Knowles?

It would be better if he stayed out of sight for a couple of days, until the killer was caught.

She picked up the phone again. "Diana?"

The voice on the end of the line mumbled a reluctant affirmative.

Loretta could hear the hostility in Diana's voice, but she ignored it. The woman had always been a frightened mouse. Tonight she was an angry mouse, which was, Loretta decided, a slight improvement on her usual state.

"No. Benjamin has not come home. He is still with his brother."

"Good!" The word was out before Loretta realised how plainly she had signalled her relief. "When do you expect him back?"

"I don't know. He wasn't here when I came home from work."

Loretta snorted. Husbands should not simply disappear. And if they did, a wife should choose her words more carefully.

"What is his brother's number? I must speak to Benjamin."

"The number? I can't—it's unlisted."

Such a stupid lie. What kind of fool did Diana think she was?

"I have to speak to Benjamin," Loretta repeated, struggling to stop herself shouting into the phone. "Rowena McKendrick is dead. They found her this morning. Bashed to death. At the centre. So you have to get in touch with your husband. At once. No matter where he is," she added in case "the brother" was a fantasy.

"But why do I have to ring him tonight?" Diana asked. At least she didn't repeat the "silent number" excuse. "Ben's got enough to worry him."

Loretta brushed that argument aside and repeated her demand. Diana had to tell her husband about the murder. She *must* ring him tonight.

"The police were asking about the committee. Where we all were on Sunday night. They will want to talk to the treasurer. You must tell him about Rowena's death," she said again, trying to phrase a warning without explaining her concern. "As he was not here on Sunday night, it might be better if he stayed away, attending to his 'family business,'" she enjoyed repeating the stupid excuse.

More protests. Diana could not understand what Loretta was talking about. Why did she have to talk to Benjamin tonight? Why shouldn't he come home?

Loretta closed her eyes. She didn't bother to respond to Diana's questions, ignored her excuses, and filled every pause with a demand that the woman ring her husband *tonight*. She would not finish the call until she got a whispered promise that, yes, Diana would talk to Benjamin.

That was all Loretta could do. If Diana knew where her husband was hiding, she would pass on the news. And if Benjamin had any sense at all, he would hear the warning behind the president's words. She had done what she could to keep the centre's affairs, as James would say, *in house*.

* * * *

Oliver Bostock stared at the phone. But he had no desire to make a call. The only person he wanted to ring would never talk to him again.

"She must have stayed behind to *tidy up*," Loretta had said.

He recognised the warning in her voice. She knew Rowena had been waiting for him. His mouth stretched in a bitter grin. Who else had guessed about the two of them? But surely even Loretta must realise that, after Rowena's death, nothing could be hidden from the police.

Murder. They would want to know everything about the victim. Victim. Rowena. What a horrible way to think of her. She'd always been so full of life. He wanted to remember her as she had been on Sunday afternoon, giggling when he promised to come back after the others had gone. He tried to picture her face, the sparkle of her eyes, and the way she shook her hair, but another image intruded. Rowena lying all night on the floor. Bloody. Bashed. And dead.

He really did love her, he thought, surprise edging through his misery. Neither of them believed the affair would last—he had already sensed a cooling off—but her death made a jagged hole in his life.

Loretta must have guessed the reason Rowena parked her car so carefully out of sight. What about the rest of the committee? And William McKendrick, how much did he know? William had a husband's right to grieve. He could sit behind closed blinds and turn day into night. He could cry aloud, wracking sobs from deep in his chest. Oliver could only show a friend's concern.

* * * *

Marion tossed all night, tangled in sweat-soaked sheets. Questions tumbled around her brain.

Rowena McKendrick had been bashed to death. After Marion left her in the building by herself. If Marion had stayed, would Rowena still be alive? Or would the killer have murdered them both?

She drifted into sleep and was in the kitchen again, staring over the monstrous barrier of Walter Edridge's back. There was a crowd of people behind her, pushing her into the room. A puddle of blood on the floor, as dark as spilled coffee, and Rowena wrapped in a green dress with her face smashed in.

CHAPTER EIGHT: MONDAY MORNING

In Brisbane, Nadine Tyson turned her small car into the yard after a hard night on the ward.

Her flat was one of four in a dilapidated block, and the only good thing about working nights was that her partying neighbours didn't keep her awake. Like them, she slept through the day. And by the end of her shift she was usually too exhausted to be disturbed by their drums, no matter what time they were played. Although she was the only tenant who owned a car, Nadine always parked at the end of the drive to leave room for visiting vehicles. This morning she edged past just such a visiting car that had been left on the patch of grass in front of her door.

The driver had known the time of her shift and had been careful not to block the drive. Last night, as she backed out, she'd been pleased by that small thoughtfulness, but this morning she frowned at the car. Why was Benjamin Knowles still here?

She opened her door to the unedifying sight of her unwelcome guest sprawled on the couch. His mouth was open, and there was an empty whisky bottle beside him on the floor.

"Why the fuck are you still here?" she asked.

The sleeper opened his eyes, grunted, and closed them again.

"I said you could stay for a couple of hours. To have a nap before driving back to Ridgeway."

She had been getting changed for work when he stumbled in, smelling of sweat and stale cigarettes, with the same story he had told, repeatedly, when he lived with her.

He wanted money. He needed the cash for one last, lifesaving bet that would clean out the bank. If she gave him a couple of hundred, she would get it back, with 300 percent interest.

Once she would have believed him. And money that should have paid their bills would be lost at the casino. She hoped his wife was less gullible.

"Christ, I'm exhausted," he had said when he saw that none of his promises would open her purse. "I can't drive back to Ridgeway like this. I'd write myself off." And he had collapsed on the settee.

He would not leave her flat without an argument and she was already running late for work, so she told him he could stay for a couple of hours before driving home.

And here he was, drunk, and still not fit to drive. And he had finished her whisky.

"I don't know what I ever saw in you," she said, loudly enough to rouse him again.

He looked up at her, like a dog caught messing the bed. "I can't go home."

"You certainly can't stay here."

She was too tired to fight. She left him and shuffled into the bedroom. The only thing she wanted to do was crawl under her doona and grab a few hours sleep. Perhaps, when she woke up, he would be gone.

A few steps into the room she stopped. Nothing was quite as she'd left it. Other hands had opened her cupboard, moved her clothes, and hunted through the undies in her drawer.

Benjamin Knowles.

He must have remembered where she hid her money when they were living together, and he'd gone through her clothes looking for cash.

She sat on the edge of her bed. Trembling. She was so angry that she struggled for breath as she remembered the bitter fights they used to have, the reason she wanted him out of her life.

When Benjamin wanted to gamble, nothing was sacred.

God help his poor wife.

"Damn you to hell," she screamed, storming into the sitting room and hauling him up by a handful of hair. "Get out."

"I can't go home."

Why not, Nadine wondered. Had Diane kicked him out? She loosened her grip on his hair, and he flopped back onto the couch, rubbing his head. She hoped it hurt.

Could she let him stay to sober up? No way. He'd still be here when she left for work . . . and when she came home.

If she were ten-feet tall and weighed a ton, she could pick him up and throw him into the street. If she had a policeman's whistle and a uniform, she could arrest him. If . . . if . . .

She went into the kitchen, took a plate from the cupboard, and broke one egg into the frying pan. She switched on the electric jug and took one mug from the shelf.

Benjamin dragged himself off the couch and followed her. He stood in the doorway like a hungry dog.

"Bugger you!" She set out another plate, added a second egg to the pan and spooned coffee powder into an extra cup. She started two slices of toast.

"Sugar?"

He nodded.

"Milk?" She poured without waiting for his reply, but the questions had served their purpose. They showed him he was no longer a part of her life. It had turned him into a visiting stranger.

He took a cup of coffee and sat down. "I really can't go home, Nadine."

She scraped the eggs onto the plates and pushed one of them in front of him as she listened, with a sinking heart, to the story of his catastrophe. Money *borrowed* from the account of some community organisation, small amounts at first, and the final large abstraction. "Judith Bostock, the secretary, has been away, in Greece, and she's coming home on Saturday. Before she left, she was asking about our account. I didn't know what to do. But when we got the government money, I saw my chance . . . I knew I could win if I had a decent stake . . ." In one disastrous session he had lost it all.

The expression "burning bridges" came to her. For an army, that wasn't only a desperate act of no return, but also the beginning of an invasion. How did people on the other side of the river feel when they saw the bridge blazing behind conquering troops?

But if Nadine thought of Benjamin Knowles as an army, he was casting himself as the victim of a malignant fate. "I knew I had to win. I've got this system, see. If I have enough cash, there's no way I can lose." He leaned forward, carried away with his story. "One more bet would have put me in the clear."

How often had she heard that?

She was tempted—God how she was tempted—to empty her purse just to get rid of him. But he would lose the money and come back for more, she thought.

What about his brother? Luke was a decent man who didn't deserve to have Benjamin dumped on him—but she couldn't have the fellow hanging around her home.

"Come on!" She yanked his arm to pull him up, but he dropped back onto the chair.

"I can't go to Luke."

"No?"

"And I'm not fit to drive." He produced this final objection with the satisfaction of a child forcing a concession from an unwilling adult. Nadine reminded herself that he was not a child, he knew exactly what he was doing and she was not . . . not . . . not going to have him spend another night in her flat.

"I'll drive your car," she said. She was achingly tired, and if she drove Benjamin's car, she would have to get an expensive taxi home, but at least she would be rid of the man.

She barely gave him time to finish his egg before grabbing his keys, bundling him into the passenger seat of his own car, and taking the wheel herself.

When they reached his brother's house, Nadine jumped out of the driver's seat and was half a block away before he had wriggled out of his seatbelt.

The shops were only a short walk down the hill. If there were no taxis on the rank, she would use her mobile phone. At this time of the day she knew both Luke and Brianna would be at work, and she wanted to be safely away before Ben realised they were not home. She had to cross the highway, and as she waited for the lights, she turned to see him leaning disconsolately against the car.

He was probably calling her a selfish bitch. Too bad.

She didn't care what Benjamin thought, but she felt bad about landing Luke and Brianna with the problem. Even if the stupid man was Luke's brother.

* * * *

75

As Brianna slammed into the driveway, she didn't recognise the car parked in front of the house.

She'd had a rotten day. A travel agent's nightmare of clients changing their bookings at the last minute, compounded by problems with the computer. She glanced at her watch. Time for a cup of tea and a rest before Luke got home.

Then she saw her brother-in-law sitting on the back step with his elbows on his knees and his head in his hands.

As she approached, he stood up. "I've been waiting for hours," he said plaintively, as she unlocked the back door.

"You might as well come in."

He followed her into the kitchen, whining about his bad luck." All I needed was a little cash. If I had the money, I would have cleaned up." She turned her back, but he went on talking. "I'd been going so well. I could have cleared my debts." Debts. Gambling. And as usual, he had lost the lot.

Two hours later Luke was equally annoyed to find Benjamin settled at the kitchen table.

His wife dragged him out of the room, and if he thought the provision of food meant she was reconciled to Benjamin's presence, she promptly disillusioned him.

"I had to feed the bugger," she hissed. "He must have been sitting in the yard all day. He looks like a bloody corpse. He spent last night at Nadine Tyson's place, and says he was too drunk to drive home this morning. He's sober enough now, and he's bloody well not staying here."

During his career with Industrial Coolant, Luke had attended a number of seminars, and the secret of selling, he had been told, is to assume the customer has already made up his mind and you're only there to finalise the sale. This was the strategy, he decided, to get Benjamin out of the house.

He marched into the kitchen and sat at the table opposite his brother, waiting for him to finish his meal. As soon as the plate was empty, he stood up, a signal for Benjamin to do the same.

"You had better be off, if you want to get home at a decent hour," he said. "Give my love to Diana."

His brother didn't move.

Luke sighed and sat down again. There would be no immediate departure. Whatever business Benjamin had in Brisbane, he was in no hurry to leave. Luke was not surprised. If Brianna had the story right, his brother had spent most of the day camped on their doorstep, instead of sobering himself up and driving home.

"I can't go back to Ridgeway." Benjamin's skinny fingers fiddled with the napkin. He crumpled it into a ball and squeezed it tightly in his fist.

"It's the money."

Luke listened to the sorry tale, though after the first few words he could guess the rest. His brother had borrowed money from some society's account.

"I thought I was finished in July. At the general meeting. Nobody challenged my report. Then there was a government grant."

"You stole that as well?"

Of course he did. Money, so easily to hand, gave him a chance to redeem his previous loss. All his problems would be solved. After one successful trip to the tables.

But he had lost the lot.

And the secretary was coming home. On Saturday.

"When Judith goes to the bank, she'll find the money's gone. And Rowena, the coordinator, will be the first to dob me in. She hates me." No doubt, in an effort to cover his tracks, Benjamin had bullied the paid staff. "I can't go home."

"You bloody well can't stay here. And you'd better phone your wife. Let her know that you're still alive."

Benjamin picked up the receiver and stared at his hand as if he had never seen it before. Luke grabbed the phone, punched in the numbers, and waited until Diana was on the line before he handed the phone to his brother.

There was a short silence. Perhaps Benjamin hoped Diana would hang up. "Diana?" he turned his wife's name into a question. It was enough to get a response. Words tumbled down the line interspersed by gasps, grunts, and groans from Benjamin.

Something was dreadfully wrong. It sounded worse than his brother's usual disasters and Luke wanted the full story, not whatever version Ben thought would rouse his sympathy. He took the phone firmly out of his brother's hand.

"Diana!"

There was a gulping sob at the other end.

Luke waited until she had composed herself. At last, between hiccups she passed on Loretta's news.

Rowena McKendrick had been bashed to death. And Benjamin must not come home. "Loretta thinks he's in trouble. She wanted to talk to him this morning, and when I said he was not here, she was furious. Tonight she rang again. But this time, she was glad he wasn't at home. She says he can't come back." More sobbing.

Luke made a sympathetic noise, and the sobs subsided to sniffles.

"When did the woman die?"

"Sunday night. Benjamin wasn't even in Ridgeway," Diana wailed. "But Loretta says the police are after him, so he can't come back. Not till they've found the killer."

Who was this Loretta person and how did she fit into the story? Luke wondered. He finished the call, ignoring his brother's frantic efforts to take the phone.

"The woman's insane," Brianna said, when he repeated Diana's words.

Luke agreed. "Ben can't just disappear. He'll have to go to the police, before they pick him up."

"I can't." Benjamin's voice rose to a shriek. "You don't understand. It's the money." He buried his head in his hands.

"For Christ's sake, man," Luke heard himself shouting, and lowered his voice. "This is murder we're talking about, not fiddling with the petty cash. Do you want to face a murder charge?"

"I didn't kill anyone."

"Nobody's saying you did. Not yet. But what else will they think if you take off? You've got to go to the police."

"But clean yourself up first," Brianna added. "In case you're stopped on the road. You look like an escaped convict."

An hour later, Luke had his brother, shaved, showered, and in fresh clothes, on his way home.

CHAPTER NINE: TUESDAY MORNING

On Tuesday morning Loretta was awake before the sun. Her night had been menaced by a formless threat that, as sleep left her, took the shape of violent death and a menacing Ray Gowd.

"You have to manage the world," James always said, "or it will manage you." Loretta never doubted the wisdom of his words, and because she was determined not to give way to fears unworthy of a Wheelwright (nee Menkes), she switched on her bedside lamp and began to plan her day.

As she leant against a pile of pillows, with her notebook and gold pen, she could have been a society hostess in some bygone age, organising the affairs of a large manor house. The only thing the picture needed was a pretty maid in a starched cap to bring the lady of the house a cup of tea.

In the absence of a maid, Loretta had to make her own breakfast. She pulled on a fluffy pink dressing gown and pattered into the kitchen, where she boiled a kettle and put two slices of bread into the toaster. When everything was ready she arranged a tray and carried it back to the bedroom.

She ate slowly, but as she nibbled the last of her toast, a glance at her bedside clock told her it would be hours before Karen Francis, the chosen recipient of her first phone call, would be at work. She used the intervening time to make a list.

Loretta was famous for her lists. There had been a time when committee hearts sank if they saw their president burrowing into her bag for the inevitable pad. In the privacy of her bedroom she still ordered her world with careful, copperplate notes, but nowadays she usually lost the paper afterwards.

Eventually, the clock's hands reached an hour when any council employee should be at work and she lifted the phone.

* * * *

Neither of the Sheas slept well.

Marion spent much of the night reliving the day before. The interview with J. R. Gowd merged with Rowena's face and her last sulky words when she shut the door on Sunday night. And as she dropped into an uneasy doze, she found herself again in the small back room, with the shadow of a killer, dark against green silk.

While Marion dreamed about murder, Stephen was haunted by a different fear. He had been shocked by the violence of Rowena's death, but he barely knew the woman, and he had not been at the centre when the body was found.

As he lay awake, he thought about Benjamin Knowles. And Antonio. Embezzlement. A position abused by the treasurer of a community group, funds stolen by a trusted accountant. The two crimes had so much similarity.

He was not involved this time, he told himself. Your wife is on the committee, said a voice in his head. Not for very long, he told himself. What had she attended—one meeting? Two at the most. Even if the story made the news, why should the papers print her name? Although she was on the committee, she was not listed as signatory for the centre's account, so nobody at the First Queensland Bank would connect her with the organisation. The bank would not have a list of committee members, they were only interested in those names registered as signatories for the account.

Why had Marion gone to the bank? What was it she said last night, talking about the embezzlement? That Loretta needed her help because the old woman was out of her depth. "Somebody had to talk to that horrible Gowd person," she said. Why did that *somebody* have to be his wife?

By the time the early morning light showed the window as a dull grey square, Stephen had examined this second embezzlement from every angle. And over breakfast, he shared his concern with Marion.

"How does the centre stand with this banking thing?"

Marion shrugged her ignorance. "After what happened to Rowena, who cares about the money?"

Stephen felt a surge of irritation. Didn't she realise the position they were in? "What about the cash box and the money collected over the weekend? That was a simple burglary," he said. "The insurance should cover it. How much do you reckon it was?"

"I've no idea. Nobody counted it, and at the moment I don't care. You're as bad as that awful manager person."

"You can't blame Gowd for being upset."

"I can, if it makes him bully an old woman." Marion slammed two eggs in front of her husband and switched on the radio to close the conversation.

The sound blasted into the room, and Stephen, thinking of their neighbours, turned it down. Marion leaned across him to switch off the set.

"We can't even listen to the news in this bloody place," she said.

* * * *

Marion stared at her cold toast and wished she could start the morning again.

If only she could wipe out the bitter words she had flung at Stephen, that had prompted his cold response.

Of course he was worried about the missing funds.

"If this gets to court, members of the committee will be in trouble," he had said. "People will ask why nobody checked the bank statements or the treasurer's report."

That had been too much. After the Melbourne debacle. She had turned on her husband.

"You should talk about slackness!" she said. Not satisfied with that retort, she had carried on, her own voice shrill in her ears . . . dragging up all the blame, resentment, and frustration she had felt since their move. Words she had left unspoken over the months spewed forth in a seemingly unstoppable, stream.

But looking at Stephen's empty chair, she thought about his words. Were they really so awful? Stephen had not been with her when Rowena's body was found, and his whole experience of the event had come from her account. Second hand. Not much more real than news on the TV.

Was he thinking about his own problems when he tried to defend J. R. Gowd? Now, in the empty room, she went over the whole, awful conversation.

For the first time since they left Melbourne, she had told Stephen how much she hated leaving the city.

81

Melbourne had done well by her. That job in a boutique, which started so casually as a student's part time work, had developed over the years as her position grew with the business. Her eye for fashion and, even more important, her feeling for what the customers would buy, made her invaluable.

And the gallery. From fashion to art had not been a big step. Marion was originally employed for her managerial skills, but over the years she had developed contacts with artists and customers and had become a recognised name in the Melbourne art world.

No wonder her mother advised against the move. As a professional photographer, Vivian had run her studio with a flair that had paid for the children's private schools. "It's the personal contact that counts," she had told Marion, when her daughter started at the gallery, "Your address book is your passport to success."

A passport not valid in Ridgeway.

As soon as she learned Stephen was being transferred out of the state, Vivian had descended on the Shea house armed with maps and timetables. Why couldn't her son-in-law work in Ridgeway during the week and fly home to Melbourne on Friday night? When Marion talked about the problems of such travelling, her mother quoted families she knew with husbands working in Singapore or Hong Kong. That was when Marion had stopped listening. Some couples might choose to live like that, but it was not what she wanted for Stephen and herself.

Because the strongest argument against commuting was one she would not share with her mother, and certainly not with Stephen. After the disaster at the bank he had been so thoroughly, and understandably, miserable that she could not bear to think of him spending the evenings by himself.

She talked about setting up a gallery in Ridgeway.

"You don't know anyone in Queensland," Vivian had said.

"Something will turn up," was Marion's confident reply.

But nothing had.

And in spite of Vivian's dire warnings, Marion had not realised how much she depended on her network of business contacts and friends. Without them, she found herself struggling to fill her day.

For months she had kept these thoughts to herself and this morning she had let them out in one angry outburst of screaming.

"If that's how you feel" Stephen had said quietly, "you'd better go back to Melbourne."

He had scooped up his car keys and walked out. Without saying good-bye.

Marion sat over her cooling coffee, telling herself how badly she'd been used, but Stephen's words rang in her ears. "Back to Melbourne." And snatches of earlier discussions that, at the time she had chosen to ignore. "Could be worse . . ." "A decent-sized city . . ."

And always at the back of her mind was the image of a green dress splattered with blood and superimposed on that, to her own self-disgust, the threatening face of J. R. Gowd accusing Loretta and herself of negligence. How could she think of money when Rowena McKendrick had been bashed to death? But she couldn't wipe it out of her mind. Embezzlement. Perhaps Stephen was right to be worried and Benjamin Knowles was her Antonio.

There was a scratching at the back door. The cat again.

"The trouble is that Stephen's worried sick," she said, as she let the animal into the kitchen. "He can't afford to be involved in another financial mess."

The cat was not interested in her problem. It twined around her legs, making a plaintive noise that should have sent her hurrying to the fridge.

"You've got your own concerns, haven't you puss?" she told it as she eventually turned her attention to the matter of milk.

Judging by the feathers she found on the front path, murder was commonplace in the feline world and the ginger cat was unlikely to be upset by a human death. As for embezzlement—that would only make sense in terms of milk or fish, and this particular tom was big enough to protect its own dinner. "Nobody steals from our ginger puss," Marion said approvingly.

The word "our" hung in the air, the casual pronoun taking her by surprise.

"You're not my cat, Ginger Meggs," she reminded it sternly. But she had given the animal a name and by doing that, moved another step closer to the relationship she denied. The phone jolted her out of her reverie.

Loretta.

Marion listened in horror as the president outlined her plan. "A meeting. Loretta, that's impossible. We can't get into the building."

And even if the police would let them use the meeting room, Marion didn't think she could face it. Not yet.

Loretta was still talking. Had Marion forgotten about the bank? Benjamin Knowles. The murder was dreadful but . . .

Marion held the receiver away from her ear. Her stomach churned as she listened to Loretta burbling on and thought of that dreadful little room. She squeezed her eyes shut, opened them and stared at a teaspoon. Teaspoon. She tried to concentrate on the small silver shape on a white plate.

"Marion?"

She shook herself back to the conversation. "We can't do anything, Loretta," she said, determined to be gentle but firm with the old woman. "We have to wait till we know more."

"We can't. We've got to have a meeting. Tomorrow night. I've been talking to Karen Francis and she's going to ring the rest of the committee."

Had the two of them gone mad, Marion wondered.

"We can't get into the building!" Marion repeated the one, insurmountable objection to any meeting.

"That's what I told Karen. I knew you'd want a meeting. But I said there'd be a problem with our room, and she's found a solution." Loretta waited for the question Marion refused to ask, and when that was not forthcoming broke her own silence with a triumphant crescendo. "We can use a council meeting room!"

"What's the point? We can't do anything without the books."

"It is all arranged," Loretta spoke over Marion's words. "The meeting is tomorrow night at eight o'clock." She put down her phone, leaving Marion to curse into her own mouthpiece.

* * * *

If Marion had spoken to Karen Francis, she would have found some support in her efforts to thwart Loretta's plans.

Because Karen also had problems.

On Monday afternoon the gods had been kind, and after the police had finished with her, she had been able to slip through the back entrance of the council building without being noticed. She shared her tiny office with the council youth worker, but the gods, in another act of kindness, arranged for Keith to be away on leave.

But on Tuesday the heavenly protection was withdrawn, and Karen had to look after herself.

She had opened her door to the demanding tone of the phone. It was still three minutes to her starting time and she could have left her answering machine to take the call, but, with the automatic response of a Pavlovian dog, she lifted the receiver.

Loretta Wheelwright.

The president didn't identify herself. She assumed, rightly, that Karen would recognise her voice and launched straight into the business of her call.

"A meeting? Tomorrow?" What did Loretta think the committee could do? The centre was a crime scene. The police had sealed the building.

As Loretta talked, Karen reached for her pad. She found herself doodling a line of circular faces that stared with wide-eyed astonishment as the president insisted Marion Shea (who knew so much about business) wanted to get the committee together, to decide what they should do about Benjamin Knowles.

Unfortunately for Karen, her reluctant agreement to an evening meeting was followed by another outrageous demand.

"We can't get into the centre," Loretta reminded her, "so we'll have to use one of the council rooms. You are the council's representative on our committee." A position the president had never previously acknowledged. "You will have to arrange it."

It was only after she replaced the receiver that Karen wondered whether the conveniently quoted *Marion Shea* knew anything about the projected gathering. But the meeting might not be a bad idea. The committee would have to be told about their treasurer's misdeeds and the sooner the better, as far as she was concerned. Let Patricia, Walter and the rest of them take some responsibility for the mess they were in.

Karen had no time to brood about the centre's financial problems. She had barely torn the doodles off her pad before she had her first visitor. One who set the pattern of the day.

Rowena McKendrick's murder had been on the evening news and the story was repeated on breakfast radio. Everybody in the council building knew what had been found inside the Arts and Culture Centre. People arriving for work greeted each other in the car park, and those lucky individuals who had been at the exhibition on Sunday afternoon repeated any small exchange they might have had with the victim. "She didn't sound frightened," one woman said resentfully. As if the coordinator should have been more subdued in the hours before she was killed.

But they only had the bare bones of the story until somebody realised the council had a representative on the committee. And it was not long before word spread—Karen had been in the building when the body was found.

Never had she had so many cups of coffee delivered to her desk or fielded so many solicitous concerns about her well-being, followed by the inevitable request for information. Eager eyes searching her face for marks of the strain she surely must have felt, after being so close to the Horrible Event. Curious ears waited for her to describe the dreadful scene.

By the end of the morning, Karen's response to her workmates questions had become so automatic she could have answered in her sleep.

"Yes, she had been at the centre yesterday."

"Yes, she was there when Rowena was found."

"No, she had not seen the body."

This last, unfortunately, was not true. Karen had followed Marion to the kitchen and, like Marion, had looked into the small back room.

"Yes the police had talked to her, but no, they didn't tell her anything."

Since this was no more than the questioners already knew, they left unsatisfied and told each other, in excited whispers, that "Karen is suffering from shock." The more knowledgeable decided she had Post Traumatic Stress, which somebody shortened to PTS, and cited an uncle's brother's friend, who was never the same after some equally horrible event.

After the tenth offer of refreshments and tenth set of enquiring eyes invaded her workspace, Karen felt Rowena McKendrick might not be the only victim of a violent attack. Perhaps her face showed the murderous thoughts, because her next visitor barely shaped her first her question before backing abruptly out of the small office. After that, whatever whispers rustled through the building, none wafted across Karen's desk, and she was left alone for the rest of the day.

Fortunately for her, the person she least wanted to meet had followed his own, often spoken, credo of going straight to the top.

While Karen was fending off enquiries, Reginald Mollison, the chief executive officer of the Ridgeway Council, was on the phone to the police station, demanding to talk to the person in charge.

The desk sergeant refused to connect him to the officers involved in the investigation, but she transferred the call to an authoritative voice, which provided enough information to persuade the CEO his importance had been recognised.

How could Reginald Mollison know the impressive voice belonged to a civilian clerk reading from the handout she had been given? Or that she had already provided the same information to the local radio station and any reporter who contacted the police?

Karen didn't have to be in the CEO's office to know what he would do when he learned about a murder, and she could have given an accurate account of his call to the station, if not of the official response.

She also knew that when he heard the whole story, he would consider the greatest disaster not the murder but the misappropriation of a council grant. Fortunately for Karen, Mollison's attention was diverted by other, more pressing affairs

87

and he did not get around to reading her carefully worded memo until she, like the rest of the staff, had gone home.

CHAPTER TEN: TUESDAY MORNING

At the Bostock garage, the radio was always tuned to the local station, and the young mechanics would turn it on as soon as they came in. They had both watched the news the night before and knew about the murder, but when the music was interrupted by another report, Damien put down his spanner and Trev swung up from under a car. Perhaps the announcer would have more information about the woman's death.

They were horrified but vaguely excited. A murder! Just a few streets away. Neither of them knew Rowena McKendrick, but since the killing happened in their neighbourhood, they took proprietorial interest in the crime.

"Some arsehole looking for cash," Trev decided. "Could of been here."

"Nah. Stocky don't leave cash overnight."

"Killer wouldn't know that."

"He'd see there's not much going on." Damian looked gloomily around the garage, if Bostock was in trouble, he'd be the first to lose his job. That was more serious than the murder of some bird they didn't know.

Trev laughed. If Damien had half a brain, he'd know Stocky was doing all right. "Pity she didn't die here," he said, banging on the counter to make his point. "If we had a bloody murder in the place, every car in Ridgeway would need repairs. So people could come and gawk at the scene."

Oliver stuck his head out of the office to glare at the lads.

"Stocky's very keen on that arty place," Trev whispered to Damien as they scurried back to work. "I bet he knew the woman."

Oliver Bostock closed the office door and sat in front of his computer, staring at the blank screen.

Rowena McKendrick was dead.

Rowena. She had been so alive, so warm in his arms. Rowena. Only last week, in the darkness of that tiny room, she had shivered with excitement when they heard voices coming, unexpectedly, into the building. There had been footsteps in the gallery and the bump of a late delivery. More canvases for the exhibition. Somebody must have given fussy Walter Edridge a key and he had come to let the carriers into the big hall. They could hear the men curse as they tried to unload and Walter kept getting under their feet. Rowena had stuffed a fist into her mouth to stifle her giggles. At last they heard the front door close behind the men, and in the safety of the now-empty building, she had let the laughter out.

Rowena was dead.

And Oliver had no mourner's right. As a friend of the family people would expect him to be upset by the death of William McKendrick's wife and it would be appropriate for him to send flowers to her funeral, but he couldn't spend his days hidden behind closed doors grieving for his love. He shaped his face into its business mask and left the shelter of his small office.

A woman drove into the garage, and he tried to concentrate on the problem with her van.

The morning dragged. He logged onto the computer, but when he tried to work on the accounts, the figures blurred.

He stood up to stretch his legs and looking through the garage door, saw a dirty young man lounging against the bowsers, with a cigarette dangling from his lips. In three long strides Oliver was outside.

"Get rid of that bloody cigarette," he growled, clenching his hands into fists to stop himself slapping the fag out of the fellow's mouth and grinding it into the ground.

The youth straightened and dropped his glowing butt into the gutter.

Oliver moved quickly to stamp on the smouldering ash. "You senseless bastard! Do you want to blow us into the next world?"

He knew what the fellow was doing. He had come to apply for a job, and by blatantly flouting the most basic safety rule, he could meet his job-search obligations without the risk of finding himself employed. That the combination of flame and fuel could cause a major explosion and kill them both was of small concern when set against the danger of having to work.

"Get out!"

The lout didn't bother to move. He watched Oliver unlock the door and as soon as it was open, pushed his way into the workshop. "Keep your hair on, mate. I only want to talk, and after what happened Sunday night, I think you'd better listen to me."

Sunday night? The words barely registered as the youth swaggered across the floor into the office, so Oliver had to follow him. The small space was crammed with the paraphernalia of business, and Oliver pushed against the youth as he put himself between the expensive computer and his unwelcome visitor. He reached under his desk and felt the comforting weight of the lead pipe he kept for just such a situation.

"Yep, I saw you," his unwelcome visitor said aggressively "So you fuckin' better talk to me. The hours I've spent in the fuckin' park waiting for your lot to leave the place so I could get into me blanket. Well, now you're going to pay."

In the garage Trev, or was it Damian, knocked something off the bench and his curses were heard above the radio.

The youth leant forward putting his face close to Oliver as he dropped his voice.

"I know what you fuckin' did, so come across."

What did this creature know? How many nights had he spent outside the building while Oliver and Rowena had their fun inside?

Oliver opened a drawer and pulled out some banknotes.

The lout gave a contemptuous sniff. "That's not enough."

"That's all the money I've got in the place. Look for yourself." Oliver leant back to let him peer into the drawer. He could see it was empty.

"You'd better get some more. I'll be fuckin' back."

Suppose he went to the police? It would be his word against Oliver's. Who would they believe—this young layabout or Oliver Bostock, a respectable business man? But the police would have to check the story and somebody was sure to mention his relationship with Rowena. If the police learned he was the victim's lover and might have been in the building on Sunday night, they would have to suspect him of her death. "I'll get more money," he said. "Come back tonight, after I've closed the garage."

"OK," the lout leaned forward again, leering into Oliver's face. "I'll wait till tonight. But you better be here. And don't think you can wipe me out, like you done that bird. There are guys that know what I saw and they know I'm coming here to talk to you, so you had better not try anything, man. You don't get rid of the Roach that easily," he said over his shoulder as he swaggered out of the office.

* * * *

After the Roach left, Oliver closed the office door.

The more he thought about the boy's words, the more convinced he was that the Roach would not go near the police; he wasn't the type to get involved with the law. But he would certainly boast to his fellows, and the story would grow with the telling until it reached official ears. By then, according to the gossip, Oliver Bostock would have been seen coming out of the building covered with blood and waving a blunt instrument.

There was only one thing to do. Oliver lifted the phone and punched in the number of the Ridgeway Police Station.

The detectives came at once. Oliver barely had time to rehearse his words before they walked into the garage. Two men in business suits. The older, Oliver noted, was beginning to put on weight, like a retired footballer. He identified himself with sharp, no nonsense words, as Detective Senior Sergeant Thomas Erbacher, and his younger companion as Detective Constable Gregory Shaw. The heavy glasses gave the senior officer a gravitas that would have sat better on a lawyer than a policeman. Oliver didn't think the eyes behind those glasses would miss much.

Oliver settled himself behind his desk, taking a small comfort from the familiar place as he offered the detective sergeant the only other chair and left the younger man standing in front of the door. Detective Constable Shaw had restless grey eyes, which shifted their focus from the papers on Oliver's desk to the faded cartoons taped to the wall until he recollected himself and made a deliberate effort to copy his senior's steady gaze.

Oliver leant forward, reaching past Shaw to close the door. The office was very small for three bodies, but by shutting out the lads' music, he was also protecting himself from their eager ears. He didn't have to be a detective himself to recognise Erbacher as an important member of the Criminal Investigation Branch.

He told the detectives about the attempted blackmail and described the Roach.

"I'm sure you know the type."

"There's plenty like him, unfortunately," Erbacher said. "You did the right thing, reporting his threats." There was a slight pause before the detective asked the question Oliver had been expecting. "Was there was any reason for the fellow to pick on you, Mr. Bostock?"

There are times when only the truth will serve. "I'd been seeing Rowena McKendrick," Oliver chose the usual inadequate words to describe their relationship but the two men nodded, knowing exactly what he meant. "I used to meet her sometimes after she finished work."

"Did you go back to the building on Sunday night? To see Mrs. McKendrick?"

"Yes . . . No. I did go back but I didn't see Rowena. It was late." Another pause while the detective waited for Oliver to explain the contradiction.

"I walked over from the garage. You know the way the centre fronts the road, with a small street on one side and the park on the other, with the grass stretching around to the back of the building?" Erbacher nodded. "There's a parking lot opening onto the street, but Rowena always left her car under the trees on the other side."

The younger detective shook his head impatiently. Of course they had been told where the woman left her car, but Oliver was having trouble explaining himself. He had to work his way into the story.

The older man gave an encouraging grunt. "That's why nobody saw her vehicle," he said—a tutor prompting a hesitant student.

"I always walked across the park. We had an arrangement. When she was able to stay at the centre, she'd turn on the light in the little room behind the hall, no-one can see that window from the street. If I saw the light, I'd go right up to the back—the kitchen—door and she'd let me in. On Sunday, she knew I'd gone out on a job, so I didn't really expect her to wait, and when I didn't see a light I didn't bother to try the kitchen door." If he had known Rowena was still there, he would have bashed down the door. And if he had been earlier, she might not be dead.

"When was the last time you saw Mrs. McKendrick?"

"Sunday afternoon, at the art show."

"What time did you leave?"

"A bit after five. It was a breakdown on the Windsor Road. A tow job. The fellow gave his name as Anderson. He had his wife and kid with him and a couple of mates."

"Did you tow the car into Ridgeway?" Constable Shaw had his notebook out to write down the names. "These— Andersons—they'll confirm your story, Mr. Bostock?"

His slight stress on the word Anderson warned Oliver that the detective would not place much value on anything they said, and Oliver's own view of the men made him doubt their usefulness as witnesses.

"It was just before the turn off to the McKendrick property. Dennis McKendrick passed me. He was on his way home."

The detectives wanted to fix the time. "You were back at the garage at what—eight o'clock?" Erbacher asked.

"That would be close."

"You fiddled about a bit. Walked to the centre, and got there around nine?"

"It might have been earlier. I got rid of the Andersons as quickly as I could, hoping to catch Rowena before she went home."

"I walked up to the centre, through the park and around the side of the building. Like I said, it was late and there was no light in the window. I thought she'd gone home. I tried to phone . . ."

"Did you get an answer?"

"No. So I went back to the garage. To pick up my van."

"You didn't go up to the kitchen door?"

"No." Oliver choked on a sob. "If I'd known something was wrong I'd—I'd have busted my way in. She might have still been alive."

"Was that when the fellow saw you?"

"No," Oliver shook his head vehemently. "If that little runt saw anyone coming out of the building, it must have been the killer, and you can bloody well shake the story out of him."

Erbacher muttered something about finding the lad.

"You can do that all right. You can pick him up tonight. I've set a trap for the rotten little shit."

Erbacher was not enthusiastic about the plan, but Oliver was emphatic. "I want the little runt charged. He demanded money with threats. Isn't that against the law? And I want to get the swine who bashed Rowena. Just let me get my hands on him." Oliver punched a clench fist into his open hand.

"The boy could have some useful information," Erbacher agreed. "Since you've already arranged the meeting, I'll have some men stand by to pick him up."

* * * *

"So we know why the coordinator stayed behind," Shaw said as the detectives walked back to their car.

"Do you believe Bostock's story?"

"On the whole, yes." Erbacher climbed into the passenger's seat and rolled down the window to catch the breeze. "We'll have to check with McKendrick."

"If that young fellow is telling the truth, the killer might be an intruder after all," Shaw said, pulling into the stream of traffic as he tentatively raised the theory his senior had discounted earlier. "Somebody thought the building was empty and had a nasty shock when the woman disturbed him."

"What about the light? It was already dark when the Sheas left, and according to the woman's story, they were the last car out of the parking lot. As soon as they were gone, the coordinator must have made her way to the little room. And she would have switched on a light."

Shaw remembered the relevant section of the forensic report. There were prints on the switches that controlled the passage lights and the ones for the kitchen and the little room behind it, but they had been smudged, as if overlaid by a gloved hand. A casual intruder would not be wearing gloves, so it looked as if Erbacher was right. Whoever killed Rowena McKendrick had planned the crime.

"It could still have been Bostock," he said. "He might have wanted his girlfriend out of the way before his wife came back."

"He'd be more likely to kill his wife, if he was still keen on Rowena McKendrick." Erbacher spoke from some experience of dealing with domestic triangles.

"And what about Knowles?"

Shaw considered Monday's interviews. After Karen Francis dropped her bombshell about the treasurer, the other woman, Marion Shea, had reluctantly confirmed the story. Yes, Benjamin Knowles had withdrawn money from their account . . . Knowles had left town, and, no, they didn't know where he was.

"Suppose the coordinator knew what he was up to and threatened to tell the committee?" Shaw asked. "He might have wanted to shut her up."

"That is a possibility," Erbacher agreed.

Earlier in the day, the detectives had visited the First Queensland Bank. Neither of them was surprised to learn the manager had spent the previous afternoon checking every transaction involving the centre. Gowd was able to give the detectives a detailed account of the treasurer's crime, including information about the government grant Knowles had transferred to an account belonging to a company he had registered some years earlier.

Since they were only interested in the murder, Erbacher had not asked the obvious question: How could the fellow get away with it?

"We'll leave that for the fraud squad to sort out," he explained, as they left the bank.

"Didn't anybody notice the money had gone?" Shaw found that hard to believe.

"From what Gowd said, the secretary of this arts and culture place was the only one, apart from Knowles, who had anything to do with the business side of things. She's out of the country, coming back on Saturday. And who do you think it is?"

Shaw mentally checked the names they had been shown at the bank. "Judith Bostock?"

"That's her. The woman whose husband was having it off with Rowena McKendrick."

"He was expecting her back at the end of the week."

With a philandering husband and an embezzling treasurer both foreseeing trouble when she turned up, Shaw wondered why Judith Bostock wasn't the one bashed to death.

"She's still out of the country." Erbacher pulled him back from this interesting speculation. "Let's take another look at the actual victim, Mrs. McKendrick. Somebody must have wanted her dead."

Back at the station, Erbacher rang Dennis McKendrick's mobile number. Yes, Dennis had passed Bostock's truck on Sunday afternoon. It looked like a tow job. "Which means we'll have to find this Benjamin Knowles," Erbacher was saying when a call was relayed from the front desk.

"It's a solicitor, from Xavier and Lyons," he told Shaw. "You'll never guess who walked into their office." Shaw shook his head. "Benjamin Knowles himself. Lyons wants to bring him in."

CHAPTER ELEVEN: TUESDAY MORNING

Stephen was not the only banker to face Tuesday morning exhausted after a restless night.

John Raymond Gowd was in his office before any of his staff. He sat with his elbows on the desk and his chin in his hands, as he tried to decide what to do.

During the previous week he had been vaguely uneasy about the centre's account, which was why he had taken the opportunity to have a casual conversation with a member of the committee. He hoped Edridge would think the topic came up naturally and the manager was simply expressing his understandable pique at the treasurer's unwelcome, but perfectly legitimate, decision to transfer so much money to a different institution.

Walter had not appeared surprised or worried by the information, but he'd shown no foreknowledge of the treasurer's action, and as they talked, it became increasingly obvious he knew nothing about the finances of the centre. "The executive committee handle all that stuff," he said, the executive committee being the treasurer, Knowles, who had arranged to transfer the money; the secretary, Judith Bostock, who was, his wife informed him, enjoying a holiday in Greece and the elderly president, Loretta Wheelwright.

Gowd was the first to concede that Loretta was a grand old lady. She was wonderful for her age and added a certain class to social events, but what did she know about handling money? After his conversation with Walter Edridge, Gowd hoped the treasurer knew what he was doing with the funds.

Unfortunately, Knowles had known exactly what he was doing.

After Loretta left with that new woman, Marion Shea, it had only taken one phone call for Gowd to discover that the target account for the transferred money belonged to a company that had been registered, three years earlier, to Benjamin Arthur Knowles, and that after Knowles' disastrous attempt to run his own business, it had been barely used until this latest deposit.

This was followed by one more, dreadful piece of information. Money had been transferred from this account to yet another, different, Brisbane bank and during the previous week it had been withdrawn as cash.

Gowd had immediately sent a flustered Bettina to collect all the centre's records, which he spread over the surface of his desk, comparing the signatures on each transaction with the ones on the organisation's file. B. Knowles was written in the same hand as the specimen, but what about the other names? The scrawls that had purported to have been supplied by the secretary and president looked disconcertingly similar and nothing like the signatures on file.

In one last, despairing effort to convince himself that he could sort out the mess, Gowd had checked the contact number for the treasurer and reached for the phone.

Knowles' wife took the call, flustered by his sharp questions. No, her husband wasn't in the house. Yes, she could give him her husband's work number, but it was no use trying to ring him at the store; he wasn't there. Because he was in Brisbane. Family problems. Gowd could not know Diana had already used this excuse, talking to Loretta, but the banker's mind did not leap to thoughts of a relative's illness or elderly parents. The man had left town.

That evening, while he slumped in front of the TV, his thoughts circled around the raided account and forged signatures, as an interview segued into a suite of advertisements followed by the local news announcing "Horrific killing . . . " Had his own preoccupation twisted the story? No. He had not misheard. The body of a woman, later identified as Rowena McKendrick, was found in a back room of a building owned by the Ridgeway Arts and Culture Centre.

Police cars and crime tape provided a sombre background to the newsreader's voice.

Gowd had yelled for his wife, who rushed in, waving a half-peeled potato, convinced that something terrible had happened in the sitting room. The sight of her husband, red faced and waving his arms, did nothing to lessen her anxiety.

"Mrs. McKendrick was bashed to death sometime on Sunday night. Police believe she surprised an intruder," the reporter on the TV was saying.

Cecily had never met Rowena McKendrick. "But her husband's brother plays golf with me," she said, as if that should have protected any member of the McKendrick family from such a melodramatic fate.

Gowd was equally shocked. There had been other murders in Ridgeway: drug-related shootings, street stabbings in the early hours, and alcohol-fuelled fights that ended in almost accidental deaths, but these dreadful events were not part of his orderly world. The fact that the victim's family belonged to the Ridgeway Golf Club brought the violence horribly close.

Cecily had gone straight to the security door to make sure it was locked, and before they went to bed, she insisted on checking every window, as if she believed the violent intruder would force his way into their lives.

Gowd had not told his wife that he was haunted by another fear. Suppose the killer was not an intruder. The death of the coordinator might be linked to the missing money and his bank, and its manager would be dragged into the mess.

So on Tuesday morning, while Marion Shea sat over a breakfast she could not eat and Loretta Wheelwright made her lists, he stared at the polished surface of his desk, as if he would find an answer to his problem written on its shining wood.

For Stephen Shea, the money missing from the centre's bank account sounded an uncomfortable echo of his own misfortune, the embezzlement that almost destroyed his career.

For Gowd, the threat was more immediate. A glance at the paperwork spread across his desk reminded him of simple precautions his staff had not taken. Nobody had checked the signatures on any of the transactions with names on the file or contacted other members of the committee to confirm their approval for such a large amount of money to be moved to a different bank. And as manager, he would be held responsible for that negligence.

Why didn't members of the committee realise something was wrong? Did any of them bother to read the bank statements?

Yesterday Mrs. Shea told him the treasurer was unavailable, but she had not explained that the reason he could not be found was because he had disappeared with their money. The secretary was out of the country, so she couldn't come to the bank. That left Loretta Wheelwright, the president.

As Gowd began to shape his argument, he was glad he would be talking to an old lady. She would be too flustered to ask why the bank had not checked the signatures before allowing the treasurer to make those large transfers.

He had Loretta Wheelwright's home address and rang the president.

Her voice on the phone was suitably frightened.

"Be here at two," he barked, slamming the receiver down with a bang that he hoped would make her eardrums ring.

* * * *

If Gowd expected to be dealing with a flustered old lady, he was going to be disappointed. Loretta had no intention of fronting him alone. She made a cup of tea to calm her nerves and rang Marion Shea.

"I've had another call from the bank. That horrible Gowd person."

There was a sob in Loretta's voice and Marion had trouble making sense of her words, but it seemed that while members of the committee had been coming to terms with murder, J. R. Gowd was checking the centre's bank account.

"He says it's our fault, the committee should have been more careful. The bank made the transfers because the forms had my name as well as the treasurer's. I told him I didn't sign anything," she wailed. "I leave that stuff to Benjamin and Judith."

Marion made a soothing noise while she considered the implication of Loretta's words. J. R. Gowd must be feeling the pressure. Problems with head office? Not yet perhaps, but there would be trouble when he reported the mess . . . Stephen's face that dreadful afternoon, saying, "They'll say I should have known." Marion felt a moment's pity for the unpleasant Gowd, he had his own demons. She shook herself. The bank would

101

have to take some of the blame for the treasurer's crime. Somebody should have checked the signatures before transferring the government grant money.

A year ago she had supported Stephen. The manager can't be everywhere, but there were certain, basic precautions that should have been taken. Gowd's staff had let him down, not with the deliberate wickedness of an Antonio, but with a carelessness that might have the same result. Mud had to stick somewhere but not, Marion decided quickly, on the committee of the Ridgeway Arts and Culture Centre.

"He wants me to come in to the bank this afternoon." Loretta sounded desperate. "He says we have to sort things out. How can we sort things out when the money's gone?" A pause. "Could you come with me, Marion, dear?"

Never had Loretta Wheelwright sounded so helpless. Never had Marion so wished she could wipe her hands of a problem. What they needed was an accountant, or a lawyer, not the manager of a Victorian art gallery. She sighed and promised to meet Loretta at the bank. At two o'clock.

"But I'm new to the centre," she said, "and I don't know anything about its finances." She cast her mind around the committee, wondering who could give her the information she would need if she had to confront J. R. Gowd. The treasurer was missing and the secretary would not be back till the end of the week. Who else was there? Karen Francis? From the little she had seen of the council's representative, Karen would not be much help. Couldn't she see something was wrong? Walter Edridge? Marion shuddered. Having Walter tell them "It's a bad business" fifty times would not solve anything. She thought of the staunch William McKendrick, but she couldn't drag him into the problem, not when his wife had just been bashed to death.

But who else on the committee was a match for J. R. Gowd?

What about William's first wife? Didn't Loretta say Agnes had been their treasurer before the divorce? They could hardly ask her to come back. Or could they?

Marion felt stupid bringing up her name, but "needs must when the devil drives" as her father used to say. To her surprise Loretta grabbed the idea. "Agnes, Agnes Willmot. That's what she calls herself now. Such a clever girl. There was never any trouble when she looked after the books. She teaches at Ridgeway College. Physics and maths they tell me, and of course that covers Roger's fees. It makes things so much easier for William."

Marion managed to interrupt the flow of irrelevant information to demand the phone number. "When Agnes was treasurer we always rang her at school during the lunch hour, that's after twelve o'clock. On her Mobile Phone." Loretta's tone gave the last words the capital letters such a technical marvel deserved. "But she'll be teaching this afternoon, so she won't be able to come to the bank with us."

Since Marion had no intention of doing anything more than listen to Gowd's planned sorting out, they didn't need Agnes at this meeting. It would be later, when they tried to clean up the financial mess, that the former treasurer would be invaluable. With a few reassuring words to the distraught president, Marion finished the call.

She went into the bedroom and faced her reflection.

"Good afternoon, Mr. Gowd," she said to herself.

"No, Mr. Gowd, we can't do anything today. No. Mrs. Wheelwright won't sign anything. We will talk to the committee tomorrow night. And we will be in touch."

Her reflection, standing in for J. R. Gowd, was properly impressed with her firmness and had it been flourishing pens or threatening forms, it would have pushed them hurriedly out of sight.

Next question, what should she wear? What outfit would be suitable for a possibly confrontational visit to a Ridgeway bank? Melbourne business suit? Too formal. Eventually she settled on dark slacks and a smart top.

Marion wondered how the manager would deal with the problem raised by Rowena McKendrick's death. Would he mouth some conventional words of sympathy or attempt to link the crime with the treasurer's embezzlement? "Just let him try that on," she thought

* * * *

Gowd ignored the social niceties. He greeted the women with a censorious frown and didn't mention the murder.

"I've been looking into your problem," he said, after settling himself behind his desk and positioning them, like defaulting debtors, opposite. Easy targets for his accusing eye.

Marion stared at him across the polished wood and raised her chin to the challenging position she had practised in front of her mirror.

Loretta shifted a little on the hard chair but, following Marion's instruction, kept her lips tightly closed.

"Raymond Gowd is a rude, ill-bred man," Marion had said when Loretta repeated the harsh words the manager used on the phone. She had chosen the terms deliberately, as the ones most likely to stiffen the old lady's spine. "He knows the bank has been very remiss. Somebody should have checked those signatures. He is trying to wriggle out of his responsibility. Leave the talking to me."

Loretta had gladly agreed. After a small, embarrassed shrug she waited, as Marion refused to give Gowd the apologetic words he so obviously expected. The silence stretched uncomfortably until the manager was forced to enlarge on his original comment.

He flourished papers as he outlined an ingenious scheme to absolve his bank from any fiscal liability for the loss of funds and made a specific reference to the centre's responsibility for the government grant. Although he did not use those words.

The complicated explanation was larded with comments about the duties of a committee and sympathetic assurances that his bank would do everything we can for you.

Loretta nodded. She started to murmur a cowed, even grateful, agreement of his terms, but remembering her promise, she waited for Marion to speak.

Marion used the lines she had rehearsed. "We can't do anything today," she said, with a firm emphasis on the final word. "The committee will have to be informed."

The manager's face soon lost its smile, and his tone moved from oily helpfulness to a businesslike growl that terrified Loretta.

Marion interrupted any conciliatory words from the president by saying that any arrangement would be for the committee to decide, "After we have checked our own records." Even Gowd had to admit that any business arrangement would have to wait until the police allowed committee members back into the building.

"We will let you know what the committee decide." Marion said, standing up and putting a hand under Loretta's elbow to help the older woman rise with her.

"Didn't anybody check the bank statements?" she asked, when they were safely away from the listening ears of the bank.

"Agnes used to go over the books with Teresa. Teresa Sixsmith. She was our coordinator before her husband was transferred to Perth. Then the committee gave the job to Rowena. Rowena left everything to Benjamin. She complained about the extra work she would have if Judith's program got funded, but I don't think she had anything to do with the government money."

"Why didn't Judith plan to use some of the grant to employ an assistant?"

"She wanted to, but Benjamin said we couldn't use the money for anything except the program itself. And we didn't really need extra staff, not if he was going to handle the business side of things."

"How very convenient for the treasurer. Didn't Karen say the secretary had been worried about the financial report?"

"Judith did make a fuss at the meeting," Loretta admitted. "But Benjamin was able to answer all her questions and she was getting ready for her holiday, so she didn't have time to look into the finances."

Was that why Benjamin Knowles disappeared, because the secretary was coming back and he knew she would want to check his books? Marion wondered.

CHAPTER TWELVE: LATER TUESDAY MORNING

After their appointment with the bank, Marion drove Loretta home and hurried back to her unit. She then phoned Agnes Willmot, the first Mrs. McKendrick and former treasurer.

Marion had not met William's ex wife, but from all she had heard that marriage should have been more satisfactory than the William-Rowena partnership. But it had crashed, while the second marriage lasted till death do us part, even if death came tragically before its proper time.

When Agnes answered the phone, she sounded as if she were talking through a mouthful of sandwich.

After she introduced herself, Marion had gone straight to the point. "I'm sorry to bother you but we are in a mess."

A questioning grunt encouraged her to continue. "It's the centre. Loretta Wheelwright thought you might help us."

There was a chuckle from the other end, "What has Loretta roped you in to do?"

Marion explained the problem—the missing money, the interview with the bank, and the fact that they couldn't get into the office to check their records because the police had locked them out of the building. "Loretta said you were treasurer before Benjamin Knowles, and she suggested I talk to you. Everything's in such a muddle, and I'm so new to the committee, I don't know where to start." Marion could hear the desperation in her own voice. "We are all upset about Rowena's death . . ."

It was an awkward reference to the tragedy, but Agnes closed the subject with a sympathetic murmur and considered the next problem. Where could they meet?

What about the Sheas' unit? The invitation, tentatively made, was accepted without fuss, and Agnes promised to call in on her way home from school.

The woman sounded competent and Marion looked forward to meeting her. But she knew she would welcome the devil himself, if he could unravel the mess.

* * * *

Agnes was also looking forward to meeting Marion Shea. She was curious about this new member of the committee who seemed to be taking charge of a difficult situation. After her divorce, she thought she could distance herself from the centre's affairs, but the committee seemed to have got themselves into big trouble and the phone call had been a welcome distraction from another problem, the dilemma posed by her ex brother-in-law.

Dennis had phoned her earlier. The call interrupted her breakfast and Agnes was so surprised to hear his voice she could not think of any appropriate words.

She had not expected him to ring. Rowena was her ex-husband's wife, and though she had been shocked by the woman's death she had not seen herself as one of the people who should be personally contacted by the family.

Besides, she knew Dennis' opinion of Rowena. No doubt he'd wear a suitably sober face to the funeral, but he could hardly pretend he liked the woman. Was he calling so they could gloat together? William's disapproving brother and the rejected former wife. But I was the one who left William.

The silence had stretched too long. An awkwardness to be bridged. There was nothing else to say, so she simply repeated his name. "Dennis?"

That was all he needed to launch into the reason for his call. "It's Roger. William was expecting him on Friday night."

Of course her son wouldn't be going to his father this weekend. Dennis didn't have to tell her the visit was off.

But that was not why Roger's uncle had called. "I'm hoping the boy will still come," he had said. "I can put him up at the cottage. Agnes, I really need his help. You know what it's like on the land, you can't put everything on hold, even when there's been a tragedy and Will won't be much use."

"Won't a sixteen year old be in the way?" Agnes asked.

"Not Roger. He would be a real help. He's a capable kid and it's his inheritance we're talking about."

Typical. The McKendricks were obsessive about the place. Even now, after his sister-in-law's death, all Dennis could think about was his bloody herd. It wasn't as if they ran a dairy farm, with cows that had to be milked.

"Things pile up." Dennis was talking into her silence. "We're starting to stock up again, and the fences need some work."

When he put it like that she could hardly refuse. She had mumbled something about "asking Roger," which Dennis took to be consent.

"Tell him I'll pick him up on Friday, after school," he said, and finished the call before she could answer.

She would pass the request on to her son. He probably wouldn't mind a weekend with his uncle, especially if Dennis needed help. That was what McKendricks did, they pitched in, and William won't be much use, to quote his brother, she thought. Agnes gave a wry smile. If Rowena's death had done nothing else, it might have shaken her former husband out of his role as the dutiful McKendrick son, trained from boyhood to run the family property. The McKendricks of Ridgeway. Agnes pictured the words scrolled across the first page of a family saga. William had grown up in his father's shadow and, after the old man died, was expected to take his place. The wail of a siren dragged Agnes back to her duties and she gathered the books for her afternoon class.

It would be interesting to meet this Marion Shea. Loretta had chosen her to cope with the latest problem and the old woman was a good judge of character when she wanted help. Look how she's got you in, Agnes told herself wryly.

* * * *

Marion waved the kettle and Agnes nodded her acceptance of a second cup.

They had, inevitably, discussed Rowena's death. Regardless of Marion's personal opinion of the coordinator and Agnes' position as the victim's husband's first wife, both had been shaken by the murder and each found it comforting to share her horror with another woman.

Over the refilled cups, Marion described the committee's problem and her second encounter with the despicable Gowd.

Agnes was suitably shocked by the manager's heartlessness. "But you gave him more than he bargained for," she said. "He knows they should have checked the signatures. I suppose you haven't got the bank statements?"

Marion shook her head. The statements were still at the centre and the police wouldn't let anybody into the building.

"The trouble is, I don't know where we stand. Loretta was in such a state when she rang. The bank is going to be difficult and the rest of the committee. . ."

"Will be wringing their hands and telling each other how awful everything is. Nothing like this has happened before," Agnes said, and Marion laughed at her impression of Walter Edridge.

"Rowena always was a lazy cow," she said when Marion described the neglected paperwork. "I'm sorry, Marion, I know the woman's dead, but it's the truth. Once Benjamin said he'd handle things, I bet she never touched the bank statements." Even allowing for the natural antipathy of a first wife for the second, Agnes had Rowena's measure.

"She didn't even open the envelopes."

As a past treasurer, Agnes had questions about the present state of the organisation, questions that led, through a description of the problems caused by the coordinator's death, to a discussion of the McKendrick situation. Agnes showed neither bitterness nor jealousy as she talked about her ex-husband.

"William met Rowena through the drama group," she said. "Dennis starred in most of the plays and William would come to the party after the show." Marion remembered Loretta's words: "Dennis often had too much to drink, and William had to drive him home."

"Rowena had some trouble in the city," Agnes continued. "I think she got dumped by the current boyfriend, so she took a job up here in real estate and she wasn't doing very well when she met William."

Marion was surprised at the extent of her knowledge.

"William has Roger, our son, most weekends, so I want to know what's going on out there. Not that Roger saw much of the new wife or much of his father either. He seems to spend most of his time with his uncle."

"Dennis lives with his brother?"

"No, but you know how it is with these family farms." City-girl Marion indicated that she had no idea. "As the family grows, they buy more land and build an extra house. Dennis has a cottage on the property."

"How come he never married? Was he unlucky in love?"

"You could say that. The glamorous Dennis McKendrick left at the church door! Not quite. But there had been all the usual fuss, engagement parties and bridal showers, the wedding invitations had gone out, and the woman called it off."

"That broke his heart?"

"It certainly hurt his pride. To reject a McKendrick! You think I'm overstating it?" Agnes laughed at Marion's puzzled frown. "You never knew old Mrs. McK, Dennis and William's grandmother. You'd think, from the way she carried on that she had royal blood, and there was some story about a Scottish earl. She filled the boys' heads with her grand ideas, so you can imagine how Dennis felt when a woman rejected the great McKendrick name. The way he carried on, it was a good thing the woman left town before he learned that he'd been dumped."

"What about your own divorce? How did the family handle that?"

"Grandma was well and truly dead by then and there wasn't a big row. William and I simply drifted apart. Dennis was upset when I walked out, but he accepts his nephew's mother as an ex-McKendrick wife. He keeps saying how pleased he is I didn't bleed old Will as if I were some kind of leech. I mean, here I am with a good job in town while they are struggling on the property." Agnes laughed. "You should have seen Rowena's face when she learned about our settlement.

"It was at a party last year, after the Christmas show. I was having a few words with Loretta when we heard Rowena sounding off to Karen. 'That Agnes is a fool,'" she mimicked Rowena's contemptuous tone. "Karen was horribly embarrassed and muttered something about 'cash poor,' which is true enough, as our little lady learned after she'd committed herself to the marriage. 'I would have made them sell a paddock or two,' she said." Agnes shuddered. "God knows what that would have done to Roger's share."

She drained her cup and was suddenly serious. "I know they're having a tough time on the land. That's why Dennis rang me today, he still wants Roger for the weekend, he says they need the extra pair of hands."

Even Marion, with her limited experience of farming, realised the work would have to be done, no matter what was going on in the family's life.

"According to Dennis, William's a mess. He hasn't been out of the house since the detectives gave him the news. He was besotted with the woman. And she wasn't worth it," Agnes added with a change of tone. "Would you believe she was having an affair?"

Marion managed to look as if Loretta had not already given her that news.

"With Oliver Bostock. He's always been keen on the ladies, and he had his eye on our Rowena, even before Judith—his wife—left for Greece." It seemed that everything, from Rowena's scattiness to Benjamin's embezzlement, somehow involved the absent Bostock wife. Her return would have finished Oliver's escapade.

"It would have fizzled out anyway," Agnes assured her. "Oliver's love affairs don't last. But somebody is sure to tell the police. They'll think jealous husband, and next thing we know, they'll cast poor William as the murderer."

Marion thought of William McKendrick storming out of the building after Rowena's dismissive taunt. He was certainly annoyed—angry—but she could not see him as a murderer.

"Of course he's not the killer." Agnes dismissed the idea. "But a jealous husband always gets the blame; half the town already suspects him. When I got to school this morning, the awful librarian woman—the Blackmore bitch—was waiting for me. 'Was William violent with you, dear?' she asked, and when I said Will wouldn't hurt a fly, she shook her head and muttered 'you poor thing', as if I was some kind of battered wife."

Agnes twisted her fingers around a biscuit, reducing it to a pile of crumbs, as if that inoffensive pastry was the Blackmore bitch.

"William's no murderer," she said. "He's a total sook. He mightn't bother to move out of the way if he were holding a knife and some fool ran into it, but that's about as far as he would go."

"Even if he was upset?" Could William be as stolid as Agnes claimed? Marion remembered his clenched fist on Sunday afternoon. "He must have some passion. He married twice."

"Was married twice," Agnes corrected her. "Two women married William McKendrick, and all he did was let it happen to him. He's a good-looking beast—not as drop-down-dead gorgeous as Dennis but very attractive in his solid way, and he finds it convenient to have a woman around. You can't blame the man if we latch on to him."

"You too?"

"I'm afraid so. It's not William's fault I read him wrong, but I would have done better with Dennis, he's the one with personality. And he's got more passion."

Marion was not sure she accepted Agnes' description of her ex-husband. What she saw on Sunday afternoon was not lack of passion but a rigid self-control. What had Loretta said about the second marriage? "He was besotted with the woman!"

Agnes was still talking about Dennis. "I'll bet he knew about Rowena and Oliver Bostock, but he wouldn't have told his brother, in case it led to another divorce."

But suppose William knew what his wife was doing when she said she had been working late? Marion wondered

* * * *

After talking to Marion, Agnes drove to the sportsground to pick up her son, and on the way reviewed an imaginary saga, "The McKendricks of Ridgeway."

Did Roger feel overburdened by his position as the McKendrick heir? she wondered, as he threw his backpack into the car and scrambled after it.

As they drove home, she pondered over her own attitude to her ex-husband's family. It had not been a bitter divorce and she was able to treat William as a friend, who just happened to be her son's father.

Beside her, Roger was unusually quiet.

It must have been a shock for him to learn that a woman he had known so well, his father's wife had been bashed to death. Today the school would have been buzzing with news of the murder.

How would he feel about spending a weekend on the property?

Sometimes she found it easier to talk in the car, when her need to concentrate on driving gave them both an excuse to let a conversation fade into silence. It was a good time to mention Dennis' call.

Roger had no trouble answering, "Uncle Den will need some help," he said.

A very McKendrick response, Agnes thought.

She had to watch the road, but a quick, sideways glance showed her son's big hands clenched in his lap.

"You'll be staying in the cottage," she told him, "Dennis doesn't think your father's up to company." The hands relaxed.

To lighten the mood she asked a question about the previous weekend, which Roger had spent with a friend. The ostensible plan had been to catch up on assignments, but she guessed the boys spent most of their time in a masculine heaven of computer games.

Usually, after he had been away, Roger wanted to know how his mother spent her weekend, and she always considered her answers carefully. The boy was transparently eager for Agnes to have fun, as if his own looming adulthood made him look at his parents as people who might have lives and feelings of their own. Did he compare his mother's lot with that of his father's second wife and think Agnes had the worst of the bargain?

But this afternoon there were no questions about her weekend, nor did he launch into a description of his own activity. Instead, he wanted to talk about his next school year.

"I'll be in your mob, Mum, for maths."

Ever since Agnes had joined the staff of Ridgeway College she and Roger avoided each other, but things would be different if he was in her class.

"Think we can cope?" she asked, her tone deliberately light as she manoeuvred into the carport.

Roger slid out, dragged his pack from the backseat, and slung it over his shoulder.

"That's not the problem," he said, heading into the house.

Such a comment should have invited questions, leading into whatever it was her son wanted to discuss. But he had chosen his moment and made the enigmatic comment when the end of the journey gave him a legitimate reason to finish the conversation. She unloaded her own bag and followed him. She'd have to wait until he was ready to talk.

While she was preparing their meal, he joined her in the kitchen.

"I've got some stuff from the university," he said. "So I can choose my subjects for next year."

He pushed the vegetables out of the way, put a bundle of papers on the table, and stared at his hands.

"I don't want to do Ag."

She'd always assumed he would take an agricultural course and that the money she didn't demand in child support would be invested in the land he would inherit.

"I thought you liked the property."

"I do," he said. "It's great to go out on weekends, but it's not a career. It's all right for Dad and Uncle Den, but . . ."

Agnes waited. She rescued a carrot that was leaning precariously over the edge of the table, washed it, and cut it slowly into strips.

"You want something different?" she prompted.

The words came in a rush. Computers. Science. He wanted to go to university.

"Then you'll need that information," she said, gathering the papers from the table and putting them into a pile, making space to chop up the chicken. "You'll have to decide what subjects to take next year."

Roger picked up the pages, put them into a folder, and carried it back to his room. Agnes measured rice into a pot and browned the chicken pieces before adding vegetables to the pan. She hoped she'd signalled approval of her son's choice.

It was only later, as she poured chocolate syrup over their ice cream that she spoke of the problem they would have to face. "Do you want me to talk to your father?"

Roger shook his head. "I'll tell him. I had been going to talk about it this weekend, but I can't now, not after what happened to Ro."

Rowena's death changed everything.

CHAPTER THIRTEEN: TUESDAY EVENING

Stephen had had an uncomfortable day. He had been shocked but not surprised by Marion's outburst.

If his wife thought she'd hidden her homesickness, she was mistaken. A happy woman does not smile all the time. A contented wife will grumble to her husband about small things and she will not always season the stories she constructs about her day with forced laughter.

For months he'd shared the pretence. He laughed at her exaggerated account of Vivian's plans, the idea she could work at the gallery during the day "and fly to Ridgeway every night in my private jet." But strip the idea of its absurdities, and it wouldn't be impossible for Marion to keep her job in Melbourne while he worked in Queensland. In a world of two-career marriages, other couples coped with the geographical separation. Stephen knew of one family where the husband managed a firm in Singapore while his wife practised law in Sydney.

And this morning, a few bitter words had raised that possibility.

"You'd better go back to Melbourne," he had said in response to his wife's tirade.

He had not gone home for lunch. That little noontime break was one of the few advantages of his new position, but today he ate a sandwich in the café next door to the bank.

The afternoon drew to its inevitable end and he had to go back to the unit. As he pushed his key into the lock, he scanned the paint on the front door, as if it could tell him what was happening inside.

He knew his wife would not have left in a huff. She would never pack her bags in a temperamental fit, scribble a note, and disappear. Whatever plans Marion made, she'd tell him about them calmly and if she did go back to Melbourne, she would leave in an orderly fashion. And he'd be left in Ridgeway. Spending his evenings in an empty room.

He shaped his mouth to his usual greeting, calling, as nearly as he could, with his normal voice.

Marion was waiting for him. Almost before he was properly inside she wrapped her arms around him, full of apologies for the morning's fuss.

"I was so frightened," she said. "I kept seeing Rowena lying on the floor. I'd never been so close to violent death."

Stephen couldn't know how carefully she'd chosen her words—an explanation for the morning's outburst that implied no previous unhappiness, as if the temporary, unjustified disgust with her new home was caused by the horror of Rowena's death.

He held her tight, helping her rebuild the brittle shell of their mutual illusion, while she told him, quivering with indignation, about the iniquities of J. R. Gowd.

"He's got to account for the funds," Stephen said, watching his wife and trying not to start an argument. "He knows his staff has let him down. Somebody should have checked the signatures."

Marion noted the hesitation. Her husband was choosing his words—as nervous as a peasant on Mount Etna's slopes. Her outburst this morning must have frightened him.

To change the subject, she told him about the best part of her day. "I've been talking to Agnes Willmot," she said.

"Willmot?" The name meant nothing to Stephen.

Marion described William McKendrick's first wife and explained her connection to the centre.

"I thought Loretta Wheelwright's crowd were William's friends. Isn't it pushing things, asking his ex-wife to get involved?"

Marion, who had supported her sister through a messy divorce, agreed. "I was embarrassed about phoning Agnes, but she had been treasurer before Benjamin took the job and Loretta was sure she'd help. Would you believe she's happy to go through the books with me to see if we can sort things out?"

Stephen leaned against the kitchen bench while Marion dredged whiting fillets in flour and laid them in the pan.

She was bringing the fish to the table when the phone rang.

"Barbara!" As Marion held the receiver, Stephen pictured their daughter in the long gypsy skirt she liked to wear in the evening. In that skirt, with bare feet and hair swirling around her

117

shoulders, she was able to relax. "Jeans are for work, Dad," she explained.

He picked up the extension to join the conversation.

"I see you've made the news up there," Barbara said, going, as was her custom, straight to the subject on her mind. "Are you OK?"

Stephen was surprised at the concern in his daughter's voice. Just because there had been a murder in the city where her parents now lived, she had no reason to connect it to them.

"That woman, didn't she work at your artsy place, Mum?"

So the national news had all the details, Stephen thought.

"The Ridgeway Arts and Culture Centre." Marion said the words slowly, Stephen knew she was giving herself time to decide how much she wanted to tell Barbara.

"That's it. And the victim, Rowena McKendrick, wasn't she the manager or something?"

"Coordinator. Yes. I was in the building when they found her."

"Ooh." Awkwardness transferred to the other end of the line. Was she wondering how to respond, whether to press for more information or move to some neutral topic?

"That must have been awful for you," she said, using her Barbara-the-vet comforting the owner of a sick pet voice.

"It was a bit grim. How are things with you?"

Given permission to talk about her own affairs, Barbara launched into her most exciting news.

"I think I've been offered a job. Oh, not until I graduate," in response to her mother's shocked gasp. "And it's not really a job, more a research place." Then she dropped her bombshell. "It's in the United States." It was something to do with a disease of sheep. Stephen tuned out the gory details of animal symptoms while his brain danced around the word "Texas." Marion made some suitable congratulatory noise, and he managed to sound enthusiastic, until Barbara started to describe the horrible ovine symptoms that would occupy her time next year.

Marion pulled a face, and Stephen held the handpiece away from his ear. Some conversations don't go well with food.

"Mum?"

Marion confirmed she was still listening, and Stephen prepared to rejoin the conversation. "I should warn you, Gran's very worried. She keeps saying you could have been killed, because you were in the building on Sunday, running that art show."

He was surprised. Marion had not told her mother about her involvement with the centre. They both knew how Vivian felt about volunteer work.

"Pete talked about what you were doing, he was boasting about how you were involved in this big event and, Mum," an awkward pause, "somehow she's got the idea you are being paid."

"And you didn't contradict her?"

"Hardly. You know how she carries on about volunteers."

Vivian had been furious when the organiser of a big charity event asked her to do the photographs, and halfway through making arrangements she discovered she was expected to donate her time. "The labourer is worthy of his hire," she had told her family, and she replayed her own heated response whenever that organisation's name was mentioned in her presence. The request had never been repeated.

Marion laughed into the phone. "Thanks for the warning. I'll have to watch my words when your grandmother rings."

Another comic anecdote for them to share, Stephen thought. Marion would use Vivian's eccentricities to carry them safely through the evening, leaving no conversational space for the difficult question. What will we do about the house next year?

He would not stay with the script.

After the morning's argument, he had realised the futility of hiding their feelings. It was a time for honest dialogue.

"We'll have to think about the house," he said, after she put down the phone. "I can't see Peter batching by himself. If the worst comes to the worst, he can have one of his mates in to share."

"No way," Marion spoke sharply.

Stephen couldn't blame her. It was one thing to leave Peter and his older sister in their Melbourne home, but a young man batching with a couple of mates—he could imagine the fate of the poor house.

"Maybe I'll be transferred back next year," he said, breaking his resolve to face their problems honestly.

He didn't expect to be called back to Melbourne, and if, by some miracle, he was offered his old job, he would turn it down. However humiliating he might find his present exile, it would be worse to go back to his old branch. In Melbourne he would have to face his peers and his former staff.

"We'll work something out," Marion said, closing the discussion.

That night, as she lay in bed, Marion realised the events of the day had left her more comfortable with herself than at any time since they left Melbourne.

She had bearded the monster that was J. R. Gowd and she was sure that, in Agnes Willmot, she had found somebody who would help her untangle the centre's finances.

Most important of all, she and Stephen were talking to each other. They still moved awkwardly around the subject of Benjamin Knowles, and she was careful how she described the behaviour of J. R. Gowd, but they were facing their problems together.

I wonder what Agnes is doing tonight? She thought sleepily, as she snuggled against Stephen. It must be lonely being on your own when things go wrong.

* * * *

It is lonely being on your own. Agnes didn't realise she was echoing Marion's thought as she tossed in bed.

She found herself thinking about the Sheas. She pictured Marion telling Stephen about the day, describing the visit to the bank and her conversation with a former treasurer.

How would he respond? Would he give an absentminded grunt, treating her words as background to his own preoccupations, or would he listen attentively, interrupt with questions, and offer his, maybe unwelcome, advice?

William had been at the preoccupied end of the attentiveness scale, but surely, when it came to his son's career, he would want to be involved. How would he react to Roger's decision? Would he see it as a McKendrick rejecting the family property? What pressure would he put on the boy to try to make him change his mind?

Should she talk to William herself or accept Roger's word that he could handle the conversation with his father?

What she really needed, Agnes decided, was a female confidant—someone she could phone for a girlish chat—the he said/she said kind of stuff that men were never able to do properly.

She thought of Marion Shea. It was hard to believe she had had just such a conversation with the woman she had met for the first time this afternoon. It was not until she described the marriage breakup to Marion that she realised how calmly he had taken her decision to leave and how little trauma either of them suffered at the end of their marriage.

She hoped William would be as accommodating about his son's choice of a career.

CHAPTER FOURTEEN: TUESDAY NIGHT

Tuesday night brought peace to the Sheas, but there was little comfort in the Knowles' house, although Diana had been as busy as Marion and her day had ended as well as anybody could expect.

As soon as his brother left on Monday night, Luke had phoned Diana to tell her Ben was on his way, and she had waited anxiously for the sound of his car.

She had paced the rooms of their small house, cursing her own impatience and forced herself to sit in front of the TV, restlessly changing channels in an effort to find something that would hold her attention.

The advertisements were strangely comforting, particularly the ones Benjamin called *shouters*, voices screaming for her to *Buy! Buy! Buy!* As if their sheer noise could drive the worry out of her mind. But there was too much time between the ads when infuriatingly calm voices told her how to build a patio or chatted about films she didn't want to see.

At last she heard the car pull up and the crunch of feet on the gravel path. She hurried to open the door and Benjamin stumbled inside. He lost his balance and steadied himself on her shoulder. She could feel him shaking.

She half supported him to the sitting room and listened to her own voice repeating the words Luke had given her over the phone, cutting through her husband's tangled sentences. Later there would be time for apologies and promises to change, but now—if they were to survive—they must conserve their strength. After learning about the murder, Diana didn't believe embezzlement was such a terrible crime.

"And you were in Brisbane all weekend?" The statement was a question, Diana begging for a reassurance her husband was, thankfully, able to provide.

"You'll have to talk to the police," she said, quoting Luke. "We'll ask the solicitor to get in touch with them."

She had made them both hot, milky drinks and helped her husband to bed as if he were the child they planned to have one day. Benjamin dropped gratefully into the role and eventually fell asleep beside his wife.

But Diana had lain awake, stiffly still. She had listened to her husband's soft snoring and made plans for the following day. It was usually Benjamin who made the plans, but he had been as limp as a discarded plastic bag and, like the bag that choked sea life through no will of its own, had drifted into a mess that could destroy their lives. Tomorrow, she would have to take control.

That evening, as Benjamin made his confession, he seemed to shrink under the weight of his own misery, but Diana felt a lightening of her own spirit. For months her husband had moved in a cloud of depression that seemed to fill the house. He sat for hours scowling over his columns of figures and responded with abrupt resentment if she interrupted him. It was a relief to know what was wrong.

So he'd taken money from the snooty centre crowd. That was going to be a problem, but she knew he had not murdered Rowena McKendrick and he could tell the police exactly where he had been over the weekend.

Was that why the Wheelwright woman had been so insistent, wanting to talk to Ben—because the coordinator had been killed after the art show? Was Loretta warning the Knowles to get their story straight?

Benjamin muttered in his sleep and Diana gave his shoulder a comforting squeeze.

Thank God he had been in Brisbane. He had not spent the weekend with his brother, but when he said he was at a friend's place on the night of the murder, she knew who the friend was. The woman he had been living with before he came to Ridgeway. Nadine Tyson. Nadine would vouch for him.

Things would be different after they got through this trouble, Diana promised herself. She was not quite sure what that different would be, but no more quiet little wifey she decided, as she fell into a restless sleep.

It was still dark when she woke on Tuesday morning, but she got up, shivering in spite of her thick dressing gown, and, like Loretta Wheelwright, began to plan her day. Like Loretta, she made a list, but unlike Loretta, Diana was not accustomed to making plans. Several times she found herself wanting to wake Benjamin, to ask his advice. Each time she settled more firmly into her chair. It's up to you, Diana, she told herself. She collected the phone book and checked the yellow pages for solicitors.

Even in the middle of their trouble she was surprised at her own daring. She was the one dealing with their problems, while her husband, the sophisticated Benjamin Knowles— manager of the white goods department of a mega store and musical star of the drama group—waited, blank-eyed, for his world to collapse.

When the sky lightened and noises in the street signalled the start of a new day, she woke Benjamin and coaxed this new, helpless husband of hers to eat some breakfast.

"You can't face the day on an empty stomach," she said.

As she made her own preparations, she looked critically at her face in the mirror—sandy lashes, blonde eyebrows, and cheeks with a natural pallor that could be mistaken for fear. Sometimes when she applied her tinted foundation, Diana wondered if she would be invisible without the cover of an artificial skin.

This morning she took extra care. She knew she was an ordinary-looking woman, compared with the crowd at the centre, even the old ones. Ordinary was all right. In the circumstances it might be good, but she didn't want to look scared. She wanted to impress the solicitor as a woman who accepted her husband's silly mistake but knew he had not killed anyone.

"A silly mistake," she shook her head at the words.

"A stupid mistake. He is dreadfully sorry." That sounded much better. It was what she'd say to the committee, if she ever got the chance.

She stroked mascara onto her lashes and darkened her eyebrows, chose a fashionable lip gloss, and added some colour to her cheeks. She felt like an Indian brave, painting his face before the fight. That is exactly what I am doing, she thought. Fighting for my man. First the solicitor and then the police.

* * * *

124

It was not easy to find a solicitor.

Few of them started work at nine o'clock. Those who were at their desks had female guardians who assured her that Mr. Smith (Brown or Robinson) was not available this morning. Diana worked despondently down her list until she reached Xavier and Lyons, where a suspiciously boyish voice said he could "see you at ten o'clock."

He spoke as if she were making the appointment for herself, which in a way, she was. She was determined to go to Xavier and Lyons with Benjamin.

"What about your job?" he spoke in sudden panic.

She kept her voice calm. One advantage of working in a medical centre, she explained, was that there were two receptionists. In an emergency, like today, Roseanne could manage by herself. Diana had often coped single handed when the other woman took time off.

Xavier and Lyons had an office in a grand old house that had been the family home of a wealthy businessman—a home to match Benjamin's dreams. Diana choked on the thought. She had never seen herself as mistress of such an establishment, and if her husband had been satisfied with the place they could afford, he would not need a solicitor.

Benjamin followed Diana up a grand staircase to the first floor, where a receptionist waited in a light, bright office with cream walls and a big window.

The girl had large earrings that dangled in front of her smooth, shoulder-length hair like ornamental handcuffs. They waited anxiously as her fingers danced over a keyboard.

There was a rectangular aquarium on a table against the wall, and as Diana watched, the small, red fish listlessly circling their glass jail, she wondered what would happen to Benjamin.

When Jonathon Lyons appeared, Diana thought he looked more like a rugby player than the dusty solicitor of her imaginings. He ushered them into a small office, where, with a few carefully worded questions, he had the gist of Benjamin's problem.

It was the same story he had told his wife, but, Diana noted, the words came more easily as he repeated the tale.

"You'll have to go to the police," the solicitor said.

"They can't hang the murder on me," Benjamin's voice was trembling. "I didn't kill that woman."

"Nooo," the solicitor said. But Diana felt the words lacked conviction. She wondered what this Jonathon Lyons was thinking as he scratched a few words on his pad. Did her husband look like a murderer?

What did a murderer look like? Diana had seen news reports, the accused going into court, their heads covered by a policeman's coat so potential jurors wouldn't see their faces on the evening news. Not that the coat would help Benjamin. What with working in a retail department and playing the guitar with a local group, plenty of people would know who he was, even if they couldn't see his face.

"Try to use the victim's name," Jonathon Lyons was saying. "Let the police see that you are shocked by the murder, and sorry for the poor woman, as I can see you are," he added gently.

Benjamin looked bewildered but Diana knew what the solicitor was trying to tell him. Don't sound hard—like a killer. "Benjamin's really very gentle," she broke into the discussion. "He didn't kill Rowena McKendrick, he couldn't do anything like that." The solicitor had to believe her, because that was part of his job. But what about the police? Diana blinked back her tears. This was no time to mess her mascara.

"Calling Rowena 'that woman' makes you sound callous," she told her husband. "It might give the police the wrong idea."

"I didn't mean it like that," Benjamin said miserably "It's just that you," turning to Jonathon Lyons, "sounded as if you were trying to shut me up. Like you thought I was guilty. And it couldn't have been me. I wasn't even in Ridgeway on Sunday night." Lyons raised his eyebrows. "I was in Brisbane, with a friend."

The solicitor wrote on his pad and Benjamin clamped his lips shut. He couldn't mention Nadine Tyson's name in front of his wife.

Diana gave an impatient shrug. "I know where you were," she said. "If you didn't stay with your brother, you were

126

with a woman. Was it the one you were living with before you met me? The police will want to talk to her."

Please God let it be Nadine, Diana thought. Make her say she was with him on Sunday night.

Benjamin gave the solicitor Nadine's name and her address. "You'll have to go to the police," Lyons said again, "and the sooner the better. Tell them exactly what you told me. And for heaven's sake don't hide anything," he added. "We're talking about murder."

As if we didn't know, Diana thought. "What about the money Benjamin took?" she asked.

"Your husband had better admit to the theft. The best thing he can do is plead guilty. He should let the police know that he will not contest the charge."

"Maybe the committee won't take him to court," Diana said hopefully. "They're supposed to be his friends."

The solicitor rested his elbows on the desk and brought his fingers together in a steeple under his chin as he considered Diana's argument. "It won't be up to the committee," he told her. "We're talking about a government grant, and some money provided by the Ridgeway Council. The committee won't have any choice—unless they're willing to make up the loss themselves."

"None of them would do that," Diana said. "What will happen to Benjamin?"

"I don't know," Jonathan Lyons spoke slowly, honestly, as he considered the options. "We can't cover up the embezzlement, but I'm sure your committee won't want a lot of publicity. Hopefully the department will feel the same way, especially as your husband admits taking the money. You are willing to do that, Mr. Knowles?"

Benjamin nodded, not trusting himself to speak.

Lyons reached for the phone. Diana could only hear one side of the conversation, but he seemed to be making some kind of bargain. "We're on our way," he said.

* * * *

127

Diana must have passed the police station many times on her way to the city's centre but she had never noticed it before. Now she was affronted by the modern façade that looked so aggressively cheerful, showing its bright face to the street. She quickened her stride as Jonathon Lyons stepped politely aside to let her pass through the door, but once they were inside she stopped, to wait beside her husband while the solicitor fronted the officer at the desk.

"Detective Senior Sergeant Erbacher," he said, with a slight stress on the man's rank. "He's expecting us."

The officer spoke into an intercom, and after a very short wait, a detective, presumably Erbacher, joined them. There was a muttered awkwardness of introduction and a what-shall-we-do-with-you? glance from the detective that left Diana feeling as useless as tits on a bull, as her Uncle Jack would have said. The detective guided her to a bench where she could wait for her husband, and she watched Benjamin's retreating back as he was escorted, with his solicitor, to an interview room. Wives are not welcome, she thought.

The officer behind the desk wrote something into his ledger. He picked up the phone, and she wondered what the call was about. Not Benjamin's case—the detectives were dealing with that.

A fly buzzed. She turned her head to watch as it circled and settled on the wall behind the bench. If somebody opened a door or window to the outside world, would it take the opportunity to escape or was it in such a deep despair that it wouldn't recognise the opportunity, and so would doom itself to spend the rest of its short life inside the building?

What was Benjamin saying to the detectives? Don't hide anything, the solicitor had advised. He wasn't like the lawyers on TV, who sat with stony faces and interrupted with "no comment" if their client started to answer a police question.

And the detective sergeant was nothing like the police she'd seen on American crime shows. He was not in uniform, naturally, he was a plainclothes detective, and he had greeted them quietly. Her husband could have been visiting the doctor.

But a doctor would only be interested in her husband's body. He would take Benjamin's blood pressure, test his

128

cholesterol, and listen to his heart. These detectives were looking for something else. They would want to know what her husband was doing over the weekend. Would Benjamin shrink into himself, as he had last night, stumbling over the words as he told her what he had done? He must be very frightened, and if he flinched away from the detective's questions, would that make him look guilty?

Diana would have to get used to this new, cowed Benjamin. He had always seemed so sure of himself. The first time they went out, to a party with the Ridgeway drama group, they sat in the car for hours afterwards and he had shared his fantasies. He told her how he was planning to start his own business. "What I'm doing now is only a temporary job," he had said, "something to fill in time while I'm organising capital. I've already got the company set up."

She had been impressed by his ambitious plans, but it was Benjamin's dream that got him into trouble. It was that company, so conveniently set up, that provided an account to hold the money he stole. Benjamin isn't really wicked, Diana told herself. He is not all that different to Loretta Wheelwright, with those bottles of wine. But taking a few bottles of moderately good wine was not the same as stealing a government grant.

The fly was buzzing behind her. She could hear it moving against the high window. She willed it to give up its hopeless quest, to accept that the glass was irrevocably sealed. Someone would eventually open the front door. Couldn't the stupid insect wait for that?

Wait.

That was what she had to do. While Benjamin stumbled through the story he told her last night. She could almost hear his stammering excuses and hoped the solicitor would interrupt—gently—to keep him on track. "They won't be all that interested in your embezzlement," Jonathon Lyons had said, "they are looking for a killer."

The door opened to admit a smartly dressed woman, who approached the counter, said something to the officer on duty, and went out again. The fly ignored the open door and continued to struggle against the barrier of a closed window.

Footsteps. The rumble of voices. The solicitor led the way into the reception area, followed by Benjamin and the detective.

Jonathon Lyons looked pleased. Did that mean the interview went well or was his expression no more than a professionally confident mask?

Benjamin should not have worn a tie. His nervous fingers had pulled it askew and his collar gaped open under it. He had worried his button while he talked, fiddling until it dangled loosely over his shirt.

"I've got to go to court this afternoon," Benjamin told Diana, staring at the floor.

"Mr. Knowles will go before the magistrate this afternoon," Jonathon Lyons explained. "The sergeant thinks he'll be bound over, on his own recognizance."

"That means I can go home afterwards. But I can't leave town, not that I would anyway—and I have to promise to be in court for the hearing. It will probably be next week."

Diana's stomach churned as she watched Benjamin going down the passage with the Detective Senior Sergeant. "Please, God, let me have him home tonight," she thought.

The solicitor took her arm, helped her off the bench, and escorted her down the steps to the street

"These detectives are more interested in the murder than Benjamin's crime," he said. "They'll be sending somebody to check with his brother and the lady friend." The unspoken hope that her husband was telling the truth hovered between them but it didn't worry Diana. The state Benjamin was in last night, there was no way he could have made up a story.

The detectives watched Diana as she left the station with the solicitor. Shaw had admired the way she lifted her chin to smile at her husband as Lyons explained the procedure.

"It's always hard on the family," Erbacher said, "but Knowles has a gutsy little wife. I'd gamble any money she was the one who found Lyons and made sure her husband took the solicitor's advice."

Shaw agreed. "The state he was in, he couldn't get himself out of bed."

He had been shaken by the interview. In spite of his years in uniform, the constable still expected villains to look like villains, not terrified small shopkeepers.

And Knowles had been terrified.

He had worked himself into such a state that, with a little prompting from his solicitor, the words had spilled out. He talked about his gambling and told them how he forged the signatures.

"I only took a little at first," he said. "Just to get me over a losing patch. I was going to put it back. Really I was." But when the cash was swallowed by the black hole of the casino, he had borrowed more. He told the detectives how he had dreaded the annual general meeting, and how relieved he had been when the committee accepted his financial report. "I wanted to give the money back," he said again, as if his good intentions would mitigate the crime. But there was nothing he could do. Not until the centre got a government grant, and he withdrew all the money, believing that one more night at the casino, would solve all his problems.

"You lost that money as well," Erbacher had cut into the tearful confession with questions about his movement on Sunday night.

Knowles was so eager to answer that he stumbled over the words. He described everything he had done over the weekend and gave them Nadine Tyson's name, address, and telephone number.

"He's not much of a criminal," Shaw said.

Erbacher laughed, "When you've sat through as many interviews as I have," he said, "you'll know how quickly these chap's crumble, once they've been caught. Knowles isn't really a criminal, just a silly little man who found it too easy to get his hands on somebody else's cash. That doesn't make him a killer."

"Unless he thought he'd been rumbled."

"Once he got through the annual meeting, he didn't have anything to worry about," Erbacher reminded him. "All the correspondence from the bank went to his box number and nobody bothered to read the bank statements."

"That's his story. Suppose the coordinator found something that gave the game away? Remember what Mrs. Shea

131

had said about the bank statements? The victim might have opened one and kept it for blackmail."

But it was hard to imagine the cowering Benjamin Knowles bashing a woman to death.

Erbacher agreed. "I think he's telling the truth. He's admitted the embezzlement, but as for the murder . . . I don't think so. Though we'll have to check with his old girlfriend."

"Do you think she would cover for him?" Shaw asked.

"Not likely. The way Knowles tells it, he must have pissed her off. He turned up at her flat on Sunday night and drank all her grog while she was at work. Our people in Brisbane will contact her, but I'd bet my last dollar she'll tell the same story."

"Suppose he had driven to Ridgeway earlier, bashed the woman and headed back to Brisbane? If the McKendrick woman had uncovered the fraud, he might have wanted to shut her up."

Erbacher shook his head. "That wouldn't solve anything. The money would still be missing. Mrs. Bostock was still going to ask questions, and he must have known the bank would eventually realise something was wrong.

"Would he be thinking so logically?" Shaw had not been impressed by Benjamin Knowles, or the committee. "If any of them had been on the ball, they would have woken up to him," he added, "I'd like to know what state the books were in, before he took them on."

Erbacher was not concerned with the centre's history. "It's enough to deal with the present problems," he said, "I'm glad we've got Knowles' statement written up and signed. It wouldn't be the first time I've had a full confession, only to have the fellow plead 'not guilty' when he got to court."

"Do you think Knowles would back down after he talked in front of his solicitor?"

"I doubt it."

"Will the magistrate let him go home?"

"I don't see why not. He won't take off again. Not now he's talked to his wife."

* * * *

All afternoon, Diana had been determinedly cheerful. She had waited nervously in the courthouse while her husband was brought before the magistrate. Everything happened as the solicitor had predicted. Benjamin stood miserably twisting his fingers while the magistrate read the charge and responded to the inevitable question with a shaky "Guilty, your honour." Lyons spoke for his client, stressing Benjamin's remorse, and reminding the court that he had voluntarily given himself up before his crime was reported to the police. When he asked for his client to be bailed on his own recognizance, Diana, a devoted fan of *Law and Order,* expected the prosecutor to object and argue that the accused should be detained in custody. But there was no objection and the magistrate agreed with the solicitor that Benjamin Knowles was unlikely to abscond.

The magistrate remanded him to a date for the committal proceedings, and he promised to appear.

To Diana's surprise, nobody mentioned the murder.

"Because it isn't relevant to your husband's offence," Jonathon Lyons said when they were safely away from the court and she raised the subject. "He hasn't been charged with that crime. I'm sure the police will check his whereabouts on Sunday night," he added cheerfully.

Usually when they were together in the car, Ben drove, but this morning he had been so nervous she had taken the keys from his shaking hand. This afternoon he had climbed into the passenger seat without comment.

When they got home, he had followed her into the house and sat at the kitchen bench watching as she prepared their meal.

Then he started to talk. For weeks he had shut himself away in silent misery. Now that he had discovered the comfort of self-revelation, words gushed out of his mouth. She listened sympathetically.

He picked at his food and was still talking as Diana cleared the plates away. He didn't stop the stream of explanation and apology until she took his arm, settled him onto the sofa, and turned on the TV.

While he obediently stared at the screen, she took sanctuary in the kitchen. She stretched out the evening duties, washing their few plates, wiping down the sink, and mopping the kitchen floor and used the time to sort out her ideas.

Benjamin had been in Brisbane on Sunday night. Of course he had. And he was drunk. That's what Nadine would tell the police. Her husband couldn't have been in Ridgeway. Not possibly.

Diana felt more like a nursemaid than a wife as she made a hot milky drink for her husband. "It's no good you moping about," she told him firmly. "What's done is done. And huddling in the corner like a load of wet washing won't help anyone."

She had never talked to him like that before. Perhaps if I had spoken up, it would have been better for us both, she wondered.

CHAPTER FIFTEEN: TUESDAY EVENING

At the end of the afternoon, as the sky darkened and the sun disappeared, the Roach leaned against a camphor laurel tree a few doors away from Bostock's garage. He saw Trev and his mate leaving, and when Oliver came out to shut the big door, he sauntered up to him.

"What've you got for me?"

Oliver felt the satisfaction of a fisherman with a bite on his hook, but he let his shoulders hunch and shaped his face into a resentful scowl, in a performance worthy of the drama group.

"There's blokes know where I am," the Roach reminded him, sounding suddenly nervous as he followed his victim into the garage.

They were alone. Oliver chuckled as he noted how apprehensively the young blackmailer looked at the various objects hanging from hooks on the wall or lying on the bench. Did he realise how easily the swords to ploughshares story could be reversed and the tools of a mechanic's trade turned weapons?

The Roach stepped quickly back into the street. "You bring the cash out here," he said.

Oliver didn't allow his face to change. The fish might be on his line, but he had to reel it in. "If I give you money, will you go away?" The words came in a nervous splutter that earned a triumphant sneer from his visitor.

The Roach stood in the yellow pool of light under a street lamp.

Did he want to be visible to passing cars in case his victim took a swing at him?

The drivers couldn't hear their conversation, and the boy didn't bother to lower his voice when he demanded, "A thousand dollars, man, to keep me mouth shut."

He leaned forward, glared at his victim, and spoke with a gangster growl.

Oliver made his stammer more pronounced as he attempted to bargain and finally agreed to tormentor's demand.

"The money's in my office."

The Roach shook his head. "You get it. I'll wait." He pulled out a cigarette, lit it, and blew a mouthful of smoke into Oliver's face.

Oliver mumbled assent as a uniformed figure stepped out of the shadows further up the street. The policeman strode purposefully towards the garage and paused, as if suddenly suspicious.

"Are you having any trouble, Mr. Bostock?"

The Roach might be waiting for the hasty denial that would send the cop on his way, but those words didn't come. Instead Oliver's complaint was short and explicit. The allegation—demanding money with menaces. The result—a chauffeured ride in a blue and white car, without the dignity of flashing light. And a short wait at the police station.

* * * *

"Demanding money with menaces? No way," the Roach said indignantly when Erbacher repeated the charge.

"That Bostock bloke, he'd say anything. Fucking murderer. He's the one you should be locking up."

After Shaw started the tape and identified everybody present at the interview, the Roach repeated his story. "I saw that Bostock bloke, goin' in to murder the tart."

"Did you see him come out?" Shaw asked.

"Nah. I was around the front. Headin' into my little place. Well I didn't know he was bashing 'er, did I?" he said in the righteous tone of one who would certainly have intervened, no matter how large the assailant, had he known what was going on.

Questions about where, exactly, the Roach had been standing and what light was available in the parking lot did nothing to help the detectives choose between this story and the account they had been given earlier by Oliver Bostock.

"How about you show us where you were hiding on Sunday night?" Erbacher suggested.

The Roach tried to give a contemptuous refusal, but the words came out in a nervous squeak that earned a cold glance from Shaw and the assurance from Erbacher that he was "in enough trouble already." He gave a sulky "OK" and allowed himself to be driven to the scene of the crime.

"Let's see if your story matches what we found. Show us where you were waiting."

The Roach slithered into the bushes at the corner of the parking lot. "I stood here for a bit. I was fuckin' fed up. Freezin' me butt off out here and them in there feedin' their faces. A mob came out the front door, but the light was still on in the building so I stayed put. After a bit, a woman comes out and goes to her car, then another one. She drops her plonk but she doesn't bother to clean up the mess. I could of cut meself on the broken glass," the Roach said indignantly. "The cars drove off, and the bird inside, she put the front light out and I thought she'd gone. I went round the back." At Erbacher's insistence, he retraced his steps and showed them where he had been standing. "I checked her car. That's what I usually do, because some nights she waits in the kitchen for her bloke."

"And you can't get under the building until she's out of the way."

The Roach wriggled uncomfortably. "Sometimes I do. I move very quiet and slip in through me hole. That's what I was going to do when he come."

"He?"

"Yeah. He come round the other side, see."

Shaw was puzzled. Bostock had told them he walked through the park. But the timing was wrong. If the victim's lover was telling the truth, he didn't reach the centre until some time after the end of the exhibition.

"You're sure about the light in the office—the one you could see through in the front window? You saw it turned off?" The Roach twisted his face, trying to decide what answer would please the detectives. "Never mind," Erbacher said impatiently. "Show us where you were standing." And, in an aside to Shaw, "Get Bostock."

The detective constable clapped his hands, and a figure came down the path and around the back of the building.

"Is that the man you saw?"

137

"Yeah. That's him all right. The Bostock bloke. He was going in through the back door. Know him anywhere I would."

The figure came closer and took off its long coat to show the uniform of an officer.

"Well it looked like him," the Roach said defensively. "And anyway, it wouldn't of been a cop, would it?" he asked, satisfied with his own logic.

Back at the station the detectives considered the boy's statement. "Nothing we didn't already know," Shaw said. "The woman was by herself at the centre, waiting for Bostock, when somebody got into the building."

"Either the back door wasn't locked or the killer had a key. We can't do anything tonight," Erbacher decided. "Tomorrow, we'll go back to the centre and have another look at that parking lot. We can check the boy's statement."

"If we release him, he will disappear." Shaw said.

They could only keep the Roach overnight if Bostock was willing to lay a charge,

"I don't think he'll do that," Erbacher said. "He won't want the story of his little game spread around the neighbourhood. And if the case does go to court, his wife will hear of his affair. There's no harm in asking, though. If the man has not gone home."

Oliver had not gone home. He was still waiting at the front counter.

To the detective's surprise, he agreed make his complaint formal. "Anything to help you get that animal. . ."

"We're holding you on the blackmail charge," Erbacher told the Roach. "Demanding money," he elaborated over the youth's protest. "It's a serious offence."

"But not as serious as murder," Shaw put in, "and you can probably clear yourself of that, if you give us a look at your clothes."

That earned a grin from his senior. "If you can search with permission," Erbacher had told him once, "that's the easiest way."

"Don't expect too much," he warned Shaw, after the Roach had been safely delivered to the custody sergeant and his clothes bundled up to go to the lab. "I doubt they'll get anything useful from those rags."

All the detectives had learned from the evening's activity was that somebody, who might have been Rowena McKendrick's killer, had been lurking behind the building and come around the side, through the empty parking lot to the kitchen door. Erbacher wanted to examine the scene again, in daylight.

"If Bostock was the murderer," Shaw said slowly, "he must be one stupid bastard."

CHAPTER SIXTEEN: WEDNESDAY MORNING

As a community development officer, Karen Francis spent much of her time applying for funds for council sponsored programs. On Wednesday morning, she was at work early, hoping to thrash out the details of a submission before the rest of the staff arrived, but no sooner had she settled behind a barricade of paper than the phone trilled at her elbow. She was tempted to ignore it, to pretend she was still at home having a last piece of toast, but her car would be visible from the windows of the main building. She picked up the receiver and admitted her presence.

It was a summons from the CEO. He must have been watching for her car and he had made the call himself.

Her memo had sparked a response, and she knew whatever arrangements she had made would be judged as The-Wrong-Thing-To-Do-You-Stupid-Girl.

It was not a good beginning to her day.

As Ridgeway had grown from the original small country town to a large inland city, the council had also expanded and, in the process, had stretched the capacity of several premises. The original council chambers, built in the nineteenth century, followed the shape of a church. Its offices were now used as meeting rooms—one of which was going to accommodate members of the committee of the Arts and Culture Centre for the evening's gathering. A square construction next door was physically joined on the second floor, but it had no architectural connection to the ecclesiastical shape, and had been intended to house an overflow of staff. This building was laughingly called "The Box."

Karen's office was in The Box—one of a row of cubicles off the main administration area. It was originally intended to accommodate one worker, but there were two desks and the large filing cabinet that held two meticulously separated sets of files.

As the city grew still larger, so did the council, and yet another building was added to the complex. This magnificent edifice housed the most important professionals involved with city infrastructure: planners, engineers, and architects and (naturally) the office of the chief executive officer.

Karen had to cross the parking lot to reach that august presence. She kept her head down to avoid the inquisitive stares of late arrivals, who would take any intercepted glance as an invitation to bombard her with questions.

At the CEO's office, she knew she was in trouble. The door was open, but Reginald Mollison didn't look up when she knocked. He made a small correction on the draft he was reading. She knocked again, more firmly, telling herself this feigned preoccupation was an old trick, stale when her grandmother was a girl.

She, Karen Francis, was an adult, a professional woman, and Reginald Mollison, for all his exalted rank, was simply a council employee like herself.

Mollison put down his pen, frowned, and nodded to a chair. It was all very well for Karen to remind herself of her professional status, but what could she do when the CEO looked down his nose, as if she were a misbehaving member of the junior school?

"Don't you take none of their cheek, my girl," is what Grandmother Joseph might have said if she had been in the room, so clearly did that oft repeated injunction ring in Karen's ears. But she was not the one who needed to recognise the position of the community development officer, and however powerful a dead grandmother might be in the spirit world, she counted for little in the council offices.

She was tempted to try her grandmother's response to pompous officialdom, mentally removing the CEO's clothes, but she decided against this exercise. On one disastrous occasion, the vision of a naked physics teacher had made her giggle helplessly in a way that didn't improve her situation.

Instead, she took the offered chair and sat, visualising a cold mountain stream, until the great Mr. Mollison was ready to speak.

"This trouble at the centre," he said. "Money missing. It's a bad business."

"Horrible." Karen answered with feeling, but unlike the man in front of her, she was not talking about possible repercussions for the Ridgeway Council.

"What's going on over there?"

He stared at her, ready to puncture any excuse she might make, as a member of the committee.

"The treasurer, Benjamin Knowles, seems to have disappeared. Loretta Wheelwright, the president, was informed by the bank that some funds had been transferred from the organisation's account," she said in a carefully flat voice.

"The council has always supported the centre," Mollison said, leaning his elbows on the desk and resting his chin on the knuckles of his closed hands. "It doesn't look good. You're on the committee." He thrust his head at her as if he wanted to bite her chin. "How did it happen?"

She didn't try to answer that question. Instead, she talked about the committee meeting the president had arranged for that evening. "It can't be held at the centre," she said, "the police have locked us out of the building."

The CEO shook his head. "We can't have your people meeting here," he said, sitting very straight behind his desk and puffing out his chest. Had he been a lizard, he would have raised a frill to make himself look hugely fearsome, as a mere human, he had to content himself with opening his eyes very wide. "I don't want the council involved in your mess."

Your mess! Your people! Karen bit her tongue. Had he forgotten he was the one who had insisted the community development officer be included on the committee? "He who pays the piper has a right to call the tune," he had quoted sententiously, as if the council's meagre contribution gave him the right to control the organisation.

"I'll tell Loretta to cancel the meeting," she said. "It means no one from the committee can talk to the bank until the police allow them to use their own building," she added, in case he had not realised the implications of his decision.

He tried to stare her down, but she willed her face to a cooperative blank. The authority—and the responsibility—was with the CEO.

142

"Since you've already made arrangements," he said grudgingly, "you might as well let them use our room tonight. But don't get the council involved in their shenanigans. And we won't be coughing up more cash," he warned.

* * * *

Fables about the ostrich trying to escape its enemies by hiding its head in the sand might have no foundation in natural history, but substitute a community development officer for the big bird and a pile of paperwork for sand, and the story has some credence.

But no amount of paper could save Karen from yet another intrusion. There was a timid knock on the wall beside her open door and a small, triangular face poked into the office. Lynette Waters.

Lynette had a problem.

She had applied for the position with the multicultural project and knew she'd done well in the interview. The Shea woman must have been impressed by her stated intention to get as much experience as possible because one day she wanted to manage her own gallery, and William McKendrick had made it clear that, as far as he was concerned, she was the best candidate. Lynette had been overjoyed and had spent the rest of the afternoon mentally composing a tactful letter of resignation from her present position. In her new role she'd be working with the council, but not as a member of Reginald Mollison's staff.

That pleasant dream had been shattered by a discouraging call from Mrs. Shea, who did not expect the program to get funding. "The department will be looking for organisations already involved with ethnic minorities," she had said, "and our centre has never worked with migrant groups."

After she put the phone down, Lynette had cursed her luck. If only they had asked her to write the submission. She knew exactly how to describe the drama group's productions as "appealing to our diverse ethnic community." And she could have used the annual art exhibition as "a reflection of the Arts and Culture Centre's support for a vibrant migrant population." Wasn't there a Chinese name on one of the paintings last year?

143

As it turned out, Mrs. Shea had been unduly pessimistic because Judith Bostock knew what she was doing. The department had liked her submission and were willing to fund the multicultural program.

At the art show on Sunday afternoon, Walter Edridge had told her the good news. "You'll hear from us officially, tomorrow, lass," he had said.

Lynette couldn't resist sharing her excitement with a few trusted workmates, but as Monday morning stretched into afternoon and the phone didn't ring, she regretted her impetuosity.

She told herself that members of the committee were busy people, that after spending the weekend working at the exhibition, they needed time to deal with their own affairs. But she wished she hadn't mentioned the job. Suppose she didn't get it after all?

On Monday night, she learned about Rowena McKendrick's death.

Lynette and her partner, Alistair, shared a house with another couple, and the early evening usually found them gathered for a communal meal. A malignant fate decreed that Alistair played squash on Monday nights, and this evening the other two were visiting friends.

While Lynette was scavenging in the kitchen for an easy snack, she had the television on in the next room to provide a sociable background noise. When familiar music signalled the local news, she took her plate into the sitting room and settled to watch the program. The first story should feature the art show, followed by something about the most recent work of the Ridgeway Council. She was interested in both items.

The announcer's face was unusually serious. "There has been a brutal murder in Ridgeway," he said. "A woman has been bashed to death."

The camera showed police cars pulling up in front of a building. Was that the Arts and Culture Centre? Lynette leaned forward for a closer look as the announcer gave the victim a name. Rowena McKendrick!

He must have made a mistake. Rowena McKendrick couldn't be dead!

Lynette had seen her on Sunday afternoon. She had made a point of talking to the coordinator, because, if her application was successful, they would be working together.

She stared at the slices of ham on her plate, at the neatly quartered tomato and the hunk of cheese. The food would choke her if she tried to eat.

According to the announcer, the police were following several leads, but that seemed to be all the information available at this time. Lynette barely heard the remaining items of news or the weather report, but she gave the screen her full attention at the end of the bulletin, when the announcer returned and repeated the main story.

There was no mistake. Rowena McKendrick had been murdered.

Over the next couple of hours the remote control gave Lynette three different sessions of news. They all confirmed the original account but had nothing new to add.

She had barely known the victim, but Rowena was part of the circle of people-like-us. She knew Ridgeway, like any city of its size, had its darker side. Drugs. Drunken brawls. Even murder. But Lynette had never been so directly connected to this violence.

She would have been surprised to know that, in another part of town, Raymond Gowd, manager of the First Queensland Bank, had had exactly the same reaction to Rowena McKendrick's death. People whose families knew his wife should not be murdered.

There was a clatter of housemates returning. They had also heard the news, and in the following discussion, Lynette's slight connection to the victim made her the centre of everybody's attention.

They spent the evening talking about the murder and asking each other what kind of maniac would do such a thing to a lovely woman like Rowena McKendrick. They also wondered why she was in the building, by herself, so late on a Sunday night.

Just as she was drifting off to sleep, Lynette had a thought that jolted her awake. Rowena's death. That was why nobody rang her about the job. She felt a surge of relief. They had not changed their minds. That thought was followed by a flush of self-disgust. How could she be so concerned about her own affairs, when a woman had been murdered?

By Wednesday Lynette was able to separate her horror at Rowena's death, her genuine sympathy for the victim's family, and her understandable anxiety about her own future.

She wanted to be reassured about her position. Surely the death of a coordinator wouldn't affect her project. According to Walter Edridge, the centre had already received the grant money.

Who could she ask about the program? A name flashed into her mind. Karen Francis. She was a member of the committee and had been on the interview panel.

That was why, on Wednesday morning, Lynette was in Karen's office, trying to find the appropriate words to start a conversation.

She didn't intend to ask Karen about the job, but if they were talking, perhaps she could mention the multicultural program. She could tell Karen how pleased she was that the department had approved the project. She imagined Karen worried about the centre and was wondering how they could manage without Rowena McKendrick. Since Lynette was already involved, why shouldn't the committee ask her to take the extra responsibility of a permanent position?

Those pleasant thoughts were dashed when Karen raised an eyebrow and had a quick but obvious look at her watch.

There would be no friendly chat with Lynette's questions dropped casually into the conversation. If she wanted to ask about the multicultural program, she'd have to raise the subject herself. She stammered a question about the project.

"Who told you the funding had been approved?"

Lynette's cheeks flamed at the icy tone.

"I know it hasn't been properly announced," she admitted. "But I saw Walter Edridge on Sunday, and he told me about the grant."

"Mr. Edridge should hold his tongue," Karen said, with a cold emphasis on the title. She checked one of her papers and, with her eyes fixed on the monitor, started tapping her keyboard.

Lynette felt herself dismissed.

CHAPTER SEVENTEEN: WEDNESDAY MORNING

The sun was shining when the detectives arrived at the centre, but the forecast warned of rain later in the afternoon. The forensic team had already searched the area, and had there been any trace of the killer, they would have picked it up.

"What do you think we'll find?" Shaw asked.

Erbacher shrugged. "I want to get the feel of the place," he said. "The art show finished just after five. If the Shea woman came out in the dark, she must have been in the building for some time after the others had gone."

A couple of early butterflies made a flash of orange. Although the spring days were warm, the nights were still too chilly for mosquitoes. Too bad. Shaw felt a dose of dengue fever was exactly what the killer deserved.

They looked around the parking lot.

Marks under a big swamp cypress were mentioned in the forensic report. They were still visible.

"It looks like the killer was waiting here," Erbacher said.

"Do you reckon he was watching the office because he wanted to catch the victim by herself? Or did he wait till he thought the building was empty?"

"Depends which lights were on," Erbacher said. He peered under the tree. "Whoever was hiding here could see the office window."

"If the woman turned off the lights, it would look as if she'd left the place."

"But anybody going around the back of the building would see a light in the kitchen," Erbacher objected.

Shaw scrambled under the stooping branches of the huge tree, but the only information the ground could give was that someone, or something, had crushed a few leaves and broken the stalk of a small weed.

Times like this, they could use the skills of an aboriginal tracker, one who would read the whole story from a few scuff marks. Perhaps they should talk to Dr Jennings, from the

Aboriginal studies department of the university. She was so proud of her heritage; did it include a tracking gene?

He laughed at himself. Dr. Jennings might have some inherited predisposition to sharp eyes, but tracking was as much a learned skill as his father's mechanical prowess. And whatever Dr. Jennings might claim, she was as much a product of the suburban life as himself and Erbacher. If they were to find Rowena McKendrick's killer, they would have to use their police training and the resource of the forensic lab.

"Let's have another look at that door," Erbacher said.

Their boots crunched on the gravel as they walked around the building. It would not be easy for a prowler to move quietly on this surface but if the victim heard a noise outside, she would probably think it was a cat.

"Bostock should have seen the car," Shaw said.

"It was dark. And he wasn't looking for a car. Their signal was a light in the window of that small back room. When he didn't see any light he went home."

"So he says."

There was a clump of bushes beside the door. "The members might be sloppy about everything else," Erbacher said. "But they take care of their plants. Did you see that notice over the sink 'Tip any clean water into the bucket, the geraniums will love you?'"

"That's what Janey does. She saves any waste water for her herbs." Shaw looked at the geraniums. The flowers were an ugly brownish red, the colour of the stain on the dead woman's dress. Was that what happened when you joined the police? Everything you saw reminded you of something horrible. Even a flower looked like dried blood. And this morning at breakfast, he had been sickened by the sight of coffee stains on the floral tablecloth.

Thinking of blood, "Did forensics check the toilet?" he asked. It would not be the first time a killer tried to wash his hands and left a fingerprint behind.

"Yes. The place was clean."

As the detectives walked back to the car, Shaw looked past the building to the park. A couple of boys were paddling in the creek.

He frowned. "Those kids should be in school." he said.

Erbacher was more tolerant. "At least they are enjoying themselves. They don't have to think about dead bodies, or a killer who might strike again."

Shaw shivered. A cloud blew over the sun and he felt a chill in the air.

"And there is something else," Erbacher said, when they were in the car. "Remember the Shea woman?"

"Wasn't she the last person to see the victim alive?"

"That's what she told us. The Sheas were the last to leave. They followed Mrs. Wheelwright's car."

"Is there any reason to doubt that?"

"No. Not exactly, but it's a bit odd. I dropped into the bank again, on my way home yesterday, I've always used First Queensland myself, so I've had a bit to do with Gowd over the years, he had finished for the day, and we got chatting." Shaw grinned at the casual *dropped in again* and *got chatting*. Was Erbacher doing a quiet check on Knowles' story? "He shared some gossip about the Sheas."

"Is there any connection with Benjamin Knowles?"

"No, but Stephen Shea is a banker. He had a senior position with Australia Central, in Melbourne, before he was sent up here. He was shunted sidewise according to Gowd. Do you remember last year, when there was that fuss in Victoria about Australia Central? Money was taken from a client's account. Shea was the manager and he didn't know they had a problem until the auditors checked the books."

"That sounds like the Arts and Culture Centre," Shaw said. "Nobody knew the treasurer had his hand in the till. And Shea's wife is on the committee. Bit of a coincidence."

Erbacher did not like coincidences. "But I don't see how it can be relevant."

Erbacher shook his head. "It's weird, the parallel between the crimes, but if Gowd's got his facts straight, Knowles started raiding the centre's account while the Sheas were still in Melbourne."

* * * *

149

On Wednesday morning, Marion was determined to make up for Tuesday's uncomfortable breakfast, and to Stephen's delight, they started the meal with a serve of strawberries. Since he didn't have a long drive to work, he didn't have to leave as early as he had in Melbourne and could enjoy a more leisurely start to the day.

That was one of the good things about living in Ridgeway, Marion decided, as she cleared away the plates and popped an overlooked strawberry into her mouth.

While the dishwasher did its duty, she checked her e-mails. Nothing. She shook herself. Barbara had spoken to them last night, what fresh news could she have?

She opened her favourite solitaire and an unseen hand dealt cards onto the screen. The first round looked good. Hearts. She put a six under the seven. Sixes and sevens, as Vivian would say when something disrupted her well-ordered world.

Those hearts should be an omen for Stephen and herself. The kids? Spades might be appropriate for Barbara, if she were going to prosper as a research vet. In Texas. Hearts could bring an overseas romance. Everybody travels more nowadays, she told herself, and imagined visiting her married daughter in the USA. As Stephen so often said, she didn't just count her chickens before they were hatched, she did her sums before the eggs were laid.

What would be her son, Peter's, card? No hearts for him, as far as she knew. How did he feel about his sister's plans? If Barbara read Peter right, and she usually did, he'd be happier sharing a flat with his mates than minding the family home. No garden. And not so many rooms to clean.

Perhaps they should rent out the Melbourne house.

Ironically, these thoughts were interrupted by the tinny rendering of "Home Sweet Home" that the Margraves had chosen for their doorbell's peal.

Marion didn't like the tune, but a tenant must accept her landlord's taste.

When she opened the door, she decided that neither of the men standing on her porch would care what music announced their arrival.

One of them must have rung the bell, but they had both stepped back, taking the nonthreatening position favoured by most canvassers. But they didn't look like spokesmen for any political party, salesmen, or members of a proselytising church.

They looked like detectives.

When she had been interviewed—it seemed an age ago— the large sergeant had said someone would check her story. She had expected another uniformed officer, but these two wore business suits. They might dress like Stephen and his coworkers, but she didn't need to see their identification to know they were from the police.

For some reason, she found their civilian clothes more intimidating than the uniforms of her earlier interview.

"Detective Senior Sergeant Erbacher," the older man presented his card in the manner favoured by detectives on TV. "And Detective Constable Shaw." The detective constable was younger than his sergeant. He fumbled with his card and looked at his senior as if waiting for directions.

"You'd better come inside." Marion felt like an aspiring actress at her first audition, reading from an unfamiliar script.

She led them into the living room, where Erbacher settled himself into a comfortable chair, as no doubt he had in many different rooms over years. The constable seemed less at ease. He chose a harder seat and twiddled his fingers until he caught her watching and was suddenly still, like a child under his grandmother's eye in church.

He pulled out a notebook, and with it on his knee and a pen in his hand, he looked more comfortable. Props are important, Marion decided, making a mental note for any film director who might ask her opinion.

Erbacher started the interview with the same questions the uniformed sergeant had asked on Monday afternoon. "What time did you leave? Who saw you go? Did you notice anything unusual?"

She mentioned a rustle in the bushes. That wasn't in the record of her first interview.

"I didn't think of it." How could she remember everything, with Rowena lying dead, in the back room?

"What time was it, when you came out of the building and heard the noise?" That was Constable Shaw. He had the point of his pen resting on the page, ready to record her answer. As if it mattered. Unless it was the murderer she heard.

"I'm sure it was a possum." She didn't want to think about a killer hiding in the bushes, watching her.

She shivered, suddenly cold in the warm room.

She had spent her teenage years reading her grandmother's treasured mysteries and knew that the second murder victim was usually a witness who could identify the murderer.

"I didn't really see anything," she said quickly. "The burglar, intruder, whatever it was, he must have come later." She stared at the constable, willing him to agree, to note with his recording pen that "the woman, Marion Shea, left the scene before the crime and could not give us any information." But the hand holding the pen did not move.

The senior detective had no more questions about Sunday night. He wanted to know about the week leading up to the art show. What could she tell him about Benjamin Knowles?

"Nothing. I hardly know the man," she said into a disbelieving silence. "I've only been on the committee for a couple of months and have only attended two meetings."

"You were very involved with the art show," Erbacher reminded her. Somebody had obviously told them about her contribution, and it would not have been the president.

"You must have seen a lot of the treasurer over the last few days," he was saying. "And you would have been working with Mrs. McKendrick. Wasn't it part of her job to arrange these affairs?"

"Benjamin wasn't involved in the show. Most of the arrangements were made during the day, while he was at work. And Rowena never did very much." Marion spoke without thinking, and wished she could swallow the words. Wasn't she the last person to have seen Rowena alive?

She felt the heat in her chest climbing up her neck to her face and knew her skin would be an ugly, mottled red.

"Did you have problems with Mrs. McKendrick?" Erbacher asked.

"No more than anybody else." Marion should have expected this interview and had her answers ready. Why was she so frightened? She had nothing to hide.

"You said you stayed behind," Erbacher quoted from an earlier interview, as if he had the page in front of him. Did he have one of those memories, Marion searched for the word . . . "eidetic." What exactly had she said on Monday afternoon?

"You offered to help Mrs. McKendrick with the cleaning up," Erbacher prompted. "Is that why you stayed behind after the others had gone?" Marion nodded. "I didn't get the idea you were a particular friend of the dead woman."

"I thought . . . I wanted . . . somehow we'd got off on the wrong foot." She might as well get the whole story out, they would hear about it anyway, if they talked to the rest of the committee. "I thought if I offered to help, after the others had gone, it would give us a chance to talk."

"You didn't stay very long." Whose report was Erbacher remembering now, as he stared into space?

"No, Mrs. McKendrick—Rowena—told me to go home. She said she'd leave the cleaning up and do it on Monday."

"You don't know why she stayed behind, after you and your husband drove away?"

"No." Marion bit off the word and stared at the detective. It was a strategy she had used effectively with people who came into the gallery just to escape the Melbourne wind. A sharp word and an icy stare were enough to persuade any scruffy noncustomer to take shelter somewhere else. Detective Senior Sergeant Erbacher ignored her tone.

At that moment all Marion's attention was on the older man. She didn't see Shaw stiffen, or note his fingers tighten as he gripped his book with a suddenly sweating hand. She thought of the detectives, like police on TV, as hardened cops, and imagined them inured to nasty homicides. She also understood that Erbacher's rank would mean he asked the questions.

She was startled when Shaw spoke. "Coming back to Benjamin Knowles," he said, "you'd been on the committee of this Arts and Culture Centre for a couple of months, you helped organise a big fund-raising event, and you didn't notice anything wrong with the finances?" Was there a note of incredulity in his voice? "You were involved in the embezzlement and bashed the coordinator over the head . . ." She could almost hear the thought.

"As I told you very clearly, a few minutes ago, I hardly knew Benjamin Knowles. We happened to be on the same committee and he was present at the two meetings I attended." Marion could hear the sharpness of her words.

Could they sense her hostility?

Shaw was asking for information about a murder. She had known Rowena McKendrick, and had worked with her.

Over the weekend, nobody acknowledged her contribution, but when the police asked about a murder—they would all remember she had been the last to leave.

"What made you come to Ridgeway?" Shaw asked

"Stephen, my husband, was transferred from Melbourne." She glared at the detectives, knowing that they knew why they had come from Melbourne, daring either to pursue the subject. To drag Stephen into the investigation. Shaw opened his mouth, as if he recognised her challenge and was prepared to take it up.

"And how do you like our city, Mrs. Shea?" That was his senior, forcing her attention back to him and changing the subject with this, the most banal of social questions.

She made the expected response and squirmed uncomfortably when he followed her answer with comments about the district's excellent facilities and the current shortage of housing.

She made a curt, ungracious response, offered no opinions and waited for the detective to return to the business at hand. But there were no more questions about Rowena's death or Benjamin Knowles' misdeeds.

Erbacher stood up, signalling an end to the interview. "Thank you for your time, Mrs. Shea, you have been most helpful."

How had she helped them? What had she said?

Or was this senior detective mocking her, trying to make her think she had given herself away. But she had nothing to hide, she thought.

Marion showed the detectives to the door and shivered as she watched their departing backs. Which was stupid, she told herself, shutting the door. She knew she was innocent. What could they possibly think she had done?

She imagined the conversation in the detectives' car. That there was financial misappropriation at her husband's bank and money was taken from a community group, after she joined the committee.

* * * *

Marion was correct in assuming the detectives had noted her discomfort, her embarrassment after the implied criticism of a murder victim, and her awkwardness when they asked about the Sheas' move to Ridgeway.

She would have been surprised by their interpretation of the little scene.

"Stupid woman," Shaw said, slowing behind an overloaded truck. "So she didn't like the coordinator, does she think that makes her a suspect?"

"You can't blame her being jumpy. Haven't you noticed how uncomfortable we make people with our questions?"

"Why? If they've got nothing to hide."

"Everybody has something to hide. Some small secret that seems huge to them. They are scared we'll ferret it out."

CHAPTER EIGHTEEN: LATER WEDNESDAY MORNING

After her unpleasant session with Reginald Mollison, Karen had marked the day Blue Wednesday on her mental calendar.

"Damn Benjamin Knowles. And damn the centre," she muttered, banging her fingers on the keyboard as if it were one of the old, manual machines. And damn Rowena McKendrick, the world's sloppiest coordinator and most inconvenient corpse. Karen Francis, an educated young woman in the civilised culture of the twenty-first century, felt a shiver of apprehension as she found herself cursing the dead. She would never say the words aloud, not even when talking to Keith, a self-proclaimed atheist.

She tried to collect herself, to prepare for the next day's meeting with the senior citizens. Their project was every bit as worthy as Judith Bostock's multicultural program, but migrants were flavour-of-the-month with the department, while programs for the elderly were less glamorous. Karen addressed herself to her computer, searching for a possible funding source.

It was hard to concentrate. She was pleased when the phone interrupted her work. Dennis McKendrick, asking if she could meet him for lunch.

Outside the sky might be overcast but in the small office Karen's mood now rivalled the sunniest day. Any concern about the problems of the Arts and Culture Centre or the displeasure of Reginald Mollison, paled into insignificance beside the prospect of spending some time with Dennis McKendrick.

Dennis' suggestion of "the usual place" might not equal the romantic overtones of "our song," but to her optimistic ear it carried the suggestion of an ongoing relationship, even if most of their previous meals had been eaten in the company of the drama group.

As she walked into The Bouvier, she felt as if her feet, in their strappy heels, were treading on the cushion of air so deceptively promised by the makers of expensive running shoes.

The restaurant appeared to reflect her excitement. Several months earlier the premises had been sold, and the new owners not only had changed its name, but they also had given the place a complete overhaul. They had knocked out walls and decorated the formerly sombre rooms with the primary colours of a child's picture book.

Karen smiled an appreciation of the new décor and looked around the room for Dennis. He had already grabbed a table.

"I see they've got rid of the Ghostly Greats," she said as she sat down. She was referring to the faded photos, which used to line the walls of the old Sportsman's Café. They would have been hopelessly out of place in the new Bouvier.

Dennis grunted. Left to himself he would have ignored the change. This was where he had always eaten when he came into town, and as long as the food was still edible, who cared about the colour of the walls? "The old place had great burgers," he said, putting his jacket over the chair to reserve their place while they went to the counter to order.

Karen knew he appreciated the huge cheeseburgers that had been a feature of the old Sportsman's Café, and she wasn't surprised when he frowned over the more expensive Bouvier offering. As usual, he ordered a burger, but his tone showed his opinion of the new, fancy menu. Karen decided to try the special quiche, served with salad and thin, crispy chips.

While they waited for their meal, Dennis explained his unexpected journey. "I didn't want to come into town today, but I had a call from the police."

Karen raised a questioning eyebrow.

"I'm an important witness. Would you believe I'm providing an alibi for Rowena's lover?" He laughed.

"The detectives talked to Bostock yesterday, because he was having it off with William's wife. Of course they know about it," he said impatiently over her protest. "People talk. And the way policemen think that makes Oliver a prime suspect. He might have wanted to end the affair and killed Rowena, to get her out of the way."

Karen shuddered. She was shocked by the idea of Oliver Bostock killing his lover.

"He didn't. Unfortunately the man is in the clear. I saw him myself, with his tow truck. Nothing, not even his lady love, can come between Bostock and a crash."

"Was it a bad accident?"

Dennis shrugged. "Who knows? I passed him just before the turnoff to our place. I had to tell the detectives it was Bostock's truck and Oliver was in it. If I'd known I'd have to alibi the rat, I might have taken the back road home."

He paused while the waitress brought their meal.

Karen was pleased to see Dennis' burger matched the old Sportsman's offering for size, and her quiche was flanked with the thin and crispy chips the menu had promised. After sampling his meal and giving a surprised approval of the new chef, Dennis continued his story. He had confirmed Oliver's alibi over the phone the day before and thought that would satisfy the police. "But they rang this morning and asked me to come into town, to sign a statement. As if I don't have enough to worry about. My sister-in-law is dead and my brother sits in the house all day, with the curtains closed and the blinds pulled down. I'm scared to leave him alone. Now the police want me to take the morning off to come into Ridgeway."

Karen was moved by the desperation in his voice. She wanted to reach over and hold the hand he had rested on the table. Too pushy she told herself. "It must be tough for you," she said.

He muttered assent. "Somebody's got to keep the place going. William really loved that woman," he added, staring at Karen as if daring her to contradict that remark. "He was besotted with her, in spite of everything."

By *everything*, Karen guessed he meant Oliver Bostock. Today was the first time she had heard him mention the affair, and she took his comment as a licence to raise the subject herself. Dennis shook his head.

"William didn't know about Bostock. I was talking about the way she treated my brother, always putting him down. Though I suppose he would have found out about the affair when Oliver's wife came back. I can't see Judith keeping her mouth shut." Dennis chewed thoughtfully while Karen

158

wondered if he had to stop himself from adding that Rowena's death solved the problem.

"Anyway, since I had to come into town, I thought I'd get in touch with you and tie up some loose ends."

She knew Dennis wouldn't make a special trip into Ridgeway just to see her, but it would have been lovely if he'd said something about the opportunity to spend some time together or even "I had to talk to somebody, and you're the only person who would understand." But no, he simply wanted "to tie up some loose ends." Hardly romantic.

"It's something Loretta said, when she rang last night." He raised his voice to a question and paused for Karen to provide more information.

"Money has gone from the centre's account," she told him flatly, "and we can't find Benjamin Knowles."

Dennis nodded. "That was roughly what Loretta said. It's a bad business. Do you realise what it means, if Knowles has taken off with government money?"

As if she had not spent most of her morning worrying about that. She started to tell him about her meeting with Reginald Mollison, but he wasn't interested in her problems. He had come to this lunch with his own agenda, and he intended to follow the script, regardless of his companion's response.

"I'm thinking about the drama group," he said. "I don't know how many members of the committee realise we're not really part of the centre. We've always used the building for our shows, and we contribute to the upkeep but . . . we don't want to get involved in your mess."

So that was why he had phoned her. He wanted to make his own position clear to the committee, and she was the most available member.

Now Dennis had delivered his message he was ready to leave and he struggled to hide his impatience while she finished her quiche. Even the intimate gesture of helping himself to a couple of chips from her plate could be read as an effort to speed the meal along.

Karen's face must have shown her feelings, because, with an all-too-obvious effort, he forced himself to relax and settle back into his chair.

159

"So you've been having problems too," he said. She was so pleased to have his attention that, after telling him about her unpleasant interview with Reginald Mollison, she also described her conversation with Lynette Waters.

"Edridge should have kept his mouth shut," he said, standing up. He handed her the bag she had hung over the back of the chair and took her arm as they moved outside.

CHAPTER NINETEEN: WEDNESDAY AFTERNOON

Shaw noted Erbacher's frown as he read the postmortem report.

"It doesn't tell us very much," Erbacher complained. "After one look at the victim, we knew she'd been bashed with something heavy."

"That was my first impression," Jamieson, the pathologist, said. "And further examination supports that idea." He had delivered his report in person, and Shaw noted, a little jealously, that his senior settled down easily to discuss the case with his old friend.

Erbacher looked at the report again. "You also said, on Monday, that you thought it was the first blow that killed her."

Jamieson nodded, "But the killer went on bashing the dead woman. Somebody really hated Rowena McKendrick."

"Or wanted to make sure she was dead. Does that sound like an intruder to you?"

The doctor shook his head. "Didn't you say one of the committee members complained about a missing hammer?"

"Edridge. He thought it might have been left in the back room, that's how he discovered the body."

"Inconsiderate of the murderer, not to put the weapon back," Jamieson said dryly.

He was also able to tell the detectives that blood from the wood around the broken lock matched that of the victim. That was no surprise.

"It's a pity the treasurer bloke is out of it," Shaw said. "According to Edridge, he didn't get on with Rowena McKendrick, and if the coordinator knew he'd taken the money, he had a great motive."

"Benjamin Knowles was in Brisbane," Erbacher reminded him. "He was certainly at the casino on Saturday night. All night. He lost his shirt. And one of the croupiers remembers seeing him on Sunday morning, about eleven o'clock. He says the man was in a dreadful state."

A uniformed constable joined them with a note.

Erbacher read it quickly.

"They've found the empty cash box in the park," he said. "But whatever the killer might want us to think, I don't believe the woman was bashed in a bungled robbery."

"No fingerprints?"

"The box was wiped clean." Erbacher frowned. "There's plenty of physical evidence—splattered blood at the murder scene, and the smashed lock, but what does it tell us? Nothing."

"If this was a TV program, there'd be a lump of mud on the kitchen floor. From the killer's boots." Shaw said.

"We'd send it to the lab and find it came some particular patch of ground," Erbacher continued the scenario, "where the murderer, and nobody else, had been walking in the rain. That would give us time to pick him up, before the last commercial break."

"The killer must have been covered in blood. If we could find the clothes . . ."

"They'll be buried or burnt," Erbacher told him

CHAPTER TWENTY: WEDNESDAY EVENING

Marion pulled into the council car park. She set her phone to vibrate and laughed at herself. The days of constantly interrupting calls belonged to a different life.

Once she was out of the car, she shivered and pulled her coat more tightly across her chest. Rain was drizzling down. Street lamps made shining pools of yellow at the edge of the parking lot, while darkness washed over the asphalt, hiding any sinister shapes that might be crouched behind the parked cars.

If she slipped into the alley that ran along the side of the building, the darkness would make her invisible, but that didn't occur to Marion. Instead she moved quickly onto the footpath, where the lights meant to protect pedestrians made her a target for watching eyes, and walked around the corner to the front of the old building. Fortunately for her, there was no killer waiting to bash her over the head.

How many of the committee will turn up? she wondered, as she stood in front of the automatic doors. Not William McKendrick, not even Loretta would expect him to come to a meeting tonight, but what about the rest of the committee? Loretta had been subdued after their trip to the bank, and a visit from the police might have shaken her confidence. But even being interrogated by a detective would not deflect a Wheelwright from her presidential duty. Other members might be less conscientious.

Karen had also used the council parking lot, but she walked down the small dark lane and would have met Marion at the door if she had not deliberately dropped back as if, Marion thought resentfully, she does not want to be seen fraternising with another member of the committee.

As soon as Marion entered the small meeting room, Loretta grabbed her arm. "The police have been talking to Oliver Bostock," she hissed. The whisper, meant for Marion's ear, travelled to the farthest corner of the room.

"Of course the police will interview Bostock," Walter thrust himself into the conversation. "The way he and Rowena

McKendrick carried on, the police would have to question him. They were a disgrace, the two of them," he added, to Marion's intense embarrassment. "Mind you, William must take some of the blame for the way his wife behaved. Only last week I tried to talk to him. I told him not to let Rowena spend her evenings in town. She never had so much work that she couldn't finish at a decent hour. It wasn't appropriate for her to be in the building at night."

"And what did William say?" Patricia Menkes asked. The others were so ostentatiously not listening Marion could almost see their ears flap as they waited for Walter's reply.

"He accused me of having a poisonous mind," Walter said indignantly. "Me! It was my duty to warn the man about his wife's indiscretion, but after the way he spoke, I was sorry I raised the matter."

"I don't think we should talk about the McKendricks," Karen Francis said.

"Why not? I expect the police are discussing Rowena and Oliver Bostock," Patricia Menkes ran a tongue around her purple lips.

The first time Marion saw Patricia, the woman had obviously fallen under the influence of an enthusiastic young beautician. She had long fuchsia fingernails that matched the top under her black pant suit, and her carefully trimmed hair was the pale, shimmering floss often seen on little girls. The hair and bright artificial nails contrasted with the old hands and a face with wrinkles that powder could not hide.

"It was," Marion had told Stephen afterwards, "a remarkable stylistic achievement. It showed the skill, if not the judgement, of a very young practitioner." None of the committee saw anything odd in Patricia's appearance. After forty years married to a Menkes, Patricia, like Loretta Menkes-Wheelwright, could afford to set her own style. If she chose to ride an elephant through the park, none of the older residents would raise an eyebrow, and as for the incomers who had flooded Ridgeway over the last twenty years, neither a Menkes nor a Wheelwright would bother about them.

Tonight Patricia's nails were chipped and her hair had lost its gleam, but her wrinkled neck supported a string of large, multicoloured, blown glass beads. During the meeting she fiddled with it nervously and Marion watched, fascinated, waiting for the string to break.

"Of course the police wanted to know why Rowena was in the building by herself," Walter was saying. "I told them I didn't know anything, but people will talk."

"In a way, it is not a bad thing that she's gone."

Patricia's words froze them into a shocked silence. "Of course we're sorry that the woman was killed," she continued, oblivious to the effect she was having on her audience, "but you have to admit she was incompetent. She had no respect for the committee." She turned to Loretta with a self-satisfied smirk, "I heard her calling you the 'doddering Duchess.'"

There was one word that would pierce even a Menkes' defence, if Marion dared use it, "vulgarity." She longed to mimic the shrill voice and throw that comment into the room. She resisted the temptation. Instead she led the way to the large table and settled herself with the obvious expectation that other members of the committee would take their places and get on with the business of the evening. They all shuffled into waiting chairs.

As president, Loretta took the head of the table, but she huddled down in her seat and made no effort to open the meeting.

She still looked like a wizened monkey. No longer the alpha female of a wild troop, but an animal that had been netted and caged and was pining in captivity.

Walter Edridge settled himself beside her, his pale face almost matching his grey, wispy hair.

Another elderly member of the committee, Erica Gossard, took the chair next to Walter. For her, any meeting was a social event, and the drama of tonight's gathering added an extra spice to the outing. She whispered excitedly into Walter's ear.

Karen Francis sat at the other end of the table. She opened a spiral bound notebook, pulled out a pen, and held it like a dagger, pointed directly at Loretta Wheelwright. Marion refused to be bluffed by the council's representative. She also took a notebook out of her bag.

There was an interruption as Dennis McKendrick walked in and excused himself to the meeting.

"What is he doing here?" came an embarrassing Menkes hiss. Marion turned her head away from the question, but Patricia leaned forward and, no longer bothering to whisper, addressed them all. "Dennis isn't on the committee. He's only a member of the drama group, and he should be at home, looking after his brother."

"I'm standing in for William," Dennis told them. "Of course he couldn't come tonight."

"Of course," Loretta nodded an agreement that accepted Dennis in his brother's place.

Karen pushed her chair to one side to make space for the newcomer, but Dennis didn't accept her invitation. He moved around the table to sit beside Erica, spilling raindrops from his wet jacket over her skirt. She shook herself angrily.

"Sorry about the water," he said. "It started to pour just as I got out of the car, and I've left my raincoat at home."

"I always keep a spare coat on the backseat," Walter Edridge told him. "You never know what the weather is going to do."

Karen rushed to defend Dennis with examples of his general preparedness. "You usually have a raincoat in your car."

Dennis scowled, showing his displeasure, as between them, Karen and Walter made him the centre of the committee's attention.

Walter would have continued chatting about the rain, but Karen brought the meeting back to the business at hand. "What will you do about Benjamin Knowles?" she asked. "Since he has stolen your money, and the government grant, you've got a big problem."

"A big problem." Walter Edridge looked around the table with an authoritative frown and stared with particular intensity at Marion.

Karen ignored him as she continued describing the consequences of the treasurer's misdeed. "You'll have to account for the money."

"You're on the committee, too," Loretta reminded the council's representative. "You're just as liable as the rest of us."

Liability! Marion thought, which was why Stephen was so upset. Was the committee responsible for the government grant money?

"And what are you going to do about Lynette Waters?" Karen continued, ignoring Loretta.

"Lynette Waters?" Most of the committee looked blank, but Marion's stomach lurched at the name. That interview!

Three of the committee had been on the panel: Marion herself, Loretta, and William McKendrick, and she had not been surprised by the lack of suitable applicants. Why would anybody with the skills needed to run such a project apply for a temporary position? She put the question to Lynette Waters, the only possible candidate.

"I'm sick of filling out dog licences," Lynette had told the panel. Yes, she understood there was only one project, the multicultural program, but if she made a good job of that—who knew what might come up? "It'll give me a foot in the door. I'm really interested in art," she had gushed, her tone giving the word a capital. "One day, I want to run my own gallery." Marion had gravely agreed that the multicultural program would be good experience for a prospective gallery owner. It was also surprisingly well paid.

"I gather you offered her the job," Karen said. She spoke in a clear, clipped tone, using her voice to emphasise the difference between her sophisticated self and the rustics who could not manage the funds so generously provided by the department and the Ridgeway Council. "Lynette Waters won't be pleased if you have to cancel the program."

This evening, Marion decided, Karen was acting a part and under the circumstances the role she had chosen for herself was particularly offensive.

"We have not made any decisions about the multicultural program," Marion said. "We couldn't offer Lynette a position because we didn't know if the department would accept our submission."

"The application has been accepted," Karen said. "The money was in your account, before it was stolen. Somebody told Lynette, and when she spoke to me this morning, she seemed to think she had the job. Where does that leave the committee?"

"You can't blame us," Patricia Menkes said, in her loud voice. "This is the first time we've met since the funding was approved. The committee has not confirmed any staff appointment, and we can't be held responsible for promises you," she looked directly at Marion, "Loretta, and William McKendrick might have made to Lynette Waters. If she wants to make trouble because she doesn't get the job, that's a problem for the interviewing panel."

Dennis shifted uneasily, but before he could speak Walter Edridge offered the opinion of a (retired) solicitor.

"I agree with Patricia. The committee can't be held responsible for anything Marion Shea, William McKendrick, or Loretta Wheelwright offered the woman. If they led her to believe she had the job," he reached back into his working years for some legal term, "they acted without proper authority."

He doesn't know what he is talking about, Marion thought resentfully.

Dennis must have had the same idea. He scowled, gripped the edge of the table, half rose, and sat. "Don't land your problems on William," he growled "My brother has enough to do keeping the property afloat without taking responsibility for your indiscretion." He looked accusingly at Walter Edridge. Like Marion, he had a good idea who had been talking to the prospective employee.

Walter muttered an incoherent protest and Erica Gossard pushed herself away from the table as if she had had enough drama for one night.

"You were never much of a solicitor," Dennis told Walter, "and since you've left work you've forgotten the little law you once knew."

Loretta flinched away from the discussion, like a small, badly frightened monkey.

My new friends, Marion thought bleakly. If this was getting to know people, she wished she had chosen a hermit's life.

The meeting continued in, a long, circular debate, with everybody repeating the few facts they knew, each trying to phrase the problem differently, as if all they needed to do, was find the right words to describe their dilemma.

Erica Gossard offered a diversion. "We've never had a murder before," she said, breaking into one of Walter's convoluted sentences.

"That's not the problem," Karen rapped on the table to emphasise her words. "Rowena McKendrick's death is a terrible thing, but the crime has nothing do with the committee. You should be thinking about the money." She slapped her notebook shut.

Everybody took that as a signal that the meeting was over. Patricia Menkes reached for her handbag and Erica Gossard pushed her chair farther away from the table.

"There is another matter we must deal with tonight," Walter Edridge said as they all stood up. They sat down again.

"We have to do something about the winos. They've made more mess in the parking lot."

Marion could not believe her ears. Rowena McKendrick had been bashed to death, the treasurer had absconded with all their funds, and Walter wanted to talk about litter.

"We can't be bothered with that now," she said impatiently.

But he would not be silenced. "It's a proper disgrace," he said, addressing Loretta. "On Monday morning, the asphalt was covered with broken glass. Those young layabouts must have been drinking all night and smashing their empties. They've got to be stopped."

"I agree," Loretta straightened in her chair, giving Walter her support. "We'll ask the police to watch the parking lot." She stood up with the satisfied air of a president who has brought at least one piece of business to a satisfactory conclusion.

Marion remembered the scene on Sunday night. Loretta dropping her bottles of wine! So the president would talk to the police and complain about winos as if she had nothing to do with the broken glass.

She was overcome with the absurdity of the situation. She looked at Dennis and saw his mouth twist into a grin that he struggled to hide. She felt her own shoulders shaking, and in spite of her efforts at self control, she found herself giggling.

The rest of the committee watched them, bewildered.

"I can't see the joke," said Karen Francis.

That was a wasted evening, Marion thought, as she drove home. She remembered a line from one of her favourite childhood books, after a trial that could have been the transcript of the evening's meeting. "They're nothing but a pack of cards." But Wonderland had been a dream and this mob was all too real.

* * * *

"How did it go?" Stephen asked when Marion got home.

"Nothing was decided; nothing has changed," she told him. "There isn't anything we can do until we have checked the books and know how much money is missing . . ."

She did not want to discuss liability. Instead, she repeated the gossip about Oliver Bostock and Rowena. "From what Walter said, I gather they were having an affair."

"So that's why she was in the building after everybody else had gone." Stephen laughed. "No wonder she was cross when you offered to help. She wasn't staying behind to do the washing up. I wonder if her husband knew what was going on."

"Walter says he tried to tell William, and got his head snapped off for his trouble."

"Walter Edridge? If he was the only source of William's information, McKendrick would be no wiser after the conversation. Australia Central handled the Edridge account, so I've had some dealings with the man. Walter would stand in the rain and wonder why he was wet. He couldn't have contributed much to the evening."

"Nobody did. We sat around telling each other that the centre was in trouble, and Karen Francis—she's the council's representative—made things worse by talking about negligence."

"Is this the first time she expressed concern, or had she spoken up before, at an earlier meeting?"

"I don't think so. The treasurer had everyone fooled, and Karen was as trusting as the rest of us."

To avoid elaborating on the financial situation she told her husband about Walter's final contribution.

"I couldn't believe it. There we were, all desperately worried about the money and he rambles on about a mess in the parking lot. And Loretta supported him. Remember that bottle she broke on Sunday night? That was the glass he was fussing about. Honestly! I caught Dennis' eye and we both got the giggles."

"Dennis might have been glad of some light relief," Stephen said thoughtfully. "It must be pretty grim at the McKendrick place." He was about to add something more but changed his mind.

"Thank God it's the end of the day," Marion said.

* * * *

As she collapsed, exhausted, into a big armchair, Loretta was also glad it was the end of the day.

Everything had happened so suddenly. One day the committee was triumphantly celebrating the most successful show they had had for years, and the next it was facing financial ruin. Because of that stupid, stupid Benjamin Knowles.

And if the Francis girl was right, members of the committee would be held responsible for the government money; they might have to replace the missing funds themselves. Would the department send a debt collector after them? Not that they would get much from Loretta. She could barely pay her telephone bill.

She made her usual bedtime drink and thought about the meeting. It was times like this she desperately missed James, and she reached for his picture. He had been a good husband. "I was a good wife, too," she whispered, thinking of Rowena McKendrick—the silly little cow.

And that idiot, Walter Edridge. She could have strangled him for saying, "I told William not to let Rowena spend her evenings in town. She never had so much work that she couldn't finish at a decent hour." Of course the woman didn't have much work, and she wouldn't have put in extra hours if her desk was sinking under the weight of her neglected paperwork. William knew that. But the McKendricks were proud. Did Walter think William would go trailing his troubles in front of his old friends?

But a few weeks after Rowena started work, he had dropped the mask with her.

"I don't want to say anything," he said. "I don't know what she would do if I confronted her. Suppose she left me for Oliver Bostock! I can't bear to lose her."

No fool like an old fool, Loretta had thought at the time, as if taking a young wife had added years to William's age. If he had asked her opinion, she would have told him to throw the woman out, but if he chose to live with Rowena's behaviour that was his business.

"She is not the first young woman to have an affair," he had said.

And not the first to have her head turned by Oliver Bostock. Loretta was very fond of Oliver, but she knew what he was like with women, "bad as his old man," as James would have said. But the affair with Rowena had lasted longer than most.

She had hoped the two of them would be discrete when Oliver's wife came home. No need to worry about that now, she whispered to her husband's photograph. But no matter what Patricia said, there was nothing good about what happened to Rowena. However stupid, incompetent, or even malicious the woman might have been, she didn't deserve to die that way.

She checked the double lock on her own door and climbed into bed but she had more than her usual trouble getting to sleep.

CHAPTER TWENTY-ONE: THURSDAY MORNING

Thursday morning saw Karen at work, but she was not proud of herself.

The night before, as she walked out of the council building she heard Loretta talking to Dennis McKendrick. What was it the president had said? Something about rats and sinking ships. And Dennis had laughed.

Of course they didn't mean her. If the centre were a ship, the council's representative was not one of the crew. She only attended their meetings because it was part of her job, to protect the interest of the Ridgeway Council. She wasn't responsible for their finances.

But suppose Loretta had been referring to her and Dennis agreed? What right did he have to criticise her, after the things he had said over lunch, when he insisted the drama group was not part of the centre? And he didn't exactly support Loretta during the meeting, when it seemed as if William could be saddled with the problem of Lynette Waters.

By the time she was ready for bed, Karen had almost convinced herself she had done all that could reasonably be expected when she warned the committee about the troubles ahead.

But this morning she wondered if she should have distanced herself quite so thoroughly from the rest of them. She had been worried about the effect the treasurer's embezzlement would have on her own career. That earlier meeting with Reginald Mollison had frightened her. He made it so very clear he considered her main responsibility, as the council's representative, was to monitor the way the committee spent any funds the council provided.

If he didn't say anything about the departmental grant for Judith Bostock's program, that only meant he hadn't heard about the money.

"Have you got a moment?" A timid voice interrupted her thoughts. Lynette Waters again. This time she used the excuse of a routine enquiry, which Karen answered easily. Yes, she had arranged for members of the Arts and Culture Centre to use a council meeting room last night because the police had locked them out of the centre. No, they wouldn't be using the room every week and there was no need to pencil in a reservation for next Wednesday.

Lynette stood by the door, leaning against the frame and fidgeting. She was trying to find the right words for her next question, and Karen, who knew the information she wanted, was not going to help her.

"This murder . . ." An awkward silence.

Had there been an extra chair in the tiny office, simple courtesy would have demanded Karen invite the girl to come in. She said a silent, grateful prayer to whichever bureaucratic god designed the space, that there was nowhere for a visitor to sit. She picked up a circular about the provision of bowling greens in council parks and studied it with frowning concentration. Lynette didn't move.

"Have they found the killer yet?" in a rush of words.

Karen shrugged, carefully refusing to look up.

"When are they reopening the centre?"

The circular offered no protection, and Karen had to face the girl. "The police have not told us."

"When I heard there was a meeting last night, I wondered what the committee decided about the multicultural program."

"We didn't discuss it. With Rowena McKendrick dead and the building closed by the police, there isn't much we can do."

She picked up her pen, scribbled an unnecessary note on the circular, and became engrossed in statistics about the use of bowling greens by Ridgeway ratepayers.

After what felt like an age, Lynette took the hint and shuffled away.

The incident emphasised the problems facing the centre. Karen had every reason to be concerned. She had spent the previous day stewing over Reginald Mollison's words and by evening had been ready to attack the people who landed her in the career-threatening mess. But was that fair to the other members of the committee? Hadn't she been as much to blame as anybody else?

Knowles was able to take the money because no one bothered to check his books. The president was little more than a figurehead, the secretary had spent the last three months in Greece, and everybody else, including herself, left all the financial business to the treasurer. Benjamin Knowles.

When he objected to the appointment of another staff member, they accepted his decision and saw his offer to take responsibility for the bookwork as a solution to the coordinator's problem. Loretta had been speaking for them all when she thanked him. How could they have been so dumb?

The more Karen thought about the situation, the more she worried about her own role. "Because," she told herself, "there were questions you should have asked and objections you should have raised."

Like other members of the committee, she had known Loretta was no longer capable of filling the presidential role, but when the woman was nominated at the AGM, she sat as quietly as the rest of them while Loretta was reelected. As long as the president was the head of the table, other members of the committee were confident the secretary and treasurer could run the organisation.

And when Judith Bostock left for Greece, these same members left everything in the shaky hands of the president, supported by that obliging and hardworking treasurer, Benjamin Knowles.

Karen had never seen herself as a hierarchical animal, but she enjoyed her comfortable salary and respected position on the council staff. She might still identify with the more idealistic girl of her student days, but with her position in the working world, her outlook had imperceptibly changed until, at this most unpropitious moment, she felt her position and salary were both under threat.

"Karen," she told herself, "you need help." Who better to steer her through treacherous waters than that survivor of many a council storm, the manager of corporate services, Rachel Cunningham.

As community development officer, Karen reported to Rachel Cunningham. If anyone had suggested she modelled herself on Rachel, she would have laughed, but she had developed a great respect for the older woman. She had taken to wearing the smart pant suits Rachel favoured and, like Rachel, lightening them with frivolous tops. Rachel chose pastel shades, but Karen, as suited her age, made a bolder statement with her colours.

If an impartial observer noted a similarity in the women's business uniforms, that same observer would be amused by the way Karen unconsciously adopted, and adapted, the strategies Rachel Cunningham used so effectively to hold her position among her male peers.

Even before she reached her present eminence, Rachel had been a formidable member of the council staff, and a number of stories had grown around her name.

One of the clerks told Karen about an episode that had given the corporate services officer an almost mythical status with the female members of staff.

"Of course Rachel wasn't nearly so important then," Anna-Beth confided, "but she never stood any nonsense, and she had a way of looking over those glasses of hers when she was annoyed that infuriated the men."

It took very little prompting from Karen to launch the girl into a story she was dying to share. It seems a group of young engineers had gone to a conference on the coast, and at the end of a long day passed an adult shop—so called because the establishment specialised in the kind of toy no parent would buy for their child.

"They must have been drinking—you know the way people do at these affairs—and they were pretty boozy when they saw this place," Anna-Beth said. "One of them wanted to go into the shop."

"Which one?"

"That's the funny thing. Nobody knows. I was talking to Johnno afterwards and he swears it wasn't him. He says he told the boys it was a stupid idea, but the others wanted to see inside and he followed the crowd."

Over the following weeks, as Karen heard different versions of the story, she learned that Johnno was not the only young man who didn't want to go into the adult shop, each member of the group had apparently been *the only one* who thought it was a stupid idea and who had *only gone along* to follow the crowd.

"It was while they were in the shop," Karen's informant was giggling so much she could hardly speak, "they saw one of those—those things—you know . . ." since Karen was obviously not going to get a more detailed description, she gave an understanding nod and Anna-Beth went on with the story. "Somebody thought it would be a great joke to buy it and send it to Rachel Cunningham." As Johnno pointed out, he had been by himself, at the other side of the shop, when the article changed hands and knew nothing about the plan. It seemed, from enquiries made later, that every young man in the group was also *by himself,* at the other side of the shop.

If it was hard to get a clear picture of earlier events, what happened next was even hazier. Somehow that large, pink object, whose function was all too obvious, was wrapped up, addressed, and posted to Rachel Cunningham, care of Ridgeway Council offices.

In spite of the disapproval each man expressed later, there had been an air of smirking expectation the next morning and such a watching, whispering, and hanging around in the corridor that even a wax mannequin would have smelt a rat. Rachel had not steered her own family through their sillier years without being able to recognise the signs of mischief brewing.

As soon as the parcel was delivered, she had guessed the reason for the general restlessness. She exclaimed with loud delight at the unexpected present and rushed into the administration area to open her gift.

She had unwrapped the pink object, waved it around and wondered, all too vocally, what it was, to the embarrassed amusement of several solid citizens who were waiting to pay their rates.

For the rest of the week, Rachel gave the trophy pride of place on her desk and responded to any suggestion she put it out of sight by informing the red-faced adviser that "Stan says it's a joke."

When questioned about the mysterious Stan, Rachel explained that he was the nephew of her brother's wife and owned a business on the coast, which "sold some very peculiar things." That was when each member of the group let it be known that he, personally, had no idea what the others had planned.

After Karen got to know the manager of corporate services, she wondered if any nephew of Rachel's brother's wife owned a business on the coast or if a fictitious Stan was Rachel's contribution to the joke.

If anybody could find a way through this present mess, that person was Rachel Cunningham, so once again Karen crossed the parking lot and headed for the main building.

Rachel was in her office and didn't appear surprised to have a visitor.

"I expect old Reggie's tearing out his hair, what's left of it," she said, grinning at Karen. "He's always been scared of the big boys, and if the centre has lost the council's funds, he'll have to do some fast talking. You'd better be careful or you'll be the one he feeds to the sharks."

At first Karen was too shaken by the idea of a Reginald Mollison scared of the big boys to consider the import of Rachel's warning. In Karen's world the position of chief executive officer was equivalent to a navy admiral, he might not match the head of a government department, but he was considerably more important than the lower levels she dealt with. It was not until her stunned brain had adjusted to a world where Reginald Mollison was a comparatively small fish that she responded to the warning at the end of Rachel's remark. Feed her to the sharks. Wasn't that what worried her? Or was Rachel talking about the police?

The older woman shook her head. "Don't worry about the murder or the police. It's the embezzlement that has our Reg jumping. And he's looking for someone to blame."

After her session with Reginald Mollison, Karen had realised that the centre's problems could pose a threat to her own position, but it was alarming to have her view confirmed by Rachel Cunningham.

"It's not fair."

Rachel raised one eyebrow. She refrained from making the obvious response, but Karen could guess what she wanted to say. Was it fair that Karen Francis should be dragged into a mess, so very much beyond her control? No. But neither was it fair that Diana Knowles share her husband's disgrace or that other members of the centre's committee be held responsible for the misdeeds of their treasurer.

And most of all, it was not fair that Rowena McKendrick, a young woman who had been so full of life, be reduced to a hunk of meat lying in a puddle of dried blood. That everything she had been, or had believed herself to be, could now be described in one word: victim.

Forget about fair. Karen listened with increasing bewilderment as Rachel talked about "damage limitation," laughing, in a particularly Rachelish way, as she mimicked Reginald Mollison's pronunciation of the jargon words. Karen giggled in response.

"The only thing that matters to our chief executive officer," she said, "is the protection of council and Reginald Mollison, and not in that order."

Karen agreed. That had also been her impression on Wednesday morning.

"Does he want you to get things under control at the centre?" Karen nodded unhappily. "And at the same time, he's telling you not to get involved in its problem?"

"Keep my feet on the ground while leaping over a fence?"

"Something like that." Rachel pursed her lips as Karen described her own performance at the meeting on Wednesday night.

"You're a member of the committee too," she said. "Even if Reggie thinks you're there to watch the council's interest."

Karen tried to think of an answer to the implied reproach, but the older woman was still talking.

"That treasurer—Benjamin Knowles—I believe he's already gone to the police. With his solicitor."

If that was what Rachel Cunningham believed, Karen was sure that was exactly what had occurred. Reginald Mollison could pick up a phone, brandish his own importance in an effort to squeeze information out of an unwilling official, and still not be told more than he could read in the local paper, but Rachel Cunningham had no need to bluster, bully, or cajole. She sat at her desk and anything she might want to know found its way to her office. In the complex interaction of favours given and received over a lifetime working for the Ridgeway Council, she had a better network than Telstra and Optus combined.

"If Knowles has confessed," Rachel said thoughtfully, "that could be in our favour."

Like Marion the night before Karen recognised the power of the pronoun, regardless of whether the *our* referred to the council's involvement or a plan of campaign restricted to the manager of corporate affairs and the community development officer. She found it very comforting.

"Judith Bostock, will be back on Saturday," Karen said, wanting to make some useful contribution to the discussion. "She's been in Greece." Feeling more explanation was required she enlarged on the significance of her comment. "Judith prepared the original submission for the multicultural project. It seemed a good idea at the time," she added defensively, remembering how enthusiastically she had backed the idea when it was originally raised.

"Mmm. Who else is on the committee then?"

Karen listed the members and Rachel pulled a face when she mentioned Walter Edridge. "That's the firm that handled Gran's estate, and we're still cleaning up the mess." Then, when Karen mentioned Marion Shea. "That new woman. Didn't she have something to do with the art show?"

Karen laughed "From what I've heard, she did most of the work, though Loretta, as usual, did the hostess bit. Apparently she managed a gallery in Melbourne before her husband was transferred to Ridgeway."

"So, really, while Judith's away, if you discount the old fogies, there are you, this Marion person, and William

180

McKendrick, and I think we can forget about William for a while."

"That's about the size of it. The centre is doomed."

"Not necessarily." Rachel leaned back in her chair and gazed at the ceiling as if expecting inspiration. "They're not a bad lot, you know," she said suddenly. "They've done some good things in their time. I'd hate to see the organisation go to the wall."

Karen agreed. "But it looks as if it's finished, after this business with Benjamin Knowles."

"I don't know," Rachel said thoughtfully. "It's not the first time a group has lost its funds. The problem is more common than you'd think, and it's usually hushed up." She stared at the window with a grin, which made Karen think that, as far as Ridgeway was concerned, this woman could probably unearth more skeletons than the local gravedigger. "Our Reggie won't want a scandal. If we can give them an excuse to hush things up," she continued, "that's what they'll do. I heard that Knowles has promised to repay . . ."

"He can't do that," Karen interrupted. "If he still had the money, he wouldn't have gone to the police. He would have put it back in the centre's account. It's gone."

"Of course he can't raise the full amount," Rachel said. "At most you'll get back a fraction, over time. But we don't have to tell the council that. Not yet. What you have to do, girl, is get things moving any way you can. You should get in touch with that Marion Shea."

"If you really think she would help, I'll give her a ring."

"Don't waste any time." Rachel tapped the desk with her pencil. "And I wouldn't let too many people know what you're doing. You don't want anyone putting their fingers in your pie before you've written your recipe."

Karen could see the sense of that. Considering the value of land so close to the business centre of the city, the CEO might be happy to get rid of the centre and sell off the building. And some of the committee would be equally as destructive in their efforts to save it.

"When you do ring Marion Shea, why not arrange to meet at Barnes?"

"The coffee shop in the department store?"

Rachel nodded. "It's a good place to talk. It's crowded at lunchtime of course, but it isn't busy in the afternoon. And it's not the usual haunt of council staff."

As Karen walked back across the parking lot, she felt like James Bond after a session with M. She was relieved to have her office to herself as she reached for the phone to call Marion Shea.

CHAPTER TWENTY-TWO: THURSDAY MORNING

Marion had never heard of Rachel Cunningham and couldn't imagine Karen, after her previous night's performance, discussing ways to save the centre. But had she been a fly on the wall at the Edridge house, it wouldn't have surprised her to hear Walter trying to dissociate himself from the committee.

While Karen was making plans with Rachel Cunningham, the Edridges were finishing a late breakfast. Margaret let her mind wander as Walter shared items from the paper spread in front of him.

"Another story about cholesterol, not that I have to worry," he gave a self-congratulatory grunt. "As the doc says, as long as you're active, and eat right, you'll keep in shape."

Margaret murmured agreement.

"I reckon Loretta Wheelwright's showing her age," Walter continued, enjoying the comparison with his own good health. "And Dennis McKendrick doesn't look so good. Not that he's old," in response to Margaret's raised eyebrow, "but he certainly seemed the worse for wear last night."

"The McKendricks have had a trying week," Margaret said tartly. "Considering his sister-in-law was bashed to death on Sunday, you wouldn't expect Dennis to be bouncing with joie-de-vie."

"That wouldn't have affected him," Walter mumbled in his own defence. "He couldn't stand the woman. Told me so himself. 'Worst thing William ever did,' he said, 'getting hitched to her.'"

"He should not have been talking like that, about his own family." Not to a chatterbox like Walter, she thought. "And even if Dennis didn't like Rowena, he will be worried about William," she said.

"I don't think Rowena is much loss," Walter harrumphed into his coffee. "As Patricia said at the meeting last night, she won't be missed on the committee. We are all sorry she was killed," he added, in response to his wife's glare. "But you have to admit she was incompetent."

Margaret refused to discuss Rowena's competence. "The woman is dead."

"Being dead doesn't make her a saint. And if you ask me, William is better off without her, the way she and Bostock carried on, there would have been trouble when Judith came back. I said as much to Dennis at the exhibition. 'Judith won't stand for such goings on,' I told him. 'And neither will William, once he opens his eyes.'"

"You should have kept your big mouth shut."

The words had no effect on Walter as he stared at the table. He frowned and pinched the tip of his chin between finger and thumb. Margaret recognised the signs. He was thinking.

She ostentatiously ignored him, stacking the dishwasher with unnecessary noise.

Walter was sublimely unaware of her mood. "If last night's meeting is anything to go by," he said, "the centre is in a mess. And suppose the Waters woman makes trouble? From what William told me after the interview, they have as good as promised her a position with the multicultural program. They shouldn't have offered the woman a job until they had the money to pay her. I'm glad I had nothing to do with the project."

Margaret remembered how annoyed he had been not to be included on the panel. "I'm the most qualified member of the committee," he had said after the meeting. "Marion might have managed a small gallery in Melbourne, but she knows nothing about Ridgeway. William has no real business experience, and as for Loretta, she'd be better employed making tea."

It was a different story now.

"Lynette was so excited when I told her the program had been approved. And why shouldn't I pass on the good news?" He asked angrily. "As far as I knew, the money was already in the bank. That Karen Francis should watch her words. Breach of confidentiality indeed. I wasn't the only person who knew about the grant. The treasurer, for one, when he handled the funds. Which he stole. And the coordinator. She must have opened the letter before passing it on to Knowles." He pinched his chin again, and Margaret waited for the next insight. "Suppose she is dead *because* she knew what Benjamin Knowles had done? She threatened to tell the committee and he killed her."

"According to Loretta, the police had him at the station but the magistrate sent him home. They don't think he's their man. But the other thing—the money. They'll still be after him for that. I'm sorry for Diana. It is going to be hard on her."

Walter was not thinking about Diana Knowles. He raised his own concern. "I was in the parking lot on Sunday night," he said, "when the killer was skulking in the bushes. Suppose he'd come after me. Loretta can call as many meetings as she likes; I'm not going near the centre until the murderer is locked away. I'm getting too old for this committee stuff."

He raised his voice to make himself heard above the clatter of plates. "Why don't we take a holiday? We could go south and visit the kids. And when we come back, I think I'll resign from the committee."

If thoughts could leap from mind to mind, Margaret's emphatic determination to keep her retired husband on the committee would have blasted its way into her husband's skull. Walter's involvement with the centre kept him fussily engaged away from home, and although she was horrified by Rowena McKendrick's death, and vaguely worried about the treasurer's embezzlement, she had no intention of letting her husband leave the committee.

What would he do with himself all day?

And as for taking a long trip south—she had a big golf tournament next month.

"You can't desert the committee, dear," she said. "They need you. Nobody else has your experience."

* * * *

Marion was not thinking of Walter Edridge or Karen Francis as she threw herself into an orgy of housecleaning. The meeting had left a sour taste in her mouth.

It wasn't Karen's doomsday talk that worried her. The woman might want to protect her own cushy job, but the council's representative shouldn't think she could dodge her own responsibility by slinging mud at the rest of the committee. Not while Marion Shea was around. Nor was she worried by the posturing of Walter Edridge, who had simply been his usual pompous self. Nor by Patricia Menkes' spiteful words.

No. The face that haunted Marion and the voice that echoed in her ears belonged to that once-autocratic president, Loretta Wheelwright. The old woman didn't really believe in the twenty-first century. She had surrounded herself with the people and institutions that had been part of her earlier years and pretended Ridgeway was still the large country town of the 1950s. The violence of Rowena McKendrick's death had shattered that illusionary world.

Marion was uncomfortably aware that Loretta lived alone in her small unit. Whatever demons haunted her on Monday night, she would have had to face them by herself. Was that why she had wanted to call a meeting, to step into her accustomed role and surround herself with familiar faces without admitting, even to herself, how much she needed them? And what comfort had they given her?

Karen had flourished her notebook, and Walter Edridge accused everybody, including the president, of slackness, while Patricia Menkes dripped poison.

But what about Marion Shea? How much support had she given the beleaguered president?

This morning, over breakfast, she had shared those feelings with Stephen.

"Loretta isn't a bad old thing," she said. "From what I've heard, she got things moving in the early days, but over the last few years she's been little more than a figurehead. William and Judith Bostock have kept the organisation going, without much help from anybody else. Now Judith's out of the country and William's in no state to be bothered with the committee. Everything's falling to pieces and poor old Loretta doesn't know what to do."

Stephen looked up from his paper as he considered the problem.

He was not particularly interested in Loretta Wheelwright, but if his wife wanted to help the old lady, she would have his support.

Marion recognised the gesture and tried to exploit it. Perhaps Stephen could offer more than encouragement. "It's the bank that is the problem. Could you—?"

"No way." Stephen choked over his coffee and put an end to the discussion by heading for the door.

As she gave the bench an unnecessary scrub, Marion cursed her own stupidity. Of course the manager of Australia Central could not talk to J. R. Gowd of First Queensland about the crimes of Benjamin Knowles.

She wondered what Loretta was doing this morning. Was she sitting by herself, brooding about the meeting, or had she picked up the phone to talk to another member of her generation—two remnants of an earlier world sharing their ignorance?

Perhaps she had shielded herself from an unpleasant reality by pushing last night's meeting into the shadowy realm *of things we don't talk about.* That was what the oldies did. Like Marion's own mother and her elderly friends, who coped with the modern world by quietly ignoring it.

It might not be a bad thing if Loretta did withdraw from the present century. There was nothing she, or anybody else, could do until they had more information.

What was it the detective said? "You were the last person to see Rowena McKendrick alive."

Except for the killer.

That uncomfortable reflection was broken by the telephone.

Was it a quick call from Stephen? Or another plea from Loretta—had the bank been hounding her again? Marion wiped her hands and reached for the phone.

Karen Francis!

If she had recognised the number, she would have let it ring. She gave a discouraging grunt and waited to see what the council representative had to say for herself.

"The meeting didn't go too well last night," Karen said.

Marion didn't reply. She let a silence travel along the line as she waited to hear a reason for the call.

"We've got to do something."

Marion made a noncommittal sound, intended to show she was still listening but had nothing to add to the comment. What was there to say?

An uncomfortable pause, as if Karen was trying to find the right words, then they came in a rush, "There might be a way through the mess."

"Do you want another meeting?" Marion made no effort to hide the doubt in her voice. They could spend more hours talking about their troubles, but at the end of the long evening, nothing would have changed.

"At the moment I'm not thinking about the committee. I'd rather have a chat with you, by yourself, to get a few things sorted out." She waited then, as Marion didn't respond. "I've been talking to people here, and if we play our cards right, we might be able to save the centre."

Karen wouldn't talk on the phone. "We ought to meet, just the two of us, and thrash things out, before we talk to the rest of the committee."

If she really wanted to get involved, Marion was willing to work with her. But when could they get together and where would they meet?

"What about this afternoon?"

She certainly wasn't wasting any time. Marion resented the assumption that she would be available at such short notice and briefly considered inventing a previous engagement. She resisted the temptation and expressed herself willing to meet the council's representative.

"We could have a coffee at Barnes," Karen said. "It's a good place to meet if you don't want to bump into council staff," she lowered her voice and Marion pictured her mumbling words out of the side of her mouth

Marion checked her makeup carefully before she left the house. David going into battle she thought as she pulled a face at her reflection.

Karen was no Goliath, but she had the full force of the Ridgeway Council—the ranks of the Philistines—behind her, and she was armed. Oh yes! She was vested with an official authority that she could wield as skilfully as any sword. Last night she had made her position plain, as the Ridgeway Council's representative, she was determined to dissociate herself from the problems of the committee.

* * * *

Two o'clock on a Thursday afternoon might be a good time to arrange a clandestine meeting in a Ridgeway department store, but it was not such a good time to find a parking spot in a downtown shopping mall.

Ridgeway, true to its name, was built on sloping ground, and Marion had to drive up a side road to enter a car park that, like the roof of the national parliament house, covered all the levels underneath. She saw a space, but while she manoeuvred around a gaggle of teenagers, a red sports car nipped into it. She had to travel down the tunnelled ramp into the bowels of the underground park.

Didn't the Francis woman watch any movies? Surely she knew that the proper place for conspirators to meet was in the municipal gardens, where they could bump into each other accidentally and share information while feeding the ducks. Or they could drive their vehicles to a deserted country road, where they could park easily.

At last she found a space and squeezed her car between a large SUV and an electrician's van.

She made her way through the mall to Barnes, noting that, thanks to the slope of the main street, an entrance from the underground park led into the second level of the store, where, according to Karen, she'd find a coffee shop.

There was a notice just inside the door, telling customers about the wonderful things they could eat in this rendezvous, but the promised feast was not immediately visible.

The tune from a James Bond film played in her head as she surveyed the array of women's clothes. Perhaps she had misheard Karen and should be hunting through a different store. She laughed at herself. This was not a spy movie. If she wanted to find the advertised café, all she had to do was ask an attendant.

A set of green patterned nails waved her through racks of swimwear to a partitioned corner, where people drinking coffee were protected from curious eyes. No doubt Karen trusted this barrier to protect her from any workmates who might be browsing among the women's clothes. And Marion had to admit the Barnes Coffee Corner was an unlikely haunt for council staff.

Karen was already settled at a corner table. She nodded a greeting as Marion went to the counter to order her cappuccino.

The display of cakes made Marion's mouth water, but she decided against having one. Karen had sounded conciliatory, even apologetic, on the phone, but if the council's representative reverted to the behaviour she had displayed at the previous night's meeting, Marion might want to leave in a hurry, and a plate of uneaten food would be a pointed reproach.

After she sat down, there was an awkward silence, which she refused to be the first to break. "I suppose you think I was a bitch last night," Karen said abruptly.

Marion mumbled a not-quite-honest disclaimer.

"I was scared. I had a rough time yesterday morning, with the CEO. He doesn't want the council dragged into our mess."

Our? Marion registered the change of pronoun. Was this the same Karen who had lectured the committee on *your* responsibility? What had changed?

"I've been talking to Rachel—Rachel Cunningham," then, as Marion looked blank, "The director of corporate services. She's a tough old bird and she's got no time for Reggie M. She doesn't want the centre to crash, and neither do I. The organisation has done a lot for the community," Karen added in an unconscious imitation of Rachel's voice.

"I don't think there's much we can do," Marion said. "Nobody on the committee knows anything about the funds, and they all seem more worried about the extent of their own liability than the survival of the centre. Loretta had a bad time at the bank and she didn't get much support last night." She gazed steadily at Karen, who shifted uneasily on her hard seat.

"Rowena . . ."

"Rowena McKendrick is dead." Marion said, spelling it out in case Karen did not fully appreciate the problem. "The coordinator has been bashed to death, the secretary is in Greece, and the treasurer has stolen our funds."

"At least Benjamin is back," Karen said. "According to Rachel he was at the police station on Tuesday and they sent him home." She pulled the inevitable folder out of her briefcase. Karen affected the persona of a modern businesswoman, but in her practiced movements Marion saw a resemblance to that social leader of an earlier year, Loretta Wheelwright. Both women—each in her own way and according to the mores of her own time—saw herself taking a leadership role.

"What about the money?" Marion asked.

"Rachel says he's confessed to taking it. She believes he'd rather be tried for embezzlement than hunted down and charged with Rowena's death."

A pause while Karen sipped her cappuccino. She wiped a smear of foam from her lips and continued. "Rachel doesn't think the department will make too much fuss about the committee's responsibility, they won't want the bad publicity. From what she's heard, the Knowleses have found a good solicitor. Benjamin is doing all the right things. He's pleading guilty, expressing remorse, and promising to make restitution. Not that he can repay the whole amount," she added, as Marion wondered about the Knowles' financial state. "Rachel says even a token offer would count for something at his trial."

Was this Rachel Cunningham an authority on all things bureaucratic? Marion hoped the woman knew what she was talking about. She selected a small tube of sugar, tore it open, and poured the contents into her coffee. That gave her hands something to do as she waited for Karen to explain the purpose of their meeting. Information about the treasurer's return could have been relayed, just as easily, over the phone.

Karen was having trouble finding words. She repeated Rachel's confident assertion that the department wouldn't want a public fuss. "So they won't come after members of the committee." That was good news. "But we're still in a bit of a mess."

Did she have to state the obvious? No matter what the department did about their grant and whatever this Rachel Cunningham might say about the centre's admirable past record,

Marion thought the organisation was finished. All that was left for them to do was to arrange an orderly demise.

Karen didn't agree. "I'd hate to see it go to the wall," she said.

Marion listened with growing disbelief as the council's representative outlined her (or was it Rachel Cunningham's?) plans for saving the organisation. She was even more surprised to hear her own voice agreeing to help.

Who else could they rely on? Judith Bostock was away, though, as Karen reminded Marion, she was expected back on Saturday. Patricia Menkes . . . Erica Gossard . . . Walter Edridge . . . as she mentioned each name Marion shook her head. "They mean well enough but . . ."

"They fuss. But they won't do anything useful. What about Dennis McKendrick?"

Marion had some doubts about Dennis. "Isn't he a bit of a lightweight?"

"Lightweight? Not Dennis." Karen was indignant on behalf of the younger McKendrick. "Dennis likes a bit of fun, that's why he joined the drama group, but he's serious about anything he considers his duty. You should see the way he looks after his brother. I know he worries about William."

"Because of the murder?"

"Even before that, the business with Rowena and Oliver. Oh, yes," in response to Marion's raised eyebrow. "Dennis knew. Most of us in the drama group saw what was going on, but we had the sense to keep quiet, not like that stupid Walter Edridge You get no thanks for passing on bad news."

"You're saying Dennis knew about his sister-in-law and Oliver Bostock?"

"He made it his business to find out. He always knew what time she came home. She had to drive past his window on her way to the big house, and Dennis used to laugh about the way the dogs barked at her car. He lives in a cottage on the property," Karen explained. "He moved out of the family home after William's first marriage."

"That's what Agnes told me." A tactful way to let Karen know she'd spoken to the former treasurer.

The other woman nodded and continued her story. "The old house was originally built for William's great uncle . . ."

Marion had no interest in these genealogical details and asked a question that brought Karen, reluctantly, to the present generation. "Dennis was really worried about what William would do, if he found out about Rowena and Oliver. And there's the problem of a divorce."

"William has already been divorced."

"He came out of that one all right. Agnes didn't demand money." (Marion was amused by Karen's definition of *all right*.) "She has a good job, and they both want to keep the property intact for their son. Dennis says William obsesses about the McKendrick name. And the law is stupid about divorce. Rowena could sleep with half the men in town and she'd still get a big settlement if William kicked her out. The McKendricks have good land, but there isn't much cash money, and a large payout could wreck the property. It isn't fair," Karen said angrily. "But that's beside the point." She pulled herself back to the business at hand. "Don't you think the centre is worth saving?"

A week ago, Marion would have given an affirmative response, but after her experience on Sunday, she had wanted to wash her hands of everything to do with the organisation. If Loretta was going to swan about like a princess at the royal garden party, let her do some of the work.

She had changed her mind again on Monday. After Loretta's desperate plea, how could she leave the older members of the committee to deal with embezzlement and murder? If she had learned anything over the last few days, it was the total inability of the Wheelwrights, the Edridges, and even the McKendricks to cope with the twenty-first century. If there had been a competent coordinator, the centre might have survived the treasurer's deprivations, but if Rowena had been halfway competent, Benjamin could never have hidden his dealings with the bank. A strong committee might be able to save the organisation even after embezzlement and murder, but none of the committee had shown that kind of strength at the last meeting. Was the centre worth saving? Karen was waiting for an answer.

"I don't know," she said, honestly.

"Rachel thinks it is."

Judging by her expression, Marion Shea from Melbourne was not impressed by the opinion of an unknown Rachel Cunningham, so Karen reported Rachel's views without further reference to their source.

Marion listened to the reasoned arguments and considered her own position.

After all that had happened in the last few days, she felt as distanced from the weekend show as from her Melbourne life. But as she invoked the self of her previous week, she remembered the frustration of working with people whose highest ambition was to repeat their previous failure. "That's the way we did it last year. And that's the way it should be done," is what those people would say. And her irritation with a coordinator who refused to do anything that was not specifically written into her job description.

But the coordinator, Rowena McKendrick, was dead. How petty those resentments seemed today.

Murder changed everything.

So did that ghastly meeting last night. After it was over, all Marion wanted to do was put as much distance as possible between herself and the incompetent, selfish, or just plain nasty members of the committee. She'd never forget Patricia Menkes' remarks.

Last night Karen Francis had shown herself one of the selfish, but today the woman was demanding Marion's support in a quixotic effort to save the centre.

Marion wondered why she was even considering the proposal.

"We'll have to cancel the multicultural program," she said, and was horrified to hear in the words, a commitment to involve herself in Karen's plans.

But Karen was not prepared to sacrifice the project.

"The way the government is pushing multicultural support, Rachel thinks the department might even replace the grant. They've already listed Ridgeway on their website, as one of the provincial beneficiaries of the funding initiative."

Marion's opinion of the unknown Rachel plummeted.

But Karen continued talking. She treated Marion's previous words as a pledge of support and moved from trying to persuade the other woman, to discussing strategy for the rescue operation.

* * * *

As Marion prepared dinner, she reflected on the afternoon.

What had they accomplished—apart from forming another committee inside the committee?

"I'll make a couple of phone calls, see if I can get a few people on side," Karen had said. "Once we've come up with some ideas, we'll talk to Loretta and Judith Bostock." In other words, they would set things up so all the committee had to do was walk through the script.

As Marion put a pie into the oven, she pondered the dramatic shift in Karen's attitude. Last night she had made it very clear that she didn't consider herself part of the group. What had that Rachel person said to make her change her mind?

Marion would like to meet this Rachel Cunningham.

And what about Dennis McKendrick? As far as Marion could see, he was the chink in Karen's armour. She was as silly as a schoolgirl about him. And she was wasting her time. In spite of what Marion had learned about Dennis' earlier engagement and the way she had seen him playing up to the ladies in the drama group, she didn't think he was the marrying kind. As she reached into the fridge for beans, she thought about the younger McKendrick.

Karen would eventually wake up to the man, but, in the meantime, could she persuade him to join the committee in his brother's place? And would he support their efforts to save the organisation? Marion remembered how strongly he had reacted at the meeting when the then-unhelpful Karen raised the problem of committee members' liability for the missing government funds. If he gave them his support, it would be because he saw that as the best way to protect the McKendrick bank account.

* * * *

Karen didn't share Marion's pessimistic view of her future with Dennis McKendrick. She had been excited by the idea of including him in their plans and furious when Marion criticised the man. Lightweight! Dennis! She had clenched her teeth and mentally counted to ten before giving a carefully moderated response to the slur.

Wait until he was involved with the centre's problems. Once Marion saw him in action, she'd have to recognise his solid worth, and she'd be the first to want him on the committee.

Karen's mouth formed an involuntary smile as she considered the implications of having Dennis McKendrick on a committee with her.

He was wary of women, and what he'd seen of his brother's wife had not improved his opinion of the female sex. She'd have to be careful not to give him the idea that she was chasing him. But if they worked together, he'd have a chance to see she wasn't like Rowena or that bitch he was engaged to years ago.

She should be grateful to that first girlfriend. If Megan hadn't turned him off women so thoroughly, Dennis would have married years ago.

Mrs. Dennis McKendrick.

She would have to keep her job. Unlike Rowena, Karen had no illusions about the financial situation on the McKendrick property. She was not after Dennis for his money; she wanted the man for his marvellous, sexy self. And if he liked the idea of a wife with a well-paying job, that was her good luck. Maybe, as the suburbs of Ridgeway stretched into farming land, the McKendrick property could be rezoned. Some developer would pay truckloads of dollars to turn it into a housing estate, and Dennis could move into town on the proceeds of the sale. She shook her head. Not Dennis. He would hang onto those family paddocks no matter how much the land was worth, and she would support his choice.

But first she had to get him onto the committee. What was the best time to phone? Early evening, she decided, when it was too dark to work outside but before he settled down to watch the news. And unless he initiated a conversation, the call would be short and restricted to the business at hand.

Karen had a moment's doubt as she remembered his comments on Tuesday, when he had distanced the drama group from the centre's problems. But he had been willing to take his brother's place at the meeting on Wednesday night, and the McKendricks would be affected if the department, or the council, decided to press for their money. As she had said to Marion Shea, the committee could count on Dennis McKendrick.

She was disappointed.

When Dennis answered the phone, she could barely hear him over a game show blaring in the background, but he didn't bother to turn down the sound.

She was determined not to yell over the noise in her ear. She waited, letting the silence stretch, while, at the other end of the line, asinine laughter was followed by an announcer's voice. She gave nothing more than her name until the soundtrack was muted.

"Yes?" The questioning syllable was no encouragement, but she forged ahead with the lines she had used so successfully with Marion Shea.

She paused, waiting for his comment, but there was no response. Not until she asked him directly, "Will you help?"

He was not encouraging. "I'll do what I can," he said. "But I don't have much time to give your committee. I'm running the whole place on my own. William hasn't left the house since Monday night. He was in such a state on Tuesday I called our medicine man and between us we got him onto sleeping pills. But they're not helping much. The trouble is, William blames himself. He thinks he should have waited for Rowena on Sunday night."

Karen snorted. If the woman had not insisted on staying in the building she'd still be alive. But they both knew why she waited behind.

"William's fallen in a heap and I'm trying to hold everything together. I've got more to worry about than the centre, and after last night, I wouldn't expect much from the committee."

197

It was no use pretending anybody had covered themselves with glory at that meeting, but with her new Rachel-inspired understanding, Karen tried to excuse the performance of the elderly members. "This business with Benjamin Knowles, it's too much for them. They're all out of their depth and worried sick about the money. But I've been talking to Marion Shea." Marion's name got no response. "And Rachel Cunningham. She knows her way around the council business and she doesn't think Mollison will go after the committee. He won't want the bad publicity. She told me that Knowles has gone to the police. Apparently he made a full confession and he is not going to contest the charge."

Karen knew her mention of money would get Dennis' attention. He had not heard about the treasurer's return and, thanks to Rachel's network, she was able to give him the latest developments in the Knowles case.

"If you're expecting Knowles to return the funds," he said, "You're in cloud cuckoo land. He will have blown the lot."

"Rachel says it's not the money that counts, it's the effort he's willing to make that will influence the magistrate. She thinks it'll give the council an excuse not to harass members of the committee. They know we don't have the money, and they'd make themselves very unpopular if they destroyed the centre. Its members have a lot of influence in Ridgeway."

"Influence! The Menkes, Wheelwrights, Edridges?"

"And the McKendricks," Karen reminded him.

"Yes. Our name still carries weight," Dennis admitted. "But I don't want it mixed up with this mess. As for the Menkes and Wheelwrights. . . they are history. Do you think people like Reginald Mollison are impressed by the old names?"

Karen laughed. By conjuring an image of the CEO, he destroyed his own argument.

"Mollison is impressed by anybody he believes to be a member of the old families," she said.

A pause. Was he searching for a better excuse?

"What about the department? The scandal won't bother them. And the woman who's been promised a job with the program?"

Karen cringed as her accusations of the night before were flung back at her. If only she had talked to Rachel earlier. She repeated the older woman's opinions and advice. "If we all pull together, we might even save the multicultural program."

After her short acquaintance with Dennis McKendrick, Marion would have realised her strongest argument was not the survival of the organisation but the need for members of the committee protect their own assets. Any indulgence the aggrieved funding bodies showed the centre would increase the odds against them holding individual members responsible for the treasurer's misdeeds. Karen had spent many hours dreaming about Dennis, but she didn't understand him.

Instead of enlarging on the way helping the centre would protect the individual members of the committee, she talked about William. "Once he is over his first grief, he'll need something to take him out of himself, and he seems to like the crowd at the centre."

"He's always been keen on A and C's." Dennis agreed. "Most of the committee are old friends. We've known the Menkes and Wheelwrights all our lives. And the Edridges . . ." Karen noted that Dennis, like almost everybody else, struggled not to forget Walter Edridge. "William enjoyed being on the committee. It gave him a bit of social life, and he's going to miss the meetings if the centre folds."

"It's not going to fold." Karen repeated the argument she had made to Marion Shea, including selected quotes from Rachel Cunningham. "Reggie M's a dead loss, but if Rachel's on our side, she's more than a match for the CEO."

Dennis grudgingly promised his support. "I'll do what I can," he said. "But with the price of petrol rising all the time, I can't be driving into Ridgeway every few days. And when the police release Rowena's body, we're going to have the expense of a funeral so cash will be tight." Dennis' tone implied that, if it were left to him, he'd cram his sister-in-law's body into a plastic garbage bag and dump her in the bush.

So, money was a problem for William and Dennis? Even without Marion's insight into the motivation of the younger McKendrick, Karen decided not to share Rachel Cunningham's opinion that individual members of the committee would not be expected to repay the money their treasurer had stolen.

CHAPTER TWENTY-THREE: FRIDAY MORNING

On Friday morning Loretta talked to Diana Knowles.

If Marion thought the president would try to shield herself from an unpleasant reality, she didn't understand a Wheelwright (nee Menkes).

Even after the events of the past week, Loretta wouldn't have recognised Marion's description of herself as *a figurehead*.

True, she had never been involved in the daily routine of the centre. She considered that to be the responsibility of the coordinator, under the general direction of the secretary.

And as far as the financial business of the organisation was concerned, that was the treasurer's responsibility. Even after learning about the stolen funds, she didn't think the rest of the committee could be blamed for anything except poor judgement in choosing Benjamin Knowles.

But a Wheelwright would not wash her hands of everything to do with the lamentable affair. The centre was in trouble, the secretary was out of the country, and it was the treasurer who caused the problem, so it was up to the president to step into the breach as her old head mistress would say. "Buck up, Loretta," she told herself in the tones of that long-dead mentor.

Fortunately, the committee's newest recruit, Marion Shea, had a wonderful head for business and was not frightened of that horrible Ray Gowd. Marion could handle the bank.

There was another problem, one that had nothing to do with the committee. The face that came into Loretta's mind belonged to a woman she barely knew, Diana Knowles, wife of the delinquent treasurer. On Monday, when Loretta rang the Knowles' house, she guessed, from the quaver in Diana's voice, that the call was an unpleasant surprise, but she had been quick to produce a plausible excuse for Benjamin's absence. Family problems. Who could argue with that?

And that second call on Monday night. Diana was obviously worried about her husband, even if she didn't know about the stolen funds. Loretta had not mentioned the money, but she had tried to make Diana understand that Rowena's death could mean serious trouble for Benjamin Knowles.

She thought when Diana passed on her carefully disguised message, Benjamin would take the warning and keep out of sight till the police had the killer locked up.

But apparently he was back in town. Patricia had come up to her in the supermarket, agog with the news. Not only had Benjamin Knowles come home on Monday night, but he also had gone to the police station the very next day with a solicitor. From the contempt her cousin put into the word, it could have been a prostitute or gambler.

"Very sensible," Loretta had snapped, pushing her trolley to the end of a different queue. Patricia might think it appropriate to gossip about the committee's affairs in the middle of a supermarket aisle, but Loretta wouldn't be drawn into the conversation.

If that silly Benjamin Knowles had suddenly developed the courage to face the police and had the sense to talk to a solicitor first, she was sure it was his wife who put the starch in his backbone. When her husband was in trouble, Diana was not a frightened mouse. But she would need support.

What should Loretta do about Diana Knowles? As usual, when she was troubled, she talked to her husband.

James smiled out of his frame when she told him about her decision to drive her old Mercedes to the Knowles' house.

Did she really want to confront Benjamin? "We'll let the lawyers handle that," he used to say, when things got sticky with the company. "Don't you worry about it, love."

Yes, the embezzlement was a problem for a lawyer, and (Loretta shuddered) the police. But Benjamin's wife? "That is my business," she told the photograph. "Tomorrow I will see Diana Knowles. But I won't go to the house," she promised. "So I won't see Benjamin." And with those words she put the picture back, sure James would approve of her plan.

* * * *

Diana didn't expect Loretta to seek her out. Her only fear was accidentally meeting a member of the committee, and she meant to keep out of the centre of town.

She was grateful for the way Ridgeway had grown. There had been a time when all the businesses were found on two main streets, everybody went to the same shops, and she would have risked meeting a Wheelwright or Menkes every time she bought a loaf of bread. Not anymore. As the city expanded, developers built shopping centres, with plenty of room for cars, in the outlying suburbs.

Since the Knowles lived in one of these new suburbs, Diana could replenish her cupboard at her usual store without seeing anybody connected with the centre.

She didn't expect to be accosted at work. Once the police were involved with her husband's crime, the committee would not want to cope with the problem themselves, and even if they took matters into their own hands, they would hardly come looking for Benjamin's wife.

But on Friday morning who should walk into her workplace but Loretta Wheelwright?

Diana was entering a patient's details onto the appropriate form when the small, elderly figure came to the counter. She didn't look up, expecting Roseanne to ask the necessary questions.

"I'm waiting for Mrs. Knowles."

She recognised the voice.

If she had been given a few minutes warning, she would have crouched behind the counter, out of sight, but it was too late for that.

"I'm working," she tried to make her own voice match the president's firm tone but the words came out in a squeak. What was the woman doing here? Had she come to make a scene, to demand that Diana produce her husband and missing funds?

There were years of social experience behind the next, reassuring words, a question about the time of Diana's lunch and the information that the two of them would be having it together, in a café of Loretta's choice. "I'll pick you up at half past twelve."

Roseanne was impressed and only a flurry of arriving patients saved Diana from the need to answer her questions.

* * * *

At half past twelve, Diana allowed herself to be loaded into the president's ancient Mercedes and driven to a small coffee shop, whose sheltered courtyard overlooked the park. Loretta chose a secluded corner where their conversation would not be overheard.

Other tables were waiting for service, but the granddaughter of one of Loretta's oldest friends came straight to them.

"Mixed sandwiches and a very big pot of tea," Loretta ordered, after she had enquired about the girl's various relations and told her the latest news about the Wheelwright sons.

After the waitress had bustled away, Diana found her voice. "I'm so ashamed," she said, choosing words to forestall the other's reproach.

"You have nothing to be ashamed about," Loretta told her, with a shake of her wrinkled head and stress on the first word. "Your husband made his own decisions. You're doing the right thing, standing by your man, but you must not carry his guilt."

Diana wondered if Loretta was speaking from her own experience. The Knowles had not been in Ridgeway long enough to know the full Wheelwright history, but from scraps of gossip Ben picked up at work, Diana gathered that in the early years of the city's expansion there had been some shady business dealings, and James' company had been involved. "Not that it seems to worry the old girl," Benjamin had said when he passed the story on.

"You're a very brave woman. Your husband is lucky to have you behind him," Loretta was saying.

Diana couldn't think of a suitable response, so she murmured appreciation of the confidence.

"I never got involved in my husband's business," Loretta said. "And neither should you."

"People will talk."

204

"Not in front of you, my dear." A smile, followed by Loretta Wheelwright's famously demolishing glare. One she intended the younger woman to emulate. It was guaranteed to silence snide remarks. Diana giggled.

Loretta was satisfied she'd made her point and as they ate their excellent sandwiches, she entertained Diana with stories about her early life when Ridgeway was a smaller country town.

CHAPTER TWENTY-FOUR: FRIDAY AFTERNOON

Friday was the end of the school week at Ridgeway College and a stream of buses and parents' cars passed the gate as Roger stood, with his pack at his feet, waiting for Dennis. The pack was heavy with books and he wished he could bury himself in assignments instead of dealing with the complicated emotions evoked by the death of his father's second wife.

His mother would soon be driving past on her way home. He was tempted to pull out his mobile, punch in a number, and ask her to pick him up. He could say he'd been loaded with extra work and couldn't afford to take the weekend off.

But he wouldn't do that. Dennis said he needed an extra hand.

From what his mother said, Roger gathered it was Uncle Dennis who was looking after things while his father was mourning. *Mourning.* Roger rolled the adult word around in his mind. What do you say to someone who is in mourning? Especially if that someone is your father. Not that he felt particularly close to his dad, he never had, not even when he lived on the property.

People don't know what to say when somebody has died, he thought, moving from his embarrassingly personal feelings into the comfortable generality that included the totality of humankind referred to as people.

Children don't. He distanced himself further by moving that population into the past, which belonged to a Roger he barely recognised.

A Roger who caught the bus to school, had a mind fully occupied by friends and games, and accepted adults as bit players in the drama centred on his own young self. That Roger should have been badly affected by his parents' divorce, by the move away from the property, and by the gradual recognition of his mother as a person in her own right and his father as a man with interests—and loves—of his own. But he had not been particularly upset. Living in town meant after-school sport, and he still spent weekends on the property.

As his world changed around him, Roger, the ego-centred child, grew into Roger the almost-adult, who found himself accepted as a useful pair of hands. His was not a reflective nature, and until this week, he had taken that development in his stride.

This week was different. Learning about Rowena's death was not a normal part of growing up. Nor was it something he could discuss with Geoffrey or Ian. His friends were sophisticated seniors who knew adults had love affairs, got married and divorced, but people you know don't get bashed to death.

Roger shivered inside his jacket. After the warm days early in the week, a stream of cold air flowed up from the south, driving the temperature down.

His mother's car passed with a friendly toot, and he lifted his hand in an acknowledging wave.

* * * *

Agnes almost pulled up, to have a last, quick word with her son, but she checked herself. The boy had his mobile phone, and before he left for school she had reminded him that, if he had a heavy assignment, he could change his mind about the weekend. She didn't expect him to use that face-saving excuse. He was a McKendrick, and his uncle had asked for his help.

How like Dennis he looked, standing by the gate in that jacket, twin to the one his uncle wore. Roger had the same slender build, and when his interest was roused, he wore an expression of such concentration he could have been a young Dennis.

The McKendricks were all obsessive. When Roger was talking about his plans on Tuesday night, she had seen the paternal grandmother looking through his grey eyes. But with Roger it was computers, not cattle, that inspired that disconcerting gaze.

What would William think of his son's plan? And Dennis? Agnes remembered how awkwardly her brother-in-law had tried to express his gratitude when she waived any right to child support. "But you won't be sorry," he had said. "It's your son's inheritance. Roger will get it all in the end."

As Agnes pulled into her own driveway, she mentally pushed Roger's problems aside and thought of the commitment she had made to Marion Shea—to look into the centre's finances.

That, on top of her usual pile of marking, would make nonsense of her son's suggestion that she have fun while he was away.

* * * *

When Dennis pulled up, Roger climbed into the truck and fumbled for words. His usual lighthearted greeting would be an inappropriate response to Rowena's death, but it would be stupid to expect Dennis to be deeply distressed by the murder of his brother's wife.

When she was alive, he had been embarrassed by his uncle's snide remarks. He knew that Dennis only came to the house when Rowena was at work.

Roger was uncomfortable with his own response to her death. He should be more affected by the tragedy, but he had not seen much of Rowena, even when he was staying in the big house. He spent most of the days outside with the men, and when they came in for meals, he and his father talked about their work. Rowena had no interest in cattle and usually drifted out of the conversation.

He shivered. Now she was dead he felt guilty. As if he had been deliberately rude. But she seemed happy enough, he told himself, and she wasn't interested in me. She could have been breaking her heart for all you knew, whispered an uncomfortable voice in his head. You never bothered to talk to her.

He looked sideways at Dennis. How did his uncle feel about the murder? Did he wish he had been kinder to his brother's wife?

"How's Dad?" Stupid question. How would you expect him to be with Rowena dead? Murdered, Roger corrected his thought. Bashed. Left lying on the floor in her own blood. He shook his head, a mannerism he had developed over the last few days, as if trying to physically change the direction of his thoughts.

Dennis growled something Roger took to mean William was very upset, was doing as well as could be expected, and would be very glad to see Roger.

A bicycle wobbled across the road, Dennis braked suddenly and Roger jerked forward.

"Sorry, Rog. Blasted kids shouldn't be on the road."

Dennis drove through a roundabout and, changing the subject, discussed his plans for the following day.

"The heifers have arrived," he said. "But they can't go into the west paddock until we've fixed the fence." A task that had been waiting for his nephew's help.

The heifers and the condition of the west paddock carried them through the rest of the journey. Roger felt strange, climbing out of the truck at the cottage instead of sliding over to the driver's seat and taking it further up the track, to the house. There was a stretcher on the veranda, and he dumped his backpack beside it before joining his uncle in the small kitchen.

Dennis threw two steaks into the pan, took down two plates, and pulled a couple of cokes out of the fridge.

Obviously Dad would not be joining them for dinner.

He tried to think of an appropriate comment but could not find the right words.

Dennis was having a similar problem. He broke the uncomfortable silence by asking about the previous weekend, and Roger launched into a description of Ian's new game. He was quickly absorbed in an explanation of the complicated rules and was blissfully unaware of his uncle's indifference to all things electronic.

CHAPTER TWENTY-FIVE: FRIDAY NIGHT

Friday night, the end of a long week. After a leisurely drink, Stephen felt comfortably relaxed as he watched Marion take a casserole out of the oven. He picked up a bowl of salad and followed her to the table.

If they were in Melbourne, he would still be driving home, and when Marion was managing the gallery, she often had a show on Friday night, which meant she spent the evening in town. In Ridgeway, the end of the day found them both with time to talk.

At first, after the move, their discussions had been constrained. Marion didn't know any of the staff at the Ridgeway branch and there was no way Stephen would discuss the undercurrent of embarrassment that attended his transfer. And without the daily contact of her work, Marion often found herself with little to say.

The centre had provided a welcome topic for their evening conversation. Even if Marion sometimes stretched her stories more than the content warranted and Stephen was more thoroughly entertained than the subject deserved, they both enjoyed the small ritual.

After the events of the previous week, the mood of their evenings had changed. Their discussions were no longer simply an excuse to relax over a predinner drink. When Marion talked about the centre, she was sharing her problems with Stephen, and he knew she needed his support. After his disastrous comments on Tuesday morning, he had been careful to put his banking persona aside and concentrate on filling his husbandly role as comforter-in-chief.

After the detectives' visit on Wednesday, he had donned his banker's hat, but only to assure her the unfortunate events in Melbourne would not impinge on the Queensland investigation of Rowena McKendrick's murder.

"They are two very different crimes," he had explained. "In Melbourne there was a senior accountant, a man well grounded in international finance, using his position to milk his employer of millions of untraceable dollars. And a meticulously planned escape."

On Thursday Stephen had been delighted to find his wife full of plans. She was her old self, the indomitable Marion Shea, ready to reduce all mountains to molehills and to destroy the moles. He didn't try to follow the intricacies of her plot but contented himself with making encouraging grunts, as he sent a silently grateful prayer to whichever gods had set his wife's feet on this path.

Thursday was, as always, followed by Friday, and as Stephen ate, he reflected on the previous week. Was it only last Sunday they had come home, laughing about the art show and the president's bottles of wine?

His thoughts were interrupted by the phone.

He noted a tightening of his wife's shoulders. Whatever the situation here and however many other calls the Sheas might expect, that first ring always triggered her alarm.

The children?

She answered with a voice carefully pitched to reassure Barbara or Peter that everything was going well in Ridgeway, and to convey her confidence in their ability to look after themselves in Melbourne.

When the caller responded, Stephen saw her shoulders relax. She hooked her leg around a chair and dragged it up to the phone.

It was not the kids.

Stephen heard a "Yes, Loretta," and grinned. Whatever disastrous plan the president was proposing, he was sure his wife would find a way to limit the damage.

As she caught his eye, he waved his hand in an air-sketched question mark. She nodded, and frowned in response to some suggestion from the caller.

Marion could read his mind. From that first ring she had been watching him. He could pretend to laugh at her fears, but as she signalled not the kids, no trouble in Melbourne, he knew she could see his relief.

And curiosity.

Was that why she repeated Loretta's name? As the president continued her outrageous plan, Marion's tone signalled increasing impatience.

Yes, the police had left the centre. She had noted the absence of crime tape when she drove past the building, but no, she had not realised they could use the rooms.

Yes, she knew Judith Bostock was expected back tomorrow.

"Why do we need a meeting?" Stephen heard the exasperation behind her words and guessed Loretta had come up with some more than usually outrageous scheme. He hoped she had called the Sheas before contacting other members of the committee, and that Marion wouldn't have to spend her evening frantically trying to undo whatever wild arrangement the old woman had made.

"First thing on Monday," she was saying, "you want a meeting with the full committee? No, I know that doesn't include the treasurer." Why had Loretta mentioned Benjamin Knowles? "You can't expect people to drop everything on a Monday morning to come to a meeting."

Loretta obviously didn't see why not. Was the president planning a gathering to welcome Judith Bostock home and tell her what she had missed by going to Greece?

"You'll do no such thing." Loretta should be careful. Stephen could hear the rising temper in his wife's voice. "Karen will be at work, Dennis has a property to run, and I'm sure the others are too busy to come to a meeting on any weekday morning," she added.

Stephen was amused by the suggestion that all the members of the committee were too busy to take time out of their crowded schedule to join Loretta at the centre. It was hard to imagine Walter Edridge with an important engagement at any time, and as for Patricia Menkes and Erica Gossard, they'd be delighted to spend a couple of hours gossiping with the returned traveller. But what would they contribute to a meeting?

From his wife's side of the conversation, Stephen gathered that Loretta was willing to change her plan. Instead of gathering the whole committee; Marion should go to the centre with her on Monday, to meet Judith Bostock.

"If it's convenient for Judith," Marion said firmly.

Stephen grinned. How would Loretta Wheelwright respond to the suggestion that anybody would find it not convenient to meet her?

* * * *

Marion would have been profoundly shocked had she known Loretta had lunch with Diana Knowles and that she planned to visit Judith Bostock before the Monday meeting.

Because, however competent Marion might be in her own world, she could never anticipate the behaviour of a Wheelwright in crisis mode. It didn't occur to her that the president would consider it her duty to support the defaulting treasurer's wife.

Loretta had not discussed the meeting because she didn't think her conversation with Diana Knowles had anything to do with the rest of the committee. Nor did she choose to share another plan with Marion.

Earlier that afternoon, she had come home filled with the satisfaction of a duty properly performed. No matter how stupid Benjamin had been, after their lunchtime conversation, Diana would know she was not without support.

Loretta intended to have a similar, private conversation with Judith Bostock, before Oliver's wife talked to anybody else, and she would use the committee's problems as an excuse to visit her friend.

It would be stupid to pretend Rowena McKendrick's death had not left Oliver in a nasty position. The police were bound to learn how often the two of them met at the centre. They would certainly want to interview Oliver's wife, and Judith should be careful what she said about the woman's death.

The woman's death. Loretta shivered. While she had been worrying about the bank, talking to Diana Knowles and ringing her friends, she had been able to shut the horror out of her mind. She had been fiddling in the office while Rowena lay, bloody and bashed, in the small back room. And she had complained because the woman was late. Late! Loretta gulped, hit by the double meaning of the word.

213

She clamped her jaws together, determined not to give way to the hysterical laughter that pushed against her teeth. A frail old woman she might be, as seen through the eyes of a Marion Shea, but Loretta Wheelwright would not lose control of herself, even in the privacy of her own sitting room.

The familiar surroundings could not protect her from her own self-accusation.

She had left the coordinator in the building, by herself, and Rowena McKendrick had been murdered.

Nobody asked Rowena to stay behind.

She was waiting for Oliver Bostock.

She did not deserve to die.

Loretta felt very old and very much alone, in a world where a woman could be bashed to death and good friends, like the Bostocks, find themselves in trouble, if they didn't choose their words carefully.

Yes, she would have to do something about Judith. Not tomorrow. Tomorrow the woman would be exhausted after her long flight, but on Sunday Loretta would visit the Bostocks.

By a huge effort of will she forced her mind away from the problems of her friends. She turned on the TV and raised the volume to a level that would have had her neighbours banging on the wall, but fortunately for them, none of the channels could hold her attention. She turned off the noise and went to bed.

CHAPTER TWENTY-SIX: SUNDAY

On Sunday afternoon Loretta climbed into her beloved Mercedes and, as she turned in the direction of the Bostock house, rehearsed the conversation she expected to have with Judith.

Oliver would have told her about Rowena's death.

Loretta frowned as she swerved to avoid an elderly dog. Rowena and Oliver Bostock. The car slowed slightly as her foot relaxed. The affair would not have lasted—a few more weeks would have seen them drift apart. Oliver wasn't built to be a faithful swain. But they didn't have those weeks. Rowena's death could not have come at a worse time.

Murder is murder, she told herself firmly, increasing speed as she steered around an awkwardly parked truck. She might not have approved of the way Rowena behaved when she was alive, but there was only one proper response to the woman's death. And Oliver's wife would have to share her view.

Loretta pictured herself punctuating Judith's shocked comments with appropriately sympathetic murmurs. After they had told each other how dreadful it was, such a horribly violent crime, they would remember the days when Ridgeway was a safer place, without these awful druggies and drunks. When nobody even bothered to lock their doors, Loretta imagined herself saying.

Judith would nod her agreement and, changing the subject, would ask about the art show. No doubt Oliver had told her about the successful event, but good news will always bear repeating, and Loretta would describe the weekend's triumph. Naturally, Judith would want to know about the multicultural program, and she would be thrilled to learn the department had accepted their submission.

That might not be such pleasant news, Loretta decided, since the money had disappeared with Benjamin Knowles. Would it be better to tell Judith about the treasurer's misdeeds before she learned the program was approved, so she wouldn't be disappointed to hear the funds had gone?

Of course the news would upset her, and that would be when Loretta could suggest a meeting the next day, just herself, Judith and the capable Marion Shea. Marion really understands business, Loretta would explain, in case Judith wondered why the newest committee member was taking such a prominent role in their negotiations with the bank.

Loretta didn't intend to spend all afternoon talking about Benjamin Knowles. That was only an excuse to visit her friend, but she would have to introduce her subject carefully. As she approached the Bostock house, she wished the street were twice as long, to delay the moment when she must face Judith.

She was relieved to see a space in the carport. So Oliver had been called out on a job. She said a grateful prayer to whichever deity sent him away from the house. It would be easier to talk about a husband's indiscretions if the man in question was not listening.

Judith answered the door in bare feet. Her hair was tied back with a length of cord and a string of shells was swinging over her shirt.

She was eager to talk about her holiday, but when the conversation turned to events at home, she seemed to lose interest.

Yes, Oliver had told her about the murder. A dreadful thing. Her mouth shaped the necessary words, but her voice was flat.

There were no questions, no shocked speculation. No wish to hear a firsthand account from somebody who was in the building when the body was found.

Perhaps it was embarrassment.

Did Judith know about her husband's relationship with Rowena McKendrick? All Loretta's social instincts told her to change the subject, and, fortunately, there was another topic at hand.

She spoke about Benjamin Knowles and the money missing from the centre's account.

That should get the secretary's attention and at the same time allow Loretta to direct the conversation to the matter she had to raise with Oliver Bostock's wife. But the woman might

216

have been an alien, newly landed from Mars—she showed so little interest in these terrestrial affairs.

"You were worried about the accounts," Loretta said, in an effort to elicit a more concerned response.

"Was I?"

"The questions you asked at the meeting."

Judith wrinkled her nose, as if trying to recall events from an earlier life. "I must have wondered what Knowles was getting up to. But I expect you've got it all sorted out, now you've talked to the bank."

What had Loretta said to give her that idea? "That's not why I came this afternoon."

Judith stretched her long legs and leaned back in her chair, waiting for Loretta to explain herself.

"I want to talk about Oliver and Rowena McKendrick." There, the words were out.

Judith raised an unplucked eyebrow. "So? The woman is dead."

"Rowena McKendrick was murdered in our building. Late at night. While she was waiting for your husband. They were having an affair."

Loretta gave the old fashioned word its full value and looked at Judith, ready for her reaction. Anger. Outrage. Embarrassment.

"Ollie told me how she died. He has already talked to the police." Judith stared at her foot, for some reason she had painted her toenails gold. She had a vine tattooed around her ankle and she circled her leg as if asking Loretta to admire it.

Loretta wanted to shake her. "Your husband was having an affair with Rowena McKendrick, who has been bashed to death." She repeated the brutal facts, thinking Judith hadn't grasped them at the first telling. "The police will ask about how things stand between the two of you. The state of your marriage. I can understand how you feel," she rushed on, determined to make Judith understand the importance of her words. "But you can't leave your husband. Not now. Not till the police find the killer."

That did get Judith's attention. She put both feet on the floor, sat up straight, and stared at her visitor.

"Leave Ollie? Why on earth would I leave Ollie?" There was a genuine surprise in her voice.

Rowena McKendrick is dead! Judith has got her husband back. Had she really been on that plane, travelling back from Greece? Or had she taken an earlier flight? A week earlier?

Judith might have been reading her mind. She laughed. "No, I didn't sneak back into the country and kill Rowena McKendrick. Look, I'm sorry the woman is dead. And it's horrible for Ollie being involved. But the police know where he was on Sunday night. Oh yes," in response to the question Loretta was too bewildered to ask, "he told me the police talked to him. They checked his story and they're satisfied."

"Will you forgive him?"

"Forgive. You mean will I play the injured wife and walk off, after taking him for everything he's got?"

Loretta nodded, although she would not have used those words.

"Of course I won't throw a hissy fit. I can hardly get all indignant with Ollie. Not when I have toys of my own."

"You?" Loretta shook her head, trying to make sense of the words.

Judith laughed. "Yes me. My generation might have missed the seventies but we grew up with the stories. We aren't easily shocked."

Loretta had been vaguely aware of the disruptive decade, but she had not imagined it impinging on her own world.

"I haven't had a lot of fun," Judith said. "Too busy with them," she waved a hand at the bookcase where an assortment of photos showed her children growing up. "Now Marta's left home," Marta, Loretta remembered, was the youngest Bostock child, "I'm having some me time."

What on earth was me-time? Loretta wondered.

"Oliver?"

"Oh, Ollie's always played around. It was never anything to break up the home, though it suited him to quote a jealous wife when he was tired of his latest flame." For the first time Loretta detected a note of resentment. As if Judith didn't mind her husband's escapades but resented being used as an excuse when he wanted to disentangle himself.

"I don't think he'd got to that stage with Rowena, not judging by the state he's in." Judith admired her toes again as she considered her husband's mental condition. "But even if he was getting tired of her, the woman's death would still be a shock."

Loretta was trying to think of a suitable response when she heard a truck pull up outside. Oliver! She felt herself blushing, as if she was the one who should be embarrassed by the Bostock's affairs.

She stood up, reaching for an excuse to leave, to Judith's obvious amusement. If this were a play, like the ones the drama group produced when she was a girl, the stage would have two entrances and characters could dodge out of each other's sight until the plot unravelled in the final scene.

But if this were a play, she would have rung the curtain down before Oliver's entrance.

The scrape of a key in the door, footsteps in the hall and Judith's unfaithful (and cuckolded) husband was in the room with them. Loretta struggled to her feet, her face hot with embarrassment as she muttered greetings and farewells. She refused the offer of a friendly drink and escaped from the house.

CHAPTER TWENTY-SEVEN: SUNDAY NIGHT

Roger spent Saturday working with his uncle, and on Sunday the west paddock was ready for the heifers.

As Dennis had explained on Friday night, the animals had been delivered early in the week but he had to pen them in the horse paddock. "With all the rain we've had," he said, "there's plenty of green pick, and I haven't had time to move them. The fence needs work, we'll have to check the pump and . . ."

These were things William had planned to attend to before the heifers arrived. But when Dennis told Agnes that William had dropped his bundle, he had been speaking no more than the truth. As far as Roger could make out, his uncle had been doing everything by himself, while William stayed in the house with the curtains tightly drawn. The fence he had been repairing when the detective called was still a tangle of wire and posts. That was Saturday's first job.

After the fence was fixed, Roger had cleaned the drinking trough while his uncle checked the pump. By the time they had removed a season's accumulation of dust and weed from the channels and checked the flow of water, the sun was low and Dennis declared the paddock ready to hold the herd.

"We can move them tomorrow," he said.

"The old man would never have had you working on a Sunday," Dennis had said, half apologetically, the following morning as they wheeled their motor bikes out of the shed.

The "old man" was Roger's grandfather, the first Roger McKendrick, a good churchman and a dutiful keeper of the Sabbath. Roger shrugged. With his father out of action, the work still had to be done. From all he had heard about his grandfather, had his wife predeceased him, her death would not have interfered with a weekday's chores. Nor would his grandmother have wished it.

The heifers were easy to move; they were accustomed to dogs and bikes.

Roger and his uncle then spent the afternoon dealing with a big gum tree that had been torn out of the ground by a September gale and was lying over a fence, roots in the air like the legs of an upturned beetle. It had to be sawed into logs, the wood carted away and stacked, and the damage to the fence repaired. That was another job that needed two of them.

"I reckon we've earned a beer," Dennis said as the old truck rattled back to the cottage. Sometime in the previous year he had decided that a nephew who worked like a man should be treated like one at the end of the day. Roger's dry throat agreed.

Tonight, as he prepared the evening meal, Dennis put three plates on the table. "I'm not much of a cook," he said. "It's steak again. OK?"

Steak was always OK for Roger. He considered the meals this weekend an improvement on previous visits. Rowena had favoured pasta and dished out salad with a heavy hand. William always praised her cooking and Roger had eaten what was put in front of him without complaint, but chewing though mounds of lettuce left him feeling like a rabbit.

"Is Dad coming over?" he asked. He had not seen his father all weekend.

"If I have to drag him by the balls," Dennis said. "It's time he had a proper meal."

Roger hoped his father would come to the cottage by himself, but when the steaks were cooked and William still had not appeared, Dennis put the meat at the side of the stove and went outside. Roger heard him starting up the truck, so he was going to drive the short distance to the house. Would he rope his brother like a recalcitrant calf and drag him to the meal for his own good?

Dennis didn't bring his brother inside on the end of a rope, but William looked as if he had been dragged out of the house. His shoulders drooped as he followed Dennis into the kitchen, and he greeted his son with an old man's voice.

When they sat down, he put his elbows on the table and rested his chin on his hands, as if he took comfort from the feel of stubble rough against his palms.

Dennis continued the conversation he had been having with Roger earlier, and tried to include William in his evaluation of pasture and the level of the dams. All he got was a grunted reply.

He pressed on, as if determined to drag his brother into the discussion, but William hunched over his plate. "I'm fed up with this place. Wouldn't it be marvellous to just walk away?"

Dennis ignored the comment, and the three of them chewed in silence.

As if starting a totally new topic, Dennis spoke about jobs piling up, "I'll be glad to have you back at work, old boy."

William shrugged and scratched his chin. "Why don't we hire some help?"

"We can't afford the wages," Dennis said and added, as if to remind his brother of the property's future. "I don't know how we'd manage without young Roger here."

The boy fiddled unhappily with his steak. It was good meat, but his uncle was no chef. Last night's slab had been barely singed, tonight its time on the side of the stove had left it charred and tough. But that was not the cause of his discomfort. Even badly cooked steak was better than Rowena's rabbit food.

"Did you hear the Smithsons were moving into town?" Dennis asked.

Roger barely knew the Smithsons, but he tried to make up for his father's abstraction by showing an interest.

"The old fellow's getting on," Dennis said, "He hasn't got a boy to take the property and the girls are both married. He told me last week that they want to move to the coast."

"Not a bad idea," William said, but Dennis ignored the interruption. "It's a good piece of land. We could do worse than pick it up."

That did rouse William. "We can hardly manage what we've got."

"There are three of us—with Roger here. He's as good as any man, and a lot better than most."

"But I'll be at school," Roger broke in. "Mum says I can't come out as much next year. Not with exams . . ."

"Exams!" Dennis snorted. "Fat lot of use they'll be. What you need is the practical stuff, and you won't learn that at school."

Roger gulped. He'd had some good times on the property and it was great to come out in the holidays, but he didn't want to make it his life. From the way his uncle was talking, he was already making plans for next year, and those plans didn't include a nephew's exams. He wriggled uncomfortably and looked across the table at his father, but William didn't meet his eyes.

"I'll have a word with Smithson," Dennis was saying.

"Next year, if I want to get into uni, I am going to need a decent score." The words came out in a rush, cutting across his uncle's speech.

"You won't have any trouble," Dennis told him. "Like I said, you're as good as a man around the place. Any Ag school would grab you. Not that you really need that stuff."

"What are you planning to do?" his father asked quietly.

Roger struggled with his steak. "I'm not sure. I'd like to muck around with science, and maybe computers. The way they handle data you can set up models and . . ."

"What about the property?" Dennis interrupted sharply.

"Farming's a mug's game," William said before Roger could answer. "Nothing but drought and debt. If Dad hadn't made me go on the land, I could have had a profession." He was no longer staring blankly at the wall. He blinked a couple of times, as if waking from an uncomfortable sleep, and looked at his son. "You'll have to make your own decision about what you want to do, Roger."

"It's a good life, on the land." Dennis said, turning away from his brother as he swung to face the boy. "That computer stuff is just a fad. You couldn't stand being stuck inside all day."

"I don't have to decide tonight," Roger muttered, sawing at his steak.

There was an uncomfortable silence.

"I see you've been tidying up the place," the boy said, desperate to change the conversation.

William raised a questioning eyebrow.

"That old drum outside. It's full of ash."

"I've been getting rid of rubbish," Dennis said. "Somebody has to clear it up." Roger thought his uncle would enlarge on the complaint, but he ostentatiously clamped his lips together and scowled at his plate.

CHAPTER TWENTY-EIGHT: MONDAY MORNING

On Monday morning, Dennis drove into Ridgeway to take Roger to school. The day had started with fog, followed by drizzle, and the boy shivered as he helped his uncle wipe the windscreen. "Spring is a dictionary definition that has little to do with the climate," Dennis said, as he climbed into the cab and activated the wipers. Roger dutifully laughed at the joke. For the first time in his life he felt uncomfortable sitting beside Dennis, and he wished it was his father driving him.

After the argument the previous night, the subject of Roger's future had been dropped by general consent, but Dennis had attacked his steak savagely and responded to any comments with an angry grunt, while William lapsed into his former state, staring, as if hypnotised, at a patch of discoloured plaster on the kitchen wall.

As soon as he decently could, Roger had given a prodigious yawn, pleaded exhaustion, and escaped to his veranda bed.

Through the open window, he had heard his uncle's opinion that "The kid has too much schoolwork" and the further complaint that "He's got everything out of proportion." It was, according to Dennis, his mother's fault, she had filled the boy's head with her silly ideas. The lad loved the property and a few weeks on the land would make him see sense.

Roger wished he could hear the words of his father's rumbled reply, but his uncle's rising tones signalled a continued disagreement. Did that mean his dad wasn't upset about him going to uni?

He would have been relieved to hear his father's last remark. "If anything happens to me, Roger will need money more than land."

* * * *

Loretta was delighted to see Dennis.

She had been making one of her famous lists, items to be discussed with Marion and Judith, when he turned up at the door.

"I had to drive young Roger into town," he said. "I thought you might like a bit of beef."

It was not the first joint she had had from the McKendrick property. She bustled to put on the kettle while he settled into the big armchair.

"How's William?"

Dennis shrugged. "Up and down. Actually that's what I wanted to talk to you about," he said, staring into his cup as if it held the solution to his problems, "I don't know what to do with the man."

Loretta paused, kettle in hand, as he struggled to find words to describe his brother's state. "I got him to the cottage for dinner last night. Roger was with me over the weekend and I thought William would make an effort, for the boy's sake, but it was like sitting at the table with a lump of wood. I think Roger's visit made things worse."

Dennis chewed a biscuit thoughtfully while Loretta waited for him to elaborate. "The boy is going through a silly stage, you know what kids are like," he said. "I'd been talking about the Smithsons. Both their girls have married city men, so Jim and Denise are selling up and moving into town. I want us to buy the place. It's a good piece of land."

Loretta nodded. Adding the Smithson's property to the McKendrick's made a lot of sense.

"William didn't think we could manage the extra land and that's when Roger dropped his bombshell." Dennis paused, as if not wanting to repeat the sacrilegious words. "He said that after he finished school, he didn't want to join us on the property."

Loretta murmured sympathetically. The McKendricks had been among the first families to settle in the district, and over the years, succeeding generations had added to their holding, but it seemed that Roger had a different dream. What a pity he was the only boy in the family.

"If Dennis had married, he might have had sons of his own." Loretta thought. She wanted to tell him he needed a wife, but she clamped her mouth shut. She remembered how furious the McKendricks had been when Dennis' prospective bride called the wedding off. Some things were better left unsaid. Safer to talk about William.

"Roger's decision. It must have upset his father."

"That's what worries me. There was Roger, about to throw his life away, and William just sat like a lump of wood. He doesn't care about anything anymore, not the property, not even his son."

William might not have been upset by Roger's plans but Dennis' voice was shaking as he described the argument. Loretta offered the only comfort to hand, a second cup of tea. He accepted gratefully.

"It's not Roger that worries me," he said. "Kids get these silly ideas. It's William . . . the way he's dropped his bundle. I don't like leaving him alone. But I had to come into town . . ."

"Rowena's death was a terrible thing," Loretta said.

"It was a nasty way to die and William is naturally cut up." Dennis reached for another biscuit. "But in the long run, it might be for the best, the way she was behaving . . . if William knew about Oliver Bostock. . ."

"It would break his heart." Loretta finished the sentence, without disclosing William's confidence. Dennis didn't need to know his brother was so besotted he would wear a cuckold's horns rather than lose the woman he loved.

CHAPTER TWENTY-NINE: MONDAY MORNING

On Monday morning Marion also noted the weather. She added a thicker top and a waterproof jacket to the outfit she had planned the night before and made a last, careful mirror check. Loretta had sounded nervous on the phone, as if she expected Judith to blame her for letting the treasurer steal their funds. But Judith's wasn't going to bully the old woman, Marion decided, choosing a businesslike shoulder bag and loading it with tools for taking notes. She hoped the sight of pen moving along paper would have its usually salutary effect on a carping critic. Benjamin had started helping himself under her watch, she would remind Judith, if the secretary started dishing out the blame.

Judith was waiting for them at the centre. Marion didn't know what she had expected from the often-quoted Judith Bostock, certainly not this long-haired, long-skirted, creature, with dangling earrings and a Greek-island tan.

Loretta led the way into the office and settled herself behind the desk with little thought for poor Rowena's ghost. Marion waved Judith to the smaller, hard-backed seat and brought a chair for herself from the next door room.

After the revelations of the previous day, Loretta was embarrassed to face Judith. In the past, an assumption of shared values made it easy to use the small change of conversational platitude, but what could she say to this woman, who had laughed about her husband's affair and spoke so casually about *me time?*

The situation was more difficult because Loretta had not told Marion about the Sunday visit. None of her business. That ruled out a number of otherwise innocuous remarks. "It was good to see you yesterday, or you were tired after your trip, are you more rested today," and left her struggling for words.

Fortunately for the president, Marion attributed the first awkwardness to her understandable reluctance to talk about their predicament.

Judith waited for the others to start the conversation, and Marion opened the discussion by describing their first visit to the bank and the discovery that, over the preceding months, the treasurer had been stealing from the centre.

The secretary was no more concerned today than she had been the preceding afternoon when Loretta told her about the theft, but she listened politely while Marion described the problem and made the expected enquiry about the state of their finances.

"If Rowena was still alive, we wouldn't have the money to pay her," Loretta said.

There was no reaction to this offhand reference to the coordinator's death. "It's a wonder the auditor's didn't notice our treasurer's depredations," Judith said, addressing herself to the business of their meeting as if murder didn't warrant even a cursory discussion.

Was that because she knew about Rowena and her husband? But as she slouched against the back of her uncomfortable chair, Judith didn't fit Marion's idea of a slighted and resentful wife. Nor was there a visible response to Rowena's name.

Marion forced herself to focus on the immediate problem. She explained that the auditors, like everything else reported at the Annual General Meeting, were a figment of the treasurer's imagination. "It's bad enough losing our own money," she said, "but Ben also stole a government grant. Your multicultural program was approved," she explained, "and he got his hands on the funds."

Judith shrugged, "So, we cancel the program."

As if that was all they had to do! Didn't she realise, Loretta asked indignantly, that members of the committee could be held personally responsible for the loss of the grant money?

Even that idea didn't shake Judith. "The department won't come after us," she said. "Think of the publicity. If Benjamin pleads guilty . . ."

"And he will," Loretta said firmly.

"There's only one thing the bureaucrats will want, and that is to keep the business quiet. It doesn't look good for the bank, the council, or the department."

That was exactly what Karen Francis had said, quoting Rachel Cunningham.

But Karen had given her opinion as a prelude to discussing plans to save the centre, while Judith presented her conclusion as the solution to their problem. Neither the department nor the council would harass the committee, so they had nothing to worry about.

"As a matter of fact," she said, standing up, "I'll have to resign from the committee. I was going to tell you at the next meeting. Now the children have left home, I'm planning to do more travelling."

With a nod to Marion and a smile for Loretta, she left the office.

"W-ee-ll," Loretta stared at the retreating back. "Judith's not herself."

Marion had no idea how the *herself* of Judith Bostock would behave, but the woman she met this morning didn't match her mental picture of Oliver Bostock's wife, secretary of the Arts and Culture Centre.

"People change," she said.

"Everything changes." Loretta's shoulders slumped and she stared at her hands, as if hoping to find an explanation written in the wrinkled skin. "The committee—we've always been such friends—and I don't understand them at all."

Marion could only agree. Was this the Judith Bostock whose imminent return had triggered their treasurer's flight? If the council closed the centre and sold the building to developers who replaced it with a shopping mall, would Judith notice the change?

"It's worse for the little wife."

"Little" was not the adjective Marion would have chosen to describe Judith Bostock. "Unfortunate, perhaps," if Loretta was referring to her husband's affair. But while Marion was trying to make sense of the morning's session, Loretta had left the Bostocks. She was talking about the Knowleses. "Diana did the sensible thing, having Benjamin go to the police." Diana Knowles? To the best of Marion's knowledge, Loretta hardly knew the treasurer's wife.

"I took her to lunch on Friday," Loretta said. "Benjamin has been a fool. But Diana will keep him in line. I told her she had our support."

Marion was shocked. So members of the committee would rally around their treasurer's wife, even after the man defrauded them!

* * * *

The morning left Marion wondering if some of the more bizarre theories of modern physics might be correct and she had slipped through some anomaly in Ridgeway's space/time into a universe that bore little resemblance to the one she knew.

Nothing she learned about Loretta's activities over the weekend fitted her expectations of an elderly person's response to a bad situation. She was relieved when she eventually reached home, to find Stephen, still his comfortably familiar self, had started his lunch.

"Would you believe Loretta's talked to Diana Knowles?" She asked, joining him at the table. "Whatever trouble that silly Benjamin's got himself into, she expects us to rally around his wife."

"Does she think the centre can withdraw the charges against Benjamin Knowles?" Stephen asked, as he buttered another slice of bread. "That would make the committee accessories to his crime."

"I was worried about that," Marion admitted. "After Judith left, we went for a coffee and I got the old girl talking. That's why I'm so late. Sometime last week she saw that nice detective, Erbacher, and told him we wanted to drop the charges. He told her we couldn't do that. He explained that Benjamin didn't steal from us, as individuals, he stole from the organisation. And we would be guilty of embezzlement ourselves if we tried to hide the theft. He said the sooner everything was straightened out, the better it would be for Benjamin."

Stephen remembered the acid remarks his wife had made after Erbacher's visit and grinned at her description of *that nice detective*. The man had obviously redeemed himself by his tactful handling of the aged president. "I gather Loretta's charity doesn't extend to replacing the money herself?"

Marion laughed. "She couldn't do that. And I don't think the others would be willing to empty their wallets to save their treasurer. They have to watch their pennies."

Most of the committee members were retired, like Walter Edridge, or, like the McKendricks, were struggling to keep a business afloat in difficult times. Stephen couldn't imagine any of them digging into their own pockets. Nor could Marion. "From what Agnes said, the McKendricks' pockets are empty. Everything they've got is tied up in the land, so there isn't much spare cash. They're having a tough time, but it's a family property and the brothers are determined to keep it going for Roger."

Stephen chewed thoughtfully. He wondered how well Agnes understood her ex-husband.

"Dennis might be determined to keep it going," he said, "but William doesn't share his brother's dream. He has decided to get out. If his son doesn't want to go on the land, he can't see much sense in hanging on. He came into the bank this morning to talk about selling his share of the property." Stephen paused. The conversation with William McKendrick had given him an idea for his own future. He selected an apple and cut it into small pieces as he explained the McKendrick's situation.

"It's a family company and there could be problems when they carve it up. I'm hoping Dennis agrees to the sale."

Marion shook her head. "I don't think there's much chance of that. According to Agnes, he's mad about the place. Do you remember that party we went to after *Pirates*?" Stephen nodded. "Dennis and I got talking, and the way he spoke about his family, I can't see him giving up their legacy." She took a piece of apple from Stephen's plate. "There could be trouble ahead, if William tries to sell McKendrick land."

"There is often trouble, when it comes to breaking up a family company. The property might be a collection of paddocks around the old homestead, but it's as much a business as a brewery, or a restaurant in town."

"It's more than a business to Dennis," Marion objected. "It's a way of life. And from what Agnes said about William, I thought he felt just as strongly about the family land."

"He might have, once. But they've had a few bad years, and what with his wife's death and Roger deciding on a different career, you can't blame William for wanting to get out."

"What if Dennis objects?"

"He could make things very difficult. He can't stop his brother selling out, but he can hold things up." Stephen paused, thinking about the old man's will. "As William explained it to me, Dennis had quite a temper in his younger days. Their father was so worried about the boys fighting that he left the oldest son a controlling interest in the property. Dennis might challenge that in court. I don't think he would win his case, but he could hold up the sale."

Marion started to make coffee while Stephen explained the complexities of breaking up a family property.

"The McKendrick situation isn't unique. As I said, there's often trouble when the father dies or one of the family wants to bail out—problems that could be avoided if people planned for their future."

"So they need a lawyer?"

"Yes. But before that, I think they need a different kind of advice." He ran his hand through his hair, a gesture Marion remembered from their younger days, when he would tug at his head as if trying to pull ideas out of his brain. He caught her eye and laughed self-consciously. "Something between a financial adviser and a mediator, to get them talking about possible problems before they come up. For example, if one brother wants to sell, and the other doesn't agree, they have to divide the property. And that can be difficult. I suggested William wait a few weeks, to give himself time to get over his wife's death. But he wants to start things rolling at once. From the way he spoke, you'd think he was leaving tonight." Engrossed in his conversation, Stephen sugared his coffee a second time and stirred it again.

Marion pictured the staunch William McKendrick. The dependable committee man, the son a father trusted to protect the family property, Agnes Willmot's phlegmatic husband, who, after the breakup of his marriage, stayed on good terms with his former wife. How did that match a William so determined to get out of Ridgeway that he wanted to start things rolling at once?

Another vision edged into her mind, one that fitted the William that Stephen described. A man whose knuckles showed white against his clenched fist before he stormed out of the office on Sunday afternoon.

What was it Karen said about the brothers? "Dennis was really worried about what William would do, if he found out about Oliver."

Was that the man Agnes called "a total sook"? And, as far as his love life was concerned, waiting to be caught?

"People change," Marion said, repeating the remark she had made to Loretta earlier.

Had Rowena's death blasted William out of his customary reserve, turning him into the impatient type? Or had he only played the dutiful McKendrick to meet the expectations of his audience, and now he was dropping the role?

"What happens if Dennis refuses to sell?"

"They'd have to fight it out in court and that would slow things down."

"It might give William time to change his mind."

Stephen shook his head. "Not a chance. The man has set his heart on getting out. The way he talks, he can't stand the place. I'd hate to be the brother who stands in his way."

Marion shivered. She stared at her half-eaten sandwich. The meat inside the bread revolted her.

Rowena McKendrick. Bashed to death.

William would never kill anyone, Agnes had said. But, from the way she spoke, theirs didn't sound like a passionate marriage. How did William feel about his second wife?

Loretta had painted a similar picture—dependable William, driving his brother home after the drama group party, and she had known him all his life. But the Bostocks were also old friends, and she had been surprised, and shocked, by the Judith of this morning's interview. She had also trusted Benjamin Knowles, and look how wrong she'd been about him. Could she be equally wrong about William?

"They're a strange crowd, those McKendricks," Agnes had said. "The only thing that matters is the McKendrick name—the McKendrick land."

But William was going to sell that land.

And Stephen said, "I'd hate to be the brother who gets in his way." Marion shuddered. Somebody bashed Rowena McKendrick, and no matter how much the committee might talk about a drug-crazed burglar, none of them really believed a stranger had killed her.

Whoever killed Rowena must have hated her. Did William know about his wife's affair?

"I'll call Dennis now." Stephen could have been reading her mind, or else he was having the same thought.

Nobody answered the cottage phone.

"Try William."

There was no answer from the McKendrick house. Or from William's mobile phone.

Stephen frowned. "He should be there. He told me he was going straight back to the property to talk to his brother. He wanted to get the business sorted out."

"When you spoke to William, how did he seem?" She tried to keep her voice flat, but she couldn't hide the fear behind her words. Stephen swallowed the last of his sandwich in one large bite. "I'm going out to the property."

Marion pushed her own plate away. "I'll come with you. If everything's OK, you'll have trouble explaining your visit, but I can do the feminine thing. 'Poor William, he's not looking after himself,'" she said in a shrill Patricia-Menkes voice. "Wait a moment." She ducked into the kitchen and pulled a frozen pie out of the freezer. "It's a pathetic offering, but it gives us an excuse for visiting."

Not much of an excuse. Even two batching men could buy a frozen pie, and Dennis might wonder why a woman he hardly knew came to the property with her husband to bring William a meal. But it was the best she could do.

Before the morning's interview, Stephen would have laughed at his wife's fears. True, she had described the scene at the art show, the way William stormed out of the building when Rowena needled him, but any man would be upset if his wife talked to him the way Rowena did in front of his friends. Like Marion, he had wondered if there were harsh words in the McKendrick house that night but, at that time, he had not imagined anything more violent.

"Rowena McKendrick had been bashed to death," Stephen thought. And the man who came into the bank that morning was nothing like the phlegmatic William McKendrick Stephen thought he knew.

CHAPTER THIRTY: MONDAY AFTERNOON

The sky was heavy with cloud as they drove out of Ridgeway. There had been a short burst of rain and the ground beside the road had darkened to mud, with small, light patches where puddles reflected the grey sky.

The Bostock truck rattled past on its way back to town. "There must be an accident ahead," Marion muttered. Their own speed increased, and she gave an involuntary gasp as Stephen swerved to avoid a log. He slowed in response and steered carefully around the hazardous bends until, like the detectives a week earlier, they were stuck behind a lurching caravan.

At last there was a stretch of straight road and an overtaking lane. Stephen's foot pressed the accelerator as he sped past the slow obstruction, barely clearing it before the road narrowed again. Marion peered through the windscreen, looking for the turnoff to the McKenzie property.

"Here!"

They swung off the highway onto a track and Stephen's hands gripped the wheel as they splashed through puddles and bumped over the uneven ground. "How did Rowena manage, driving on this track at night?" Marion wondered.

Their way was blocked by a gate. Marion climbed out of the car and cursed shoes not made for tramping in the mud. Her fingers slipped on the wet metal as she struggled with the catch.

Stephen drove through the gate and waited while she slammed it shut and scrambled back into the passenger seat.

After going through another gate, equally hard to manipulate, they drove around a small cottage.

"That must be Dennis' place," Marion said, remembering what Agnes had told her. "William lives in the main house."

Stephen nodded as they followed the route that had taken Rowena so annoyingly close to her brother-in-law's window. Now, in the early afternoon, there were no dogs to bark and, Marion noted, no vehicles. Dennis was probably out working—but what about William? Like his brother, he could be anywhere on the property.

She was pulling her mobile out of her bag to try his number again, when they saw a large timber house that had been hidden by a clump of trees. Stephen stayed on the well-worn track that ignored the front door and led around the side of the building to a flat, cleared space in front of a tin shed.

Marion noted a tractor, well past its use-by date and beside it, the late-model Holden William usually drove into town. Somewhere, she was sure, there would be working vehicles, a truck or two, and a tractor in better condition than the derelict on display.

There were parallel ruts in the mud. Something with large tyres had been driven away, after rain had softened the dirt. "Sherlock Holmes," she mocked herself.

The pie on her knee had thawed and the cardboard was damp in her hands. Perhaps she should leave it in the car and Stephen could say he had dropped by, on his way to somewhere else, with a question for William about the property. He had to be going to some engagement that involved his wife, or why was Marion in the car with him?

If either of the men were home.

She started to speak, but Stephen almost dragged the door off its hinge as he sprang out. She put the pie on the driver's seat and followed him. "What now?"

No answer. All Stephen's attention was on William's car. And she saw what was wrong. A dark line snaking from the exhaust to the front window. A hose.

She could hear the engine running as Stephen struggled with the Holden's door. An elderly heeler was lying beside the wheel, it stood up and nosed his legs, pushing him into the side of the car. He reached out a hand to steady himself, bent and straightened, gripping a rock.

He smashed at the window, breaking the glass and, oblivious of sharp edges, pushed his arm inside to release the lock. The whole car rocked as he jerked at the door, opened it and switched off the ignition. He dragged something out. William. As unresponsive as a log of wood. He might have been dead.

She rushed to Stephen as he laid the unconscious man on the ground and crouched over him, blowing air into his mouth.

The rhythm of saving a life, head down—blow, head up to suck in air and head down again, blowing into the patient's lungs. The chest began to move and Stephen straightened his back.

William opened his eyes. Gasping and coughing. The dog pushed its nose into his face and Stephen pulled it away, gripping the back of its neck as it tried to snap. William moaned.

"We'll have to get him sitting up," Stephen said, grasping his shoulders while Marion wrapped her hands around his waist and pushed. Between them they raised the half-conscious man, dragged him over to the shed, and propped him against the wall.

Marion left Stephen holding him while she went back to their car for her mobile phone. They needed help.

She punched numbers and, at a spoken response, gave directions to the property. Half remembered stories whirled in her brain. "They won't come. They'll think it's a hoax call. They'll want a street number," she thought. She forced herself to speak calmly and was given comforting words in response. The ambulance was on its way.

"It would have to drive out from the town," she thought. She stared around the empty paddock and the muddy track. How long would it take?

Williams face was an unnatural, rosy pink. Was that a good sign? His body was shaken by dry retching. Stephen grabbed his shoulders and pulled his head forward.

Still not fully awake, William wrapped his arms around the dog, taking comfort from the animal.

Stephen gestured to Marion to take his place, and she held William steady against the shed while he went to the Holden. He leaned into the car and reached across the driver's seat to scrabble on the floor. He backed out and stood up, holding a piece of paper and a small bottle. Sleeping pills. "He must have swallowed the lot."

William gurgled, as if starting to speak, closed his mouth, and squeezed his eyes shut.

Stephen shook him until he opened his eyes again. "For God's sake—we've got to keep him awake."

The note fluttered out of Stephen's hand and Marion picked it up. "I'm sorry, but she didn't deserve to live. I couldn't help . . ." The words were scrawled across the page, as if the writer had passed out. Already affected by the pills

She pulled her husband away from the gasping man and showed him the note.

Stephen took the paper out of her hand.

There was the roar of a vehicle. A truck came around the trees and pulled up behind William's car. Dennis.

He started to climb out and saw the Holden's door swinging open, the broken window, and the hose, still dangling from its exhaust like a hungry snake.

"William! What the hell has he done?" he screamed. In three strides, he was beside Stephen. His eyes moved to his brother, leaning groggily against the shed.

He turned back to the truck, but Stephen moved in front of him. Dennis swung a fist, knocked him to the ground and scrambled into the cab.

Marion screamed as the engine roared. The truck jerked, crashing through a fence as it headed across the paddocks, through the scrub, into the hills.

Stephen stood up, holding his face. William groaned.

Marion had dropped her phone. She scrabbled in the dirt, picked it up and punched triple 0 again. This time she asked for the police.

* * * *

It seemed an age before help came. Marion struggled between the two men. Stephen was shaken and dazed, and William kept drifting out of consciousness. Somehow she had to keep him awake.

At last, a shriek more welcome than an angel choir. The ambulance.

Strong hands and confident voices as the crew took control. Marion watched the quick, practised moves. Oxygen for William. A stretcher.

"He'll make it," the woman said, years of experience behind her words.

Her companion took the bottle out of Stephen's hand and read the label. He looked at the hose but didn't waste time on questions. Marion watched as, with practiced hands, they manoeuvred William into the ambulance.

"What about him?" the woman asked, pointing to the still-dazed Stephen.

Marion was about to explain about Dennis—the assault—when the police arrived, in their brightly marked car. With a few words they sent the ambulance on its way.

The sergeant, an older woman with many interviews under her belt, listened to Marion's incoherent account and, by skilful questioning, was able to get most of the details of this bewildering afternoon. She moved away to use her phone, but from fragments of conversation with her partner, Marion knew the hunt was on for Dennis McKendrick.

She left the sergeant talking into her phone and followed the ambulance to the hospital with Stephen, not fit to drive, slumped beside her in the passenger seat.

* * * *

Erbacher and Shaw were at the hospital.

William had been in no state to talk, so they waited to interview the Sheas. Marion could only tell them what she had seen, but Stephen showed them the note he found in the car.

"So, McKendrick tried to top himself," Shaw said, scanning the scrawled words. "Set up the hose, turned on the motor, and flaked out. Now we know who killed the wife." He made no effort to hide his contempt for William McKendrick. He thought of the woman they had found in the small room. Whatever reason her husband thought he had, nobody deserved to die like that.

The way Shaw looked at the scrawled words reminded Marion of Gowd looking at another piece of paper. She thought of Dennis rushing away from the scene.

"Are you sure William wrote that?" she asked.

The men stared at her and Stephen took the note.

He frowned. "Those *r*'s and *t*'s. I've seen Williams writing at the bank, and I think he made those letters differently."

"We'll have the experts take a look at it," Erbacher promised. "But don't forget the man was under stress, and if he

241

had taken the drug, probably already half asleep. It looks as if he passed out before he finished the letter."

"The shape of a person's letters doesn't change," Stephen insisted. "Especially not if he's drugged."

"We'll need a sample of the man's writing."

That was no problem. Marion had the notes William made, when they were organising interviews. "At least the program had some use," she added, turning to her husband with what Shaw assumed was a private joke.

"If it wasn't for that business with Dennis McKendrick, hitting me and taking off, " Stephen said, "I might swallow my doubts about the letter. It's very plausible. A jealous husband bashes his wife to death, and unable to live with what he had done, tries to kill himself."

"We'll see what the brother has to say." Erbacher promised. "He won't get far. The police can move quickly in a case like this. There will already be roadblocks in place. Tell me what happened again."

"Dennis came tearing up, saw William was recovering, hit me, and drove away." Stephen rubbed his face and winced as his fingers touched a tender spot.

Marion enlarged her husband's response with conjecture and indignation that fizzled into bewildered exhaustion.

* * * *

"But what I don't understand," Shaw said, after a doctor had checked Stephen and sent the Sheas home, "is why they were at the McKendrick place. Since when have bankers made house calls?"

"Who knows what prompted them to go visiting," Erbacher said. "It is lucky they were there. Though, from what I've heard about these later cars, gassing yourself is harder than it used to be."

Shaw suspected his senior was quoting the paramedics, who had talked knowingly about "new models, catalytic converters," and "would have knocked him out eventually."

"At least we know what happened to Mrs. McKendrick."

"I'm not so sure," Erbacher said. "There are several possibilities. McKendrick might have bashed his wife to death and tried to kill himself, or somebody else killed the woman, and the husband couldn't face living without her. Or, if Shea is right about the 'suicide' note, a second murder was intended to explain the first."

CHAPTER THIRTY-ONE: TUESDAY MORNING

"An unsuccessful murder or attempted suicide?" Erbacher raised the question again the following morning, as Shaw drove them to the McKendrick property. "And still no sign of his brother," he added.

Somehow Dennis McKendrick had avoided yesterday's roadblocks and the well-publicised state-wide search. That was why the detectives were followed by the detective team, who were coming, with their own van, to examine the site again.

Shaw grunted. "Fellow must be hiding in the bush."

Erbacher agreed. "Backcountry's riddled with tracks. We'd need an army to cover them all."

Shaw couldn't forget how easily he had accepted the idea of a drug-crazed intruder. He hadn't even seen that tiny splash of blood behind the broken lock. "I guess I'll never make a detective," he said ruefully.

"You knew how important it was when I mentioned it," Erbacher reminded him. "With a bit of experience under your belt, you'll be first rate." Shaw reddened at the unexpected praise.

They turned off the highway, onto the track that took them through the inevitable gates and past the cottage to the original big house. Like the Sheas the previous day, Shaw drove around the side and pulled up in front of the shed. He saw the old tractor that appeared to have rusted into the ground, and the Holden, the hose still connected like an obscene tail. He parked beside a third vehicle, a truck that showed the scars of years spent bumping through the scrub.

"Oy there!" The large man, shoulders bulging out of a blue singlet, was leaning against the back door of the house. He was not a McKendrick, but as the detectives climbed out of the car, he stepped forward, fists balled, demanding to know their business.

The dog beside him gave a warning bark before it appeared to remember the detectives' first visit and trotted over to greet them as friends.

To Shaw's surprise Erbacher didn't ask the stranger's business. Instead, he introduced himself and showed his identification with one hand, while using the other to scratch the old dog's ears.

The man relaxed. He gave a friendly grin and told them he was "Alf, from Smithy's place. Your fellows, the uniformed officers sent out yesterday, asked the boss to keep an eye on things, feed the dog, and check the herd—you know." Erbacher gave an encouraging grunt. "And Smithy thought about rustlers. Once they heard the place was empty they'd be out with a truck—and good-bye cows. So he told me to come over with me swag. 'Make the place look lived in, Alf,' he said. 'I can manage on me own for a couple of days.' He cleared it with Mrs. McK."

"Mrs. McKendrick?" Shaw had a sudden incongruous picture of this Smithy, in torn jeans and singlet hovering over an Ouija board.

"Not the dead woman," Alf laughed at the detective's all too obvious bewilderment. "The first one. William's ex."

Another approving grunt from Erbacher.

"Didn't he see anything odd about a neighbour 'clearing it' with William's estranged wife?" Shaw wondered.

"And I rang the hospital meself last night," Alf was saying. "In case old Will was fretting about the place. He's happy to have me here."

It seemed William McKendrick might be too dazed to answer the detectives' questions, but he was able to talk about his property.

The explanations were cut short as the forensic team drove up and parked beside the detective's car.

* * * *

"We did well out of that," Erbacher said, after the house, the cottage, and land around the shed had been thoroughly searched and they were following the forensic van back to the main road. Like Roger on Sunday night, the team had noted the remnants of a fire in the old drum, but, unlike Roger, they had scrabbled through the ash to find lumps of blackened metal that were still recognizably buttons and charred scraps of cloth that must be from the same garment.

"You certainly got the old chap on side," Shaw said.

"Sometimes you learn more if you don't push," Erbacher explained. "Alf seemed like a decent chap. He's the sort that wouldn't break the law himself, but he mightn't go out of his way to help the police. Ask too many questions and he'll just clam up."

* * * *

Other people were asking questions. And with less information than the detectives, they answered each other with more confidence.

After hearing the news on Monday night, Lynette Waters told her housemates that William McKendrick must have bashed his wife after finding her in bed with his brother. "And then he tried to kill himself."

"She wasn't found in her bedroom," Alistair objected.

"So, he waited till he could get her alone, and away from the house."

In spite of Alistair's protest, the others found the story plausible, and passed it on.

By Tuesday afternoon the stories had grown. In the council offices one popular explanation had the McKendricks dealing drugs and getting on the wrong side of big city boys, while another story involved a lover from Rowena's past.

The only person who would not discuss the subject was William McKendrick himself. He responded to all questions with a blank stare, tightly closed lips, or, if he was feeling especially communicative, a muttered "I don't remember."

"He must have some idea," Shaw said impatiently, as they edged into the midday traffic after a second—fruitless—visit to the hospital.

"Blood's thicker than water," Erbacher said dryly. "We won't learn much from William McKendrick. But if those buttons could talk, they'd tell us what was burnt."

He held a piece of the metal on his palm and rubbed his fingers over it, feeling the raised pattern. "They are not ordinary buttons, not something used to fasten a man's work clothes. They might have come from an expensive coat . . . a coat that had been worn in town . . . that somebody might recognise . . ."

The buttons might not have a voice, but a human could speak for them, if that person was an observant woman who knew something about clothes.

Shaw thought of the Sheas. The banker had been right about the suicide note, and his wife seemed like a smart woman, the best of that Arts and Culture crowd. She might recognise the buttons.

Erbacher accepted his suggestion without argument; perhaps the senior sergeant really did think he had the makings of a good detective. A phone call with a carefully worded request was followed by a visit to the Shea's unit.

Marion was happy to help.

Erbacher's "We would like your opinion on some evidence," made her feel like a consultant. The talented Mrs Shea. "Expensive," was the word she used when she saw the pieces of metal. "They wouldn't belong to William. Not his style." She squeezed her eyes shut trying to visualise the buttons against cloth.

"A coat," she said suddenly. "Raincoat." There had been the party, after a play. "Dennis! He had been talking like a farmer, about his land, but it was raining and when he put on his coat, with those fancy buttons, it didn't look like something a farmer would wear.

Which only goes to show," as she had said to Stephen afterward, "you can't judge a man by his clothes."

"Dennis McKendrick again," Erbacher said to Shaw, as they drove back to the station. "We'll have to wait till we can talk to him."

CHAPTER THIRTY-TWO: WEDNESDAY MORNING

Nobody would be talking to Dennis McKendrick.

On Wednesday Erbacher got a call.

"Bryson, from Hadley Downs," he told Shaw. "They've found the other McKendrick."

Two bushwalkers had found the truck, crashed into a tree. Questioned about the condition of the driver, the caller had been incoherent. But his companion, taking the phone, was able to give clearer account. There had been a body in the cab—it looked like a man—and, yes, he was dead.

"It's definitely McKendrick's truck, Bryson checked the rego. And if Dennis McKendrick was driving, we can guess who tried to kill William."

"So that's why he won't talk?" Shaw shook his head as he tried to make sense of the McKendrick's world. "You don't rat on your brother, even if he tries to murder you. I wonder which one killed the wife."

"We know it wasn't her husband. Oh, yes," registering Shaw's surprise. "He was at home on Sunday night. Phone records show he had a call, on his landline, at the critical time. We followed it up and the caller swears he spoke to McKendrick, something about a delivery."

"Why didn't McKendrick tell us earlier?"

"He said we didn't ask."

"But when he said he was home that night, while his wife was bashed to death in town . . . you'd think he'd mention the call."

Erbacher could only agree. "It looks like his brother killed the woman. After he passed Bostock with the Anderson's truck, he knew she would be at the centre by herself. He took the back roads into town, waited in the bushes till the others had gone, and bashed his sister-in-law. But Lord alone knows why."

* * * *

If the detectives had spoken to Agnes Willmot, they might have learned the reason for the crime.

She had presented a sphinx face in the staffroom, but over a cup of tea with Marion, she talked about the murder, and the two McKendrick men.

"Dennis was crazy about the family land," she said. "But from what Roger said, William had lost interest in the place. He called farming a mug's game, and when the boy talked about going to uni, said he'd have to decide for himself."

"How did Dennis take that?"

"Roger said he was wild. And if William threatened to sell up . . ." As Marion knew he had. "For Dennis, that would have been the end. He was obsessed. It was the grandmother's fault." Agnes paused, while Marion poured a second cup of tea. "I didn't know her very well, but from what I've heard, she had one subject of conversation, the importance of the McKendrick family. And their father was almost as bad."

"What does Agnes think happened?" Stephen asked, when Marion reported the conversation.

"She says Dennis knew about Rowena and Oliver Bostock. If Judith came back and made a fuss, William would learn about his wife's affair. There would be a mighty row, and if that was followed by divorce, Dennis was sure she'd get a settlement. The way things are financially, the brothers would have to sell McKendrick land."

"So Dennis murdered his brother's wife to save the property." It made sense, in a convoluted way. "But why did he try to kill William?"

"To remove another threat to the estate." She described the lunchtime scene as Agnes pictured it. William saying he wanted to get off the land, and Dennis, pretending to agree, suggesting a drink while they worked out how to split the property. A drink doctored with sleeping pills. "And when William was unconscious, Dennis wrote the suicide note, dragged his brother to the car, and ran a hose from the exhaust. All to keep the property intact for his nephew."

"But Roger didn't want to go on the land," Stephen said. "That's why his father decided to sell."

"Dennis was obsessed." Marion repeated Agnes' word. "All those years, he was the one who loved the property. And he convinced himself that if William died, Roger would forget about leaving and take his proper place as the McKendrick heir."

CHAPTER THIRTY-THREE: WEDNESDAY EVENING TWO WEEKS LATER

Two weeks later, members of the Ridgeway Arts and Community Centre committee were able to meet in their own building. The main purpose of the evening was to replace the treasurer. After some gentle persuasion from Marion, Agnes agreed to take the job.

"So, it's business as usual at the A and C," Marion told Stephen when she got home. "Judith was at the meeting."

"The elusive Judith Bostock. Has she recovered from her Greek idyll?"

"Not really. She still wants to travel. She talks about the simple life."

"Very seventies. How does Oliver react to that?"

"As far as I can gather nothing's changed. He has his interests and leaves his wife to hers. What with the business and their children, neither wants to separate. As Judith says, the marriage is convenient for them both. Loretta's still reeling from a comment she made about toys of her own."

Stephen laughed and hugged his wife. "I'm glad you don't share those ideas," he said. "But if Judith leaves the committee, they'll have to find somebody to take her place."

"Uh-uh."

There was an uncomfortable pause and an embarrassed grin.

"You're going to take it on?"

Marion shrugged. "Somebody has to do it. And when Walter Edridge volunteered, Karen positively screamed my name."

"Perhaps you can bring them into the modern world."

"I doubt that," she said. "But I can help them cope with it. Not that I feel competent. I didn't even guess about Dennis."

"I don't see how you could. I know, after you recognised the fancy buttons, you remembered that meeting on Wednesday night, Dennis coming in wet. And Karen's remark about the coat he usually had in the car."

Marion laughed. "You can't call every man without a coat a murderer. Or assume he'd put it on to protect his clothes from splashes of blood. No there was something else, at that meeting in the council rooms. I told you how old Walter carried on, grumbling about the broken glass, and the druggies." Stephen nodded. "Loretta was all solemn and indignant and I couldn't help giggling; I knew she was the one who made the mess. Dennis was laughing with me, but none of the others could see the joke, because they had gone home before she dropped the wine.

"So, he must have come back to the centre after the show, and the noise we heard while I was getting into the car was him, lurking under the trees." She shivered. "How about your day?" she asked, with a determined change of subject.

"Particularly good. I had a meeting with William and Agnes, about Roger's future. Would you believe that Dennis has saved the property after all. Insurance. Because his death was, officially, an accident, there will be a large payout. William is talking about scaling down and maybe getting a manager, so Roger won't be tied to the place. And neither will he."

"His friends will never believe it. William McKendrick choosing to leave his land."

"His friends didn't know him very well, did they? Any more than they knew other members of the committee, like Judith Bostock. Though, for someone so disengaged from the scene, she seems to have had a huge effect on them all."

"Judith really was the catalyst," Marion said," Benjamin expected her to check the books. That was why he tried for one big win, to repay the money he 'borrowed' from the centre account."

"And, according to your friend, Agnes, Dennis expected a scandal when Oliver's wife came home, one that would lead to another McKendrick divorce."

"And the funny thing is, Judith had lost interest in the centre, and had never been bothered about Oliver's affairs. She was no threat to Benjamin or Dennis. They've known Judith for years. How could they get it so wrong?"

"They got it wrong because they've known her for years. People change. Look at you, taking on the secretary's job?"

Marion saw his point. Who would have believed, a few weeks ago, she would immerse herself so thoroughly in the problems of the old fogies?

Stephen was following his own thought. "That was the trouble with the McKendricks, they didn't have any plan for breaking up the estate. It's something that should have been settled before the old man died. You know," he leant forward, more engaged than Marion had seen him for months, "these family businesses—people need help setting them up, someone to talk them through the problems . . ."

Marion could see where the conversation was leading, a new role for a banking man, adviser-come-family-counsellor.

Stephen was about to enlarge the idea when his thoughts were interrupted by a rumble of tyres on the gravel outside, followed by the slam of a car door. The sounds reminded Marion of the proximity of neighbours and the inadequacies of their shared garden space.

"Maybe we can sell the Melbourne house," she said.

Stephen stared at her, but before he could reply there was a scratching at the kitchen door. Ginger Meggs. Marion let him in and opened the can of tuna she had bought that afternoon. "Now we're settled in Ridgeway," she said, "we'll need a proper home for our three cats."

* * * *

While the Sheas contemplated their future, Loretta Wheelwright found one of her lists. "Ring Oliver Bostock."

She puzzled over the words, why did she want to ring Oliver? The business with the bank had been sorted out. The new secretary, Marion Shea, and the returning treasurer, Agnes Willmot, seemed to have the measure of that horrible Gowd.

"Ring Oliver Bostock."

It couldn't have anything to do with Rowena's murder, nasty business though it was. In her efforts to protect Oliver, and her concern about William, it had never crossed Loretta's mind that Dennis McKendrick might be the killer. When she learned the truth, she allowed herself to grieve for the boy she had known. But there was nothing she could do for Dennis.

"Ring Oliver Bostock."

Of course! They would have to do something about Benjamin Knowles and his brave little wife. Loretta picked up the phone, changed her mind, and put it down.

There was no hurry. Benjamin still had to face court and possibly prison. The problem of what happened afterwards, that would have to be handled carefully. Oliver Bostock would have to believe the decision to give the delinquent treasurer a job was his own idea.

She was ready to climb into bed, but before she could settle there was one last small ritual. She reached for the photo beside her bed. "Jamie," she whispered to the picture, "did we do well?"

Light from the bedside lamp glinted off her husband's face, making the eyes sparkle. Loretta gave a contented sigh.

~

About the Author

Robin Hillard grew up in the Western Australian goldfields and has spent many years living in provincial cities and country towns of varying sizes during a career spent teaching in Australia, England, and Canada.

She has now settled, with her husband, in Toowoomba, also known as the "Garden City" of Queensland. It is also well served with antique shops—providing the inspiration for Archie's Antiques—while Robin's own fertile mind and interest in the strange and curious have created "Archie's Antiques Mystery Puzzles."

Toowoomba also provides the basis for the Australian town of Ridgeway, which features in her murder mystery/cozy novel "Ridgeway Murder."

You can read more about Robin at the Cyberworld Publishing website.

Robin likes to receive feedback and appreciates reviews being posted on distributor and book review websites.

Cyberworld Publishing

All books available in e-book and paperback.

Books by Robin Hillard

Ridgeway Murder*

Archie's Antiques Mystery Puzzles Book 1 (E-book only

Archie's Antiques Mystery Puzzles Book 2 (E-book only

Archie's Antiques Mystery Puzzles Books 1 & 2 (Paperback only)*

Books by Peter Tonkin

Football Mambo*

Books by Olivia Stowe

Mystery Romance

Restoring the Castle*

The Charlotte Diamond mystery series

By The Howling (Book 1)*

Retired with Prejudice (Book 2)*

Coast to Coast (Book 3)*

An Inconvenient Death (Book 4)*

What's The Point? (Book 5)*

White Orchid Found (Book 6)*

Curtain Call (Book 7)*

Horrid Honeymoon (Book 8)*

Making Room at Christmas (Seasonal Special)

Cassandra's last Spotlight (Seasonal Special)

Charlotte Diamond Mysteries Bundle 1 (Books 1&2)

Charlotte Diamond Mysteries Bundle 2 (Books 3&4)

Charlotte Diamond Mysteries Bundle 3 (Books 5&6)

The Savannah Series

Chatham Square*

Savannah Time*

Olivia's Inspirational Christmas collections

Christmas Seconds (2011)*

Spirit of Christmas (2010)*

Books by Stephen Bush

No Regrets

My Sister's Funeral: A Murder mystery*

Books by Gina Drew

The Koniotis Mysteries Series: each book in this six part Cyprus set series, which travels from the islands past to its future, stands alone, but they are also all connected in various ways and form the different parts of one story.

Laughter's Echo*

Salted Away*

Mouflon Brigade*

Amathus Armageddon*

Bogus Bills*

Homewrecker*